"PLEASE GIVE ME MY CLOTHES AND LET ME GO."

Fitzroy laughed and tossed Jessie a garment that had been lying across the foot of the bed.

"This is all I get to wear?" Jessie stared at the gauzy chemise.

Fitzroy smirked. "Yep. But don't worry. We've got too many scantily clad females running around this place to ever let it get cold."

"What kind of place is this, anyway?" Jessie pleaded.

"You *really* haven't figured it out yet?" Fitzroy asked, grinning...

LONE STAR

The Exciting New Western Series from the Creators of Longarm!

WESLEY ELLIS

LONE STAR
AND THE OPIUM RUSTLERS

A JOVE BOOK

LONE STAR AND THE OPIUM RUSTLERS

A Jove Book / published by arrangement with
the author

PRINTING HISTORY
Jove edition / September 1982

ISBN: 0-515-06227-8

Jove books are published by Jove Publications, Inc.,
200 Madison Avenue, New York, N. Y. 10016. The words
"A JOVE BOOK" and the "J" with sunburst are trademarks
belonging to Jove Publications, Inc.

PRINTED IN THE UNITED STATES OF AMERICA

LONE STAR

AND THE OPIUM RUSTLERS

Chapter 1

The sunlight dancing across the choppy blue waves of the bay made Jessie Starbuck squint. She was standing on the open deck of the Oakland ferry as it plowed its way across the water toward the wharves of San Francisco.

The ferry was crowded. There were cattlemen in dusty denims, Stetson hats, and worn leather gunbelts, all of them were rough old boys, coming into the city to sell their beef. There were Kansas and Nebraska homesteaders in overalls and straw hats, their complexions the sunbleached color of wheat, here in San Francisco to sell their crop and enjoy a once-in-a-lifetime fling away from the farm, the wife, and the kids. There were a great many derbied businessmen who had come from no farther than Oakland, and who were making their daily commute to their offices in the city.

It made no difference where the man was from, or where he was going. Regardless of whether a fellow wore High Plains spurs on his high-heeled boots, worn, muddy workshoes, or shiny patent-leather, city-slicker office slippers. To a man, they all paused to stare at the leggy silhouette of the young woman in her twenties. Jessie Starbuck could turn any male's head!

Jessie leaned forward, planting her elbows against the varnished wooden railing, to watch the big gulls wheel and soar in a clear, bright turquoise sky studded with puffy white clouds. Her green tweed skirt and matching hacking jacket—both so comfortable during her long hours spent in the saddle—also kept her warm against the stiff, salty breeze that was just now making her long blond hair dance and whip. Her tresses had

1

more than a hint of copper-red glint, brought out by the sunshine. The copper highlights sparkled when Jessie turned her head to watch the horses on board as they nervously stamped their hooves against the gently swaying deck of the ferry. Jessie had high, full breasts, and a slender waist accented by the snug contours of her buttoned jacket. The curve and swell of her firm, plushly rounded bottom was deliciously sheathed in green wool, the way the round curve of a six-shooter's cylinder is hugged by the soft leather of a custom-molded holster.

Jessie was never offended by the glances of men. Far from it! She accepted the looks, smiles, and even whistles as the compliments they were intended to be. After all, if the Lord hadn't meant for a woman to be the most fascinating work of art a man could contemplate, he wouldn't have made people the way they are. Truth to tell, Jessie herself enjoyed indulging in an occasional fleeting and decorous glance at a well-built male who happened to be sauntering by in a pair of snug trousers—not that she would *ever* admit that to a soul . . . After all, there were some things a lady just did not talk about, not even in the cosmopolitan, international port that was San Francisco in 1880.

Besides, if any fellow forced unwanted physical attentions on her, Jessie knew how to handle the situation. She had her double-barreled, .38-caliber derringer. Its ivory grips were just now pressed against the ivory flesh of her thigh; she carried the deadly little gun in a tiny stitch of a leather holster held in place by an elastic garter, which hugged her thigh just above the top of one of her silk stockings. But the odds of her having to draw her derringer were slim, for she had Ki.

Jessie turned her gaze away from the fast-approaching San Francisco hills, to search the deck of the ferry for her companion and bodyguard. A sudden tap on her shoulder made her spin about in surprise. Then she smiled at the wiry, dark-complexioned fellow standing before her.

"Ki," Jessie laughed. "You startled me—"

"I'm sorry, but did you not wish for me?" Ki asked, his almond eyes wide, perplexed, as if appearing in response to a silent wish were the most natural thing in the world.

But, as Jessie had to remind herself, Ki was able to do so many incredible things . . .

He had been born in the Japans, the only child produced in an ill-fated marriage between an American businessman and

2

adventurer, and a noble-born Japanese woman. Ki had the height, build, and handsome features of his father and the thick, shiny, blue-black hair and almond eyes of his mother. He had journeyed to American while still in his adolescence, but not before the completion of ten years' worth of study of the martial arts of his mother's culture. Ki was a samurai, a master warrior.

"Since you know so much, answer me this," Jessie quietly began, while her fingers absently tugged straight the lapels of his blue-gray tweed suit jacket, and then rose to straighten the bow of his black shoestring tie. "Tell me, Ki . . . is his *kami* watching over us on this trip?"

Ki frowned as he patiently endured Jessie's fussing at him. A gust of wind suddenly snatched his Stetson off his head. The hat sailed out over the railing of the cruising ferry, but before it could fly out of reach, Ki's right arm shot out even faster than the wind, to snatch his hat back—the movement was so fast that the cloth of his sleeve made a sound as sharp as the crack of a whip, and yet the rest of Ki's body had remained so motionless that Jessie's fingers never slipped from the smooth silk of his tie.

Their eyes met. Ki winked.

Jessie giggled and gave him a quick hug from which he gently disengaged himself. How aware Jessie was of the fact that presuming to adjust Ki's tie was very much akin to reaching through the bars of a tiger's cage in order to smooth the big cat's fur. But Ki, who with just his bare hands could kill a man, or even that tiger, in the blink of an eye, was always patient and gentle with her. As far as her *touching* him, well, she considered their relationship like that of brother and sister. Ki had grown up with her; she had been just a colt of a girl when her daddy had hired the then-adolescent samurai to be her protector.

"Well? Answer me," Jessie demanded, a half-smile darting at the corners of her lovely mouth.

"You speak of Alex Starbuck's *kami*," Ki replied. "The spirit of your father."

"San Francisco is where my father's business empire really began," Jessie said. "Of all the places we've been, and all that we might eventually get to, San Francisco was the business site most dear to my father."

"With the exception of the ranch in Texas—"

Jessie's voice was far away. "I wonder . . . The Starbuck

3

spread—our home—was the culmination of everything he'd worked for, but San Francisco was the bright beginning."

"Then San Francisco will be the most important battleground to your father's enemies—and yours," Ki reminded her, but Jessie was no longer listening.

The ferry's paddlewheels had slowed, to allow the boat to coast into its slip. The ride was almost over.

Jessie and Ki had disembarked from their Central Pacific train in Oakland, had been shepherded, along with their luggage, to the ferry slip, and had boarded the sidewheeler dubbed *Alameda I*. The big ferry had given a mighty shudder, belched one thick, black plume out of its tall smokestack, and backed away from the Oakland pier, to carry its multitude of passengers across the bay. Now the ever present bay breeze was flattening the ferry's furl of smoke, so that it trailed behind the squat-bottomed boat the way a black satin hat ribbon will trail behind a matron hurrying off to do shopping for her family.

There came a loud *thwak!*, and then there was silence as the Alameda's steam plant shut down. Looming above the ferry's smokestack was the squat, wooden clock tower of the city's Ferry Building, a long, barnlike structure owned and operated by the Central Pacific and Southern Pacific railroads.

As the gangplank was set into position, Jessie hurried to be among the first in line to leave the ferry. "Come on!" she scolded Ki. "I want to see everything! My memories of this city are so vague, they're more like dreams. I was so young when we moved to Texas—"

"Wait," Ki shouted. "I must see to the luggage." But Jessie was already racing down the gangplank, much to Ki's amusement. He trudged after her, leaving their baggage for later. Jessie was like a little girl rushing toward a wide-open candy store. Ki wanted to be there to witness her reaction to the interior of the Ferry Building. He watched as Jessie rushed in, only to stop, literally awestruck.

"The cable cars!" she exclaimed. "This is where they keep them!"

But she would have had to scream to be heard. The Ferry Building was a madhouse.

The walls of the place, which seemed as high and wide as a Colorado canyon, were rainbow-colored, with gaudy posters advertising North Beach breweries and honkytonk bars, downtown restaurants and hotels, and the rail-roads' faraway des-

4

tinations of Chicago, St. Louis, and New York. There were throngs of people hurrying along in that urgent way Jessie had always considered unique to citizens of large cities. Swarms of porters were shouting for the attention of those ferry passengers with luggage, and, not to be outdone, a half-dozen ragamuffin newsboys were hawking as many different newspapers.

Off to one side of the cavernous building stood dozens of cable cars. Many of them were shaking and rumbling, reminding Jessie of a herd of cattle about to stampede. "Market Street! Clay Street! California Street!" shouted the conductors, the clanging bells of their brightly painted, candy-colored cars adding to the din. There was the shrill, steam-whistle blast of a departing ferry, and the pungent aroma of snorting horses, who shook their bridles in impatience to collect a fare and draw their cabs out of this foul-smelling place so filled with the machines that many people were saying would soon render horsedrawn vehicles obsolete.

There was so much to take in, so much to listen to and see, that Jessie—spinning around like a top—suddenly grew dizzy. Ki came up behind her placing his firm hand on her elbow to steady her.

"I see that as usual, *you're* totally in control," Jessie remarked wryly. "But your Stetson is out of place here. We'll have to get you a derby."

"Do not forget that it was this city where I arrived as a young man, when I stepped off one of your father's clippers. It was in that first office of your father that I presented myself to him for hire."

"Just because he'd owned the clipper that transported you," Jessie marveled, shaking her head.

"It was an omen," Ki said, quite earnestly. "A sign. Such things are not to be ignored. Surely your father's housekeeper, Myobu, taught you *that* when she taught you the arts of the geisha?"

"Yes, she did," Jessie smiled. "Among other things . . ."

"I remember your father's office quite well," Ki continued, smiling now himself, as the memories came back to him. "He had only one floor in a frame building on Pacific Street, overlooking the wharf."

"Now the Starbuck home office takes up an entire block-long building," Jessie remarked proudly. "We took over one

5

of the banks that went bust after the Comstock Lode began to fizzle."

"California Street!" shouted a conductor.

"That's where our office is located!" Jessie cried out. "Oh, let's ride the cable car there!"

"I am afraid your ride will have to wait," Ki laughed. "I must see to the luggage before the ferry carries it all back to Oakland."

"Well, I'll ride it on my own," Jessie countered. "I can certainly take care of myself as far as—"

"Look there," Ki interrupted.

Standing with the rest of the cabbies was an elderly fellow dressed in a frayed, blue serge suit, and a lopsided, black leather visored cap. Above his head he held a square of cardboard on which was written, in uneven block letters, MISS JESSICA STARBUCK.

"How do you do, Miss," the old fellow said as Jessie and Ki approached. "And you, sir, how do *you* do? Mr. Lewis, of the Starbuck Import and Export Company, has engaged me to drive you to your hotel, wait for you while you refresh yourself, and then take you to Mr. Lewis's office for a meeting at three o'clock."

"You certainly know a lot about Mr. Lewis's affairs," Jessie observed. Arthur Lewis was an old family friend. He had been with Alex Starbuck from the beginning, and he was vice-president in charge of Pacific trade. In reality, Lewis just about totally ran all of the various enterprises comprising the Starbuck dealings with the Japans and China.

"Begging your pardon, Miss Starbuck," the cabbie said, doffing his worn cap. "My card—" He held out a small white rectangle. "Thaddeus Simpson is the name. And like it says there—" He tapped the card Jessie held. "Driver for hire."

Jessie eyed Ki, as if to say, *A cabbie with a business card?*

"This is San Francisco," Ki reminded her.

"Mr. Lewis keeps me on retainer," Simpson explained. "I don't carry no other fares but the folks he wants me to carry. He gets an awful lot of business folks come to see him, you know," he added sagely. "He's made you both a reservation at the Palace Hotel, Miss. And we ought to be on our way, if you're to have the time to rest a bit before going—"

"—to the meeting. Yes, thank you, Mr. Simpson," Jessie

6

laughed. "Oh, well, I guess my cable car ride will have to wait."

"You go along," Ki said. "I'll get a porter to fetch our luggage, and then take another cab to the hotel. That way you will have more time to rest."

Ki watched until Jessie was safely inside Simpson's hack. The cabbie clucked his horse into a brisk walk toward the daylight-flooded, high-arched portals of the huge building.

Ki turned to summon a porter. Through experience, both he and Jessie knew how to travel lightly. Ki had one bag for this trip, and Jessie one trunk of clothing.

A somewhat surely-looking porter appeared, and Ki gestured toward the bags and said, "To a cab, please."

Then he turned and began to walk before the porter, whose luggage cart had wheels that squeaked like mice as he followed. Suddenly the porter stopped, grabbed Ki's arm, and spun him around, to peer angrily at his face.

"Say, you're an Oriental, ain'tcha?" the porter glowered. "A Chinaman—"

"I am Japanese," Ki corrected him gently.

"Jap or Chinaman, it don't make no difference to me," the porter growled. "But I'll take my money in advance, seeing that I'm not dealing with no white gentleman."

Ki felt his temper rising, but he got control of his anger, reminding himself that this fellow was not worth crushing. "Here is your money, then, in advance," he said, being careful to keep his voice level as he handed the porter his coins.

Mollified, the porter began pushing his noisy cart once again. "That's the way I like it," he nodded. "Money in advance from Chinamen. I'm a member of Mr. Kearney's Workingman's Party of California," he boasted.

"And what is that?" Ki asked, now genuinely curious. He had already waved away the man's previous insult, the way he might a bothersome fly.

"What, you don't know?" the porter snorted. "You'd better find out, else you might get hurt, Chinaman—"

Ki reached out to gather up some of the porter's jacket front. He then lifted the man into the air, using just one hand. "I am *not* Chinese. Understand?"

"Put me down, dammit!" the porter squealed, his shoes dancing on thin air.

Ki gave him a little shaking, the way a terrier might shake

a rat. "Do you understand?" he softly repeated.

"Yes," the porter pouted. "Yes . . . *sir*."

Ki put him down. "I have already paid you," he said softly. "I wish to hear no more insults. Fair enough?"

The porter said nothing, but glumly went back to pushing his cart. Ki chose to interpret his silence as acquiescence.

"No! Please, no! Somebody help me!"

The woman's wail came as shrill and shockingly sudden as a steam-whistle blast from one of the ferryboats. Ki whirled around in the direction of the cry. He saw two men closing in on a solitary woman traveler. The bigger of the two hoodlums had locked his burly forearm across the woman's throat, while his smaller friend waved a length of iron pipe in her face.

"Let her go!" Ki shouted, and began racing toward the scene.

"My purse!" the woman cried. The little fellow had taken it. He'd tucked it under his arm as he began to run toward the cable cars. The big one released the woman in order to confront Ki's charge.

"What have we got here? A hero, is it?" the big man laughed. He was dressed in tattered denims, his shirt sleeves rolled up to display the knotted masses of his muscles. His hands were large, his splayed fingers grimy and padded with calluses.

Ki saw that the woman, brandishing her umbrella, had set off after the other robber. Ki attempted to swerve around the larger man, in order to pursue the one who had the woman's purse.

"Oh, no you don't," the big man laughed, crabbing sideways, to block Ki. He was bald, and wore a thick black beard, and had one gold earring in his right ear. His smile revealed a mouthful of gold teeth that matched the earring. "My friend will do the lady right proper," he nodded. "And I'm going to do you," he growled. He rushed forward, his fists balled, windmilling right and left.

Ki brought his own hands up to distract the robber's attention, and then executed a *mae-geri-kekomi,* a forward foot-thrust. His ankle-high, black Wellington boots allowed his foot the proper mobility. His foot-strike caught the man squarely on his bearded chin. The fellow's knees buckled, but he shook off the effects of the kick and aimed a roundhouse right at the side of Ki's head.

Ki sidestepped outside the swing. He clamped his right hand

around the other's outstretched wrist, and slammed the heel of his left into the other's elbow. There was an audible crack, and then the big man fell to the floor, howling in agony.

"Oh, God! Oh, you broke my arm!" The robber's face, beneath his beard, had gone white as a sheet. He writhed about, cradling his elbow and moaning.

"You!" Ki commanded, pointing a finger at the porter. "Stay with my luggage."

The porter nodded. "Yes, sir!" He himself had grown a shade paler as he looked down at the big bruiser crumpled on the floor, and thought about how he had so impudently sassed the soft-spoken, rather thin-looking gentleman who had put the lug there.

Ki was already in the midst of the empty, currently out-of-service cable cars. There were at least thirty of the cars scattered about on a crisscrossing network of track. He peered under the first few, his frustration rising. The one who had the purse could be hiding anywhere—assuming he was even still in the building...

"Over here!" came a woman's shout.

Ki hurried around the side of a pink cable car emblazoned with the words HYDE STREET. He saw the woman who had been robbed bent over at the waist, prodding beneath the car with her umbrella. "He's under here!" she declared triumphantly.

Ki had a moment to admire the woman's shapely backside before she straightened up and hurried away. The robber slid out from beneath the cable car, the purse still clutched in his left hand, and that deadly length of pipe still in his right. He was dressed in denim pants and a floppy canvas jacket, and was about five nine, but his wiry body was far from puny. Ki knew that this one would be twice as quick as his larger, lumbering partner, and that would make him twice as dangerous.

"I'll bash your head in," the purse-snatcher snarled. "Then I'm gonna do the same for you, lady," he warned the woman.

Ki had grown weary of the game. He reached inside his jacket and extracted one of his *shuriken* throwing blades from the sheath sewn into the lining of his garment. The four-inch, hiltless blade flew from his fingers to pin the pipe-wielder's loose sleeve to the wood-paneled side of the cable car.

The pipe fell from the surprised man's fingers and rolled out of sight beneath the car. Dropping the purse, the little man

9

shrugged out of his jacket and ran off, leaving his garment hanging the way a lizard leaves behind its severed tail.

Ki wiggled his blade out of the cable car's paneling, letting the robber's jacket fall to the floor. He slipped the *shuriken* back into its sheath, and then bent to retrieve the lady's purse.

"Thank you so much," the woman enthused. "You have been so kind, so brave—"

"I am glad that I could be of help," Ki said, bowing slightly. Now that the woman was speaking normally, and not in a series of frightened exclamations, Ki could detect a European accent. The woman's voice was lilting and quite pleasant, as was the rest of her. She was wearing a tightly fitted, high-necked dress of dark blue velvet. It emphasized the elegant lines of her body. Her hat was cut from the same velvet as her dress, and was perched on her mass of auburn curls. The hat was tipped at a rakish angle that made her look quite cosmopolitan, and more than a bit daring. That daring look was only heightened by the lascivious sparkle in her catlike eyes as she looked Ki up and down.

"I must go now—" Ki began.

"No! Wait!" the woman exclaimed. "I mean . . ." Her white gloved hands rose to her rouged cheeks. "I mean . . . I do believe that with all this excitement, I'm beginning to feel faint." Her long lashes began to flutter as she swayed toward Ki, falling into his quickly outstretched arms.

The warmth of her this close to him, and the sweet scent of her perfume, made Ki himself feel like swooning. This close to her, Ki could see the faint crow's feet around her eyes, and the slightest hint of a burgeoning double chin. She was in her late thirties, Ki reckoned, but still a lovely woman. She had about her that fecund ripeness, that promise of bursting sweetness, that only the most mature, late-summer fruit can have.

"Perhaps my hero would like a kiss in reward for his valor?" she murmured.

Ki gathered her in his arms, and pressed his mouth against hers. She tasted vaguely of cinnamon; there was a hint of tobacco. Her kiss was heady, as intoxicating as wine. Her thighs, beneath her velvet dress, locked about Ki's leg. One dainty, white-gloved hand dipped to stroke him, bringing him rapidly erect within the confines of his trousers.

"I wish to thank you more profusely," she breathed into his

10

ear. "We are alone here. We could slip into one of these empty cars—"

There was no denying the urgency in her husky whisper, and there was no denying the randy, bucking urgency Ki himself felt in his loins. He swept her off her feet and into his arms, and strode with her toward the pastel-pink Hyde Street car.

"You are so strong," she warbled, nuzzling her upturned nose and full lips into Ki's neck. "I hope you are strong down *below,* as well . . ."

Inside the car, a canvas tarp had been draped across several rows of seats. The effect was that of a makeshift tent; the sheltering tarp would afford them some measure of privacy.

Ki unsnapped several seat cushions and scattered them on the floor beneath the tarp. The woman had set down her purse and umbrella, and had peeled off her white gloves and her dress as well. Now she stood before Ki in just her black corset, silk stockings, and high-heeled, high-buttoned shoes. She tugged down on the corset, to allow the lush, creamy globes of her breasts to bounce free. Her large, pink nipples stiffened, as if in anticipation of Ki's approach.

Once more she fell into his arms, moaning as Ki sucked first one turgid nipple and then the other, shifting quickly from right to left, and then back again, pausing only to skate his moist tongue about the dark rosettes that framed those delectable, fleshy nubs.

"Hurry," she begged. "Undress, and then let us scurry into the cozy nest you have built for us."

As Ki shucked his suit jacket and pulled loose his tie, she got down on all fours to crawl into their canvas-roofed hideaway. Ki himself let loose a soft moan as he watched her fine, round buttocks, lewdly jutting out from beneath the bottom of her tight corset and the tops of her stockings, wiggle and jiggle as she disappeared, headfirst, beneath the tarp.

By this time, Ki was down to just his longjohn bottoms. He heard a gasp, and then a sigh of satisfaction, and looked down to see her head poking out from beneath the canvas, her wide purple eyes taking in his broad, sinewy shoulders, corded arms, and washboard-rippled belly.

Ki crawled in with her beneath the tarp. The air was already rich with the flowery scent of her perfume and the musky

11

fragrance that no chemist can duplicate, but which comes only when a woman is aroused and ready for her man.

"We do not even know each other's names," Ki mused as she planted kisses across his chest.

"No names, *liebling*—I mean, darling. It is always more exciting for me when it is—how do you say it?—*ungenannt*. Anonymous."

"But—"

"No more questions," she hissed, her lips moving down his belly. "Questions and familiarity spoil it for me."

And then her lips moved down past his belly, to encircle and warmly, wetly enclose the tip of his throbbing erection, and then no questions seemed important or, indeed, even possible. He intended to hold off, but her head began moving up and down, and she reached between his legs to tickle, palm, and finally squeeze him. His intentions faded against the intense, shuddering rush of his orgasm.

She swallowed it all greedily, and sat back on her haunches, licking her lips the way a cat licks its whiskers after finishing a saucer of cream. Her look of smug satisfaction turned to one of startled amazement, however, as Ki gently pushed her back and moved himself between *her* legs. He was still as hard as a rock.

"Oh, *liebling*, you are an incredible man!" she gasped as Ki penetrated her. She locked her legs around his waist. "Hard now, darling. Very hard," she breathed into his ear. "I want to feel it against my backbone!"

Ki set himself an easy, steady rhythm, his supple hips working like a bucking mustang's. As she raked his back with her fingernails, he thrust harder, enjoying the small squeaks and squeals of pleasure/pain he was eliciting. He was normally a quite gentle, quite tender lover, but there was something about this mysterious feline female, some innate cruelty that brought out a matching cruelty in him.

Her moans and tremulous sighs were coming ever faster now. Ki slid his hands down to her upraised legs in order to caress her feather-lightly with his palms, enjoying the silky variations in texture as he went from her stockinged thighs to her bare backside.

"Soon I shall come," she sighed, her tongue moist and hot in his ear. "But you must hurt me. I need this!"

12

"I cannot—" Ki managed as he felt his own orgasm rising within him. "I will not do—"

Suddenly she dug her nails into the tender skin of his armpits. The sensation was not one of painful pleasure, but almost of excruciating agony. Her touch was not the touch of a playful lover, but of a cougar unsheathing its claws. Gritting his teeth to keep from crying out, Ki instinctively struck out. His palm came smacking down, hard across the tautened flesh of her right buttock.

She yelped in pain and slid her legs even higher up Ki's back. Then she yelped in a quite different manner as she convulsed into a series of shattering orgasms that left her lying limp.

Ki withdrew as soon as her legs relaxed their scissors-hold around him. He had not come, and no longer had the desire to experience his personal pleasure with this woman. Her predilection for pain did not shock, but merely saddened him. He was an experienced lover, and had been trained in the sexual secrets of the Far East. While it was not particularly to his taste, he was well aware that there was nothing at all unusual or uncommon in the incorporation of the fantasy of pain into lovemaking. But there was a vital difference in the spicy passion evoked by the teasing spank, the tickling scratch, the gentle nibbling of teeth, and that dark surge of emotion generated by the bruising fist, the skin-shredding claw, the maiming bite.

Now Ki gazed into the violet eyes of this woman as the last echoes of her pleasure faded from her wet center, and she began once more to comprehend the material world. What he saw in her eyes, suddenly glittering like ice, was not only cruelty, but *evil* as well. He shuddered as a chill crept along his spine like a droplet of freezing water. *Evil.*

"You see how it is with me, *liebling,*" she said matter-of-factly, as Ki slid out from beneath the tarp to begin dressing. "You see why I love only strangers, and never, *never* twice. In my work, I command many people. I control their very lives. This I enjoy. But when it comes time to make love, I find that it is *I* who must be taken in hand...*brutally,*" she snarled. "But only for that instant," she warned, leaving the tarp and reaching for her dress.

Ki said nothing, but only watched as she raised her arms above her head to slip on her garment. The cherry-red imprint

13

where his palm had landed still glowed in stark contrast to the milky paleness of the rest of her buttocks.

That was all right, Ki sourly thought to himself. Droplets of blood were still oozing from his armpits. The sting and color would fade from her backside long before the lacerations she had inflicted upon him would heal. But of course, that was the way she had planned it. It was what she had counted on, trusting that he *would* not, *could* not go too far for her liking. For her sake, Ki hoped that her ability to evaluate the personalities of her sexual partners remained canny. Otherwise she might one day find herself with a body as scarred as her soul.

She fixed her hat in exactly the same saucy tilt as before, and bent to pick up her umbrella and purse. The snap on the latter came undone as she rose, so that the purse's contents spilled across the floor of the cable car. Ki, finished dressing, stooped to help her gather up her things. The purse's contents included coins and paper currency, both domestic and foreign, a gold pillbox engraved with the initials *G.K.*, and the woman's Prussian passport, which had flopped open. She snatched the document quickly from Ki's hand, but not before he'd gotten a glimpse of her name: Greta Kahr.

She was scowling as she tucked her purse under her arm, gripped her umbrella, and took her leave of the car. "I owe you one favor for helping me with those robbers. Here it is. Do not attempt to find me, *liebling*. Never again can I make love with you." She tottered down the steps of the car and walked quickly away.

"I do not wish to find you," Ki muttered to himself. "And as for making what you call 'love' to you, who would ever want to?"

He set his Stetson on his head and left the cable car. He fully expected to find the porter still guarding his luggage, and he was not disappointed. The man chattered on excitedly about how the police, and then two stretcher-bearers, had come to take away the hoodlum whose arm had been broken. There had been enough witnesses to what had happened so that the police considered it an open-and-shut case of a good Samaritan coming to the aid of a lady in distress.

"Did you get the other one, as well?" the porter asked as he loaded Ki's luggage into a waiting hack.

"Yes, I did," Ki replied, hoisting himself into the cab.

"And I bet you got something from the lady, right?" the

14

porter asked shrewdly. "A nice bit of reward, eh?"

Ki tossed him an extra few coins to make up for the time he'd spent waiting. "I certainly got more than I'd expected— and more than I'd bargained for," he added quietly.

Ki latched the hack door closed. He was not smiling as the cabbie flicked his whip above the horse's head, and the hack lurched on its way.

Chapter 2

The Starbuck Building was of granite, and stood on bustling California Street. It was as massively forbidding as a mountain. The huge institution's halls were paved with marble, and its bannisters and fluted gaslight fixtures were of polished brass. Interior doors paneled with frosted glass lined the corridors, which were decorated with costly sculptures and oil paintings in gilded frames, imported from Italy and France. The hushed murmur of countless voices filled the still air of the place, combined with the staccato clicking of typewriters and the metallic rasping of hand-cranked adding machines.

Jessie had dim memories of skipping up and down these marble-floored hallways long ago, a fine handmade doll imported from the Japans clutched in her arms. But then she had been just an oblivious little girl. Now she was an adult, and as she listened to the sound her own heels made as they clacked along the corridors, and as she spied the dignified, pinstriped-suited gentlemen who were all standing in their office doorways gazing at her as she passed by, Jessie found herself rather intimidated by it all.

Until she reminded herself that she owned the place, and that all of these people worked for *her*.

She and Ki were fifteen minutes late for their appointment with Arthur Lewis, the man who, under Jessie's auspices, ran the Starbuck interests up and down the West Coast and in the Orient. Ki, for some mysterious reason he refused to divulge, had been extremely tardy in arriving at the hotel with their luggage. Jessie had planned on changing out of her green tweed

17

traveling suit before going to see Arthur, thinking it a bit too rustic for the occasion. When Ki had finally arrived, it was already close to two-thirty. Jessie had been forced to scramble to unpack her trunk. Fortunately the services offered at the exquisite Palace Hotel were simply unbelievable. A uniformed employee had whisked away, and then quickly returned, freshly steam-pressed, the light blue linen dress and matching shawl she was now wearing. The service had also cost the unbelievable sum of forty-five cents, but Jessie, who had been taught early on by her father that money was to be enjoyed but not wasted, had already promised herself that the various treats only to be found in a big city like San Francisco were too good to be denied.

Jessie was certainly not angry with Ki for his delay, whatever the reason, but she was concerned with his subdued, saddened manner. She wished there were some way she could coax her companion into unburdening himself to her, but she knew her wish was futile. Ki kept his thoughts to himself. Perhaps it was seeing San Francisco again after so many years that was making him sad . . .

Arthur Lewis's pink-faced clerk ushered them right through the executive's outer office and into his private study. Both Jessie and Ki were relieved to see that the stuffy European trappings so apparent in the rest of the building were absent here.

Lewis's office was carpeted in wall-to-wall gray wool. The walls were painted white, and were bare except for several strikingly bold, Japanese brush paintings. Lewis's desk was of mahogany. The big easy chairs scattered about the room were of matching wood, and upholstered in rich brown leather. End tables held jade ornaments and fine vases. Bright sunlight flooded through the room's large windows, and the air itself was fragrant with the smell of freshly brewed green tea sending up clouds of steam from a Japanese teapot. Next to the pot were four matching, handleless cups.

"Arthur," Jessie said, smiling, "how pleasant this room is."

Arthur Lewis stood up and came around his desk, a big grin on his handsome, lined face. "All that European stuff is for the clients and customers," he winked. "These days a San Franciscan isn't impressed unless he can surround himself with junk from what the furniture dealers like to call 'the Continent.'" He paused to look Jessie up and down. "My God, girl.

18

You've grown into a beauty. I see your mother in your eyes, and in that reddish-gold hair of yours."

Jessie blushed. "You look just the same as ever," she said shyly.

Lewis's laugh was deep and rich. "Then your memory isn't what it ought to be." He fingered his bald head, which was fringed by a horseshoe of gray hair. "For instance, I used to have hair up there." Next he patted his protruding belly, encased in a vest of gray silk that nicely matched the gray herringbone wool of his suit. "I used to be as thin as your friend Ki here, as well."

Lewis turned to Ki and executed a formal bow. He kept his knees straight and his palms on his thighs. The angle of his back and the way he kept his eyes level with Ki's were both exactly right in terms of Japanese protocol.

Ki returned the bow, and as they straightened up, Lewis remarked, "Not bad for a barbarian, eh?"

Ki smiled. "It was quite excellently done, my old friend, Arthur."

Lewis guffawed. "Hear that Jessie! Ki said it was excellent! And he smiled! This fellow *must* be glad to see me." He shook his head. "My bow *ought* to be excellent; I've certainly practiced it enough down through the years. Don't forget, Alex Starbuck and I were mates together on one of Admiral Perry's ships back when the United States broke open the Japans. Yes, Alex and I were just lowly sailors, but he told me then what he aimed to do with his life, and I, thank the Lord, had enough common sense to stick with him."

"Come now, Arthur," Jessie argued. "My father had total confidence in you. He often told me that he could never have moved to Texas if he hadn't had your capable help to depend on."

"You make an old man happy, child," Lewis said softly, his light blue eyes suddenly grown shiny. "Last time I saw you, you were little enough to sit on my lap."

"I don't think I can do that anymore," Jessie laughed.

"And you used to call me 'Uncle' . . ."

"That I can do, *Uncle* Arthur," Jessie smiled.

"Thank you, child. Now! both of you sit down!" Lewis poured them all a cup of green tea and sat down behind his desk. "I'm so glad we can talk together so easily, Jessie. Even after all these years."

"Well, we haven't seen each other for a long while, it's true, Arthur—*Uncle* Arthur," Jessie corrected herself. "But there has been all that correspondence between us since my father's—"

"Death," Lewis quickly interrupted.

"No, Arthur. Let's call it what it was," Jessie firmly corrected him. "It was *murder.*"

Lewis frowned, then sighed. "I see your mama's spark more plainly now, Jessie. And I see in you your father's iron will and intelligence."

"In the telegram you sent last week, you spoke of an urgent situation that required my personal attention, but there were no details," Jessie said. "Tell me what is going on."

Lewis nodded. "Let's start from the beginning. The mainstay of the Starbuck business is still the Pacific trade. It's from *this* end that we get the working capital necessary to fund the Starbuck ventures into other areas. Our lumber mills in Oregon, for example, the cattle ranch in Texas, where you and Ki reside—"

"Yes, Uncle," Jessie patiently said. "And there's the recent merger with that textile concern in New England. I negotiated that myself, you know." She winked at him. "Really, Uncle. I'm no longer that little girl who sat on your lap."

"No . . ." Lewis sounded rueful. "Well, I'm aware that you're on top of things, Jessie, so I guess I'd better get to the point. We need—our clippers need—San Francisco's port in order to continue to do business. The port is now regulated by a corrupt city official named Harris Smith. It's up to this Smith fellow to say when we get to unload our cargo, and when our ships can sail again. Why, he even gets to decide how much duty we have to pay on our goods! This official, or his minions, tie our goods up for ninety days at a time, making us pay penalties to our customers' for late deliveries. When he does lift his embargoes, he charges us three times the proper duty rates."

"Can you not complain to a higher authority?" Ki interrupted.

Lewis smacked his desktop with the flat of his hand. "Sure, I can *complain* all I want, Ki. But it gets us nowhere. The city government looks the other way concerning things like this. Smith's job as waterfront commissioner is a patronage position. He's appointed by the mayor."

"And the mayor won't fire him?" Jessie asked.

"Unfortunately the mayor is under obligation to two powerful shady interests in this city," Lewis explained. "These two interests wish things to stay exactly as they are on the waterfront. The first interest is one of the Tongs."

Ki frowned. "That is bad for us, Arthur." In response to Jessie's confused look, Ki said, "*Tong* means 'association' in Chinese. They were once family associations that looked after the interests of their family members when the American authorities would not. But the name has recently been taken by bands of ruthless criminals who now control all commercial activity in the Chinese community."

Lewis nodded and went on, "There are five of these associations—called 'families'—in San Francisco. The one that controls the waterfront is called the Steel Claw Tong."

"Why should they affect us?" Jessie asked. "I thought you said they only worked in the Chinese community."

"Unfortunately," Arthur Lewis said, "the Steel Claw Tong has its steel claws in quite a few other places as well. Their main 'businesses' are the opium and slave traffic. The slaves—women, you can guess for what purpose—and the opium have to be brought into the country, and it isn't the Chinese who run the ships. The Steel Claw Tong owns opium dens and brothels. This Smith fellow is paid off to look the other way as the Tong brings in its dope and female slaves, and meanwhile, he harasses *us* in our entirely legitimate importation of silks, spices, and jade."

"But Arthur, I'm confused," Jessie blurted. "I understand why the Tong would bribe Smith to let them smuggle in what they want, but who would pay him to make business difficult for us . . ." Her voice trailed off as her green eyes widened in comprehension.

Lewis gestured toward her with his chin, his voice filled with admiration as he told Ki, "She's *sharp*."

"Indeed she is, Arthur," Ki smiled back.

"Now I understand your urgent telegram," Jessie muttered, her face set in determination. "And the need for secrecy. The cartel is involved in all this, correct?"

"Absolutely," Lewis replied. "Once again they are trying to destroy the Starbuck organization."

"How did you ever get wise to them, Uncle?" Jessie asked. "It was clever of you, I'll say that!"

21

Lewis positively blushed with pleasure at the compliment. "I hired a private detective in order to see whether I could flush out any incriminating evidence on Commissioner Smith. It was my intention to take whatever evidence I could get on him directly to the newspapers, and in that way, force the mayor to discharge him, despite the wishes of the Tong. The private detective is still working on that angle, but while he was investigating Smith, he came upon the cartel's involvement in the situation."

"What do they hope to get out of it?" Jessie asked. "Besides my ruination, that is," she wryly added.

"And why would the Tong, traditionally a closed group, wish to associate themselves with the Prussians?" Ki interjected.

"One at a time," Lewis chuckled. "The detective—his name is Moore, by the way—found all that out as well. He's quite bright, but extremely insolent, I must add. Fairly slight fellow, considering the rather dangerous nature of his work . . . Anyway, Moore has discovered that the Tong is playing along because the Prussian cartel is providing them with a controlling interest in a bordello being operated here in San Francisco for very rich and powerful white clients. No Tong family has ever been able to extend its slimy tentacles outside of Chinatown. For the Steel Claw Tong to achieve such expansion would put them far ahead of the other four families. As far as the cartel is concerned, you both know that Prussia, England, and the other European powers have a foothold in the Orient, alongside the United States. The Prussians send their goods into the Japans, and import Japanese raw materials to Europe, but they haven't been able to touch the trade franchise *we* have here in America. With the help of the Tong, and through them, with Commissioner Smith's help, the cartel means to so disrupt our seagoing trade that we lose our import/export licenses in the Orient. If that were to happen, it would tear out the heart of the Starbuck empire."

Jessie nodded. "Our organization would be crippled, all right. The Prussians could move right in on us, just as they've always wanted." Jessie paused a moment to think about it. "And it wouldn't just be in the Orient. The Prussians could take over right here in America, as well."

Lewis, his lips pursed, leaned back in his chair, silently nodding in agreement. "I'm a businessman," Lewis murmured.

"But this isn't about business, it's about war. We've got to stop them, but I don't know how. That's why I sent for you, Jessie."

"What is the name of the Tong leader?" Ki asked.

"That I still don't know," Lewis answered. "It's incredibly difficult for a non-Chinese to get any information at all on the Tong. Wandering the streets of Chinatown is like walking down a maze of mirrors. All you ever see is your own white image reflected back at you. Anyway, I've got Moore working on it."

"And the cartel representative's identity?" Jessie asked sharply.

"That too remains a mystery," Lewis sighed. "I knew their old man quite well. Used to have a none-too-friendly-but-obligatory drink with him now and then. The cartel considered him adequate for paying Smith his bribes, and for balancing the ledgers at that bordello I mentioned, but Moore found out that cartel headquarters in Prussia considered their man not cutthroat enough to handle the next phase of their plan to crush us. Who the new man will be, and when he's supposed to arrive, Moore hasn't yet discovered."

"This fellow Moore seems to have quite an inside with our enemies," Jessie mused. "How did he manage it?"

Lewis blushed, the mottled pink that suffused his cheeks rising all the way up and across his bald dome. Just then there came a knock at his door, at which he seemed inordinately grateful. "I think I'll let Moore himself explain that, if you don't mind, child." He called out, "Come in!"

Both Jessie and Ki turned to watch Lewis's private eye enter the office. He was, indeed, as Lewis had described him, a slightly built fellow for the sort of rough-and-tumble work Jessie associated with the job of a private investigator.

"Miss Jessica Starbuck," Lewis began, rising to his feet, "may I present Mr. Jordan Moore. Mr. Moore, Miss Starbuck."

Moore approached to shake hands with Jessie. He was about five feet ten inches tall, Jessie guessed, and weighed about one hundred and forty pounds. She wondered fleetingly why a stiff San Francisco breeze hadn't already blown him out to sea.

"And this gentleman here is Miss Starbuck's companion," Lewis continued. "His name is Ki."

Moore grinned as he stuck out his hand in Ki's direction. "What do I call you for short?" he asked.

Ki smiled back at the slender man. "Whatever you call me,"

he said softly, "I should do it very politely if I were you, Mr. Moore."

"Certainly, *Mister* Ki," Moore replied, his inflection just polite enough so that Ki wasn't quite sure if he should take offense.

"Please sit down," Lewis said hurriedly, taking Moore by the elbow and guiding him to an armchair some distance away from Ki's. "Cup of tea?" he asked.

"Thank you, no," Moore replied. He took a moment to align the razor-sharp creases in the trousers of his black wool suit, and then sat down. He balanced his derby on the head of a porcelain figurine of a sword-wielding samurai.

Jessie held her breath as she watched Ki stiffen with anger over Moore's flippancy, then she herself grew angry. *What arrogance!* Moore ran his hand through his thick black hair, which he wore combed back, but without oil, and gave his derby a tap, to make it bob up and down on the samurai statuette's tiny head. He then beamed his wide grin around the room, like a child looking for approval, Jessie contemptuously thought. His green eyes—the color of emeralds, the color of her own eyes, she realized distractedly—sparkled with amusement. Why, the man was in his thirties, but he acted like an insolent adolescent!

"You've come up with quite a good deal of information for us, Mr. Moore," Jessie began. "I'm quite pleased with your work."

Moore glanced questioningly at Lewis.

"Miss Starbuck is *my* employer," Lewis said. "Need I say more?"

Moore shook his head, smiling to himself. Once again, Jessie felt her anger flare, and then she grew doubly angry as Moore—still grinning—gazed at her until she had to blush.

"I hope you have no qualms about working for a woman," she declared.

"On the contrary, Miss Starbuck," Moore replied, his voice clear and pleasant. "A private investigator often finds himself working for a woman, but usually on cases involving a husband's infidelity. Such women are rarely as beautiful as yourself..."

"Can we keep our minds on business?" Jessie asked curtly.

"Certainly," Moore chuckled. He reached inside his jacket to remove a tiny black notebook.

24

As he flipped through the notebook's pages, Jessie asked, "Have you found out the name of the head of the Steel Claw Tong?" She noticed that not only was Moore's suit black, but so were his boots, vest, tie, and derby. His white shirt only emphasized the starkness of his garb, and the brilliant sea-green of those eyes of his, set in his handsome, clean-shaven face...

"The leader's name is Chang Fong," Moore began, reading from his notebook. "He's in his early fifties. Chang came to Chinatown when he was ten years old, from the Kow Gong district of Canton. He got himself a job working in a fish market for five dollars a month—and on that, this ten-year-old supported a passel of much older uncles and cousins evidently too lazy to earn their own way—"

"Excuse me, Mr. Moore," Ki interrupted. "Allow me to correct you. Chang's relatives were most likely not too lazy, but too *old* to adapt. They came from a culture where the ripeness of their age would have afforded them much respect."

"But they weren't *in* their culture. They'd come to America," Moore pointed out.

"Indeed, but for elders to learn English, to accept menial jobs..." Ki shook his head. "It was up to young Chang to support his elders. Honor demanded it."

"Indeed..." Moore said softly. He peered at Ki's face, scrutinizing his features, and then he smiled, and nodded to himself. "Thank you for the correction, Ki," he said earnestly. "It helps me understand Chang. Anyway, ten-year-old Chang was soon making ten dollars a month, as the store's manager. Meanwhile, he was attending a Sunday school run by the Methodist mission, in order to learn English."

"Why didn't he go to public school?" Jessie asked.

Lewis and Moore exchanged embarrassed looks. "Jessie," Lewis sadly began, "Chinese children are not allowed in our public schools."

"But the Chinese pay city taxes, don't they?" Jessie demanded indignantly. Lewis shrugged and looked down at his desk, as Ki chuckled sadly.

"Chang found himself a couple of hatchet men to make sure that the nearby fish stores didn't do so well," Moore resumed. "By the time he was in his twenties, he owned those stores, as well as the one he used to work at. He got himself a few more hatchet men, and then began to extort protection money from both legitimate and illegitimate businesses in Chinatown.

25

Chang's gang was still not a Tong, still not one of the official five," Moore pointed out. "That had to wait until he had enough income to buy himself a chunk of city hall, and of the police. Once that was accomplished, he was able to move against the man who did hold Tong status, from Chang's district of Canton. Legend has it that Chang personally killed the man, not without suffering an injury in return, an injury that gave him his nickname, as well as the name of his Tong. Now he was official, and that allowed him to take over the opium and slave traffic." Moore closed his notebook. "Do you mind if I smoke?" he asked Jessie.

"Not at all." After a moment she asked, "What was his injury?"

Moore extracted a long, thin cheroot from a leather case. "Pardon me?"

"You mentioned that Chang suffered an injury that gave him his nickname . . ."

"Oh, yes . . ." Moore thumbnail-flicked a match and puffed his cheroot alight. He exhaled a perfect, blue-gray smoke ring, and while contemplating it, he said, "His rival managed to lop Chang's right hand off. Now he wears a five-taloned metal gauntlet where his hand used to be, and is known as the Steel Claw." He took another puff of his cigar. "I understand that it is a formidible weapon . . ."

"Just incredible!" Lewis beamed. "You are to be congratulated, Jordan. To have learned so much about the head of a Tong! How ever did you pry the information out of Chinatown?"

"I didn't, Arthur," Moore smiled. "There's no way a Caucasian can get anywhere in Chinatown, these days. The Chinese are too wary, too frightened." Moore scowled as he flicked his cigar's ash into a sand-filled, standing ashtray next to his armchair. "You can blame Dennis Kearney for that."

"Earlier today, Mr. Kearney's name was thrown into my face," Ki said.

"And so it would be," Moore replied sardonically. "Pardon my curiosity, but are you—"

"I am of Japanese heritage," Ki explained patiently. "And I should think curiosity was a requirement of your profession," he added, his smile fleeting but unmistakable.

Moore's easy grin reappeared. "Kearney's a soapbox orator who has managed to get himself a following made up primarily of unskilled workers. These men are being forced out of their jobs by Chinese who are willing to work for a pittance. The Chinese and Japanese aren't the only targets of Kearney's Workingmen's Party. He often rants about the wealthy as well. His followers are mostly decent folks, angry and bitter over their economic situation, but decent nonetheless. Unfortunately, some bad apples have caused a few ugly incidents. There have been lynchings in Chinatown, and just recently, a poor Japanese fellow was clubbed to death in Japantown."

"I didn't know there was such a place," Jessie said.

"Yes, there are some ten thousand Japanese living together in a neighborhood huddled on the fringe of Chinatown," Ki informed her.

"As compared to the fifty thousand Chinese living in Chinatown," Moore added.

"Well, then, if it wasn't in Chinatown, where *did* you find out so much about the Tong?" Jessie demanded.

Once again, Lewis blushed. Why, even the ever-brash Moore seemed slightly embarrassed, from the way he lowered his eyes in order to avoid Jessie's frank stare. "Will you two stop acting like bashful schoolboys and come out with it?" Jessie groaned, totally confounded.

"I already explained to her about the . . . bordello . . ." Lewis shrugged. "Just come out with it, man."

"Well, the bordello is where I did most of my investigating," Moore began, his voice tentative. "This is difficult to explain to a woman. I decided to pose as the wastrel son of an Oregon lumber tycoon. Fortunately, San Francisco is large enough, and I'm obscure enough, so that I was able to infiltrate the right after-hours clubs with my cover intact in order to meet the people who could get me into that bordello. I threw around a lot of money—*your* money, actually, Miss Starbuck." Moore chuckled. "I made it known that I was looking to smuggle Chinese coolies into Oregon to work at my father's lumber mill. In that way I gained an introduction to Chang himself." Moore shuddered. "I must say, looking into the old devil's eyes, and seeing that steel claw of his, certainly made me wonder if I was going to have to move out of San Francisco after this job is finished. Anyway, many of the city's so-called leaders—business executives, government officials, and so on—frequent the bordello, which, by the way, is extravagantly, wonderfully luxurious . . ." Moore's voice trailed away.

"I expect we'll see the costs of those luxuries on your expenses bill," Jessie murmured hotly. "Would you mind telling me what my money bought?"

"Yes, *ma'am*," Moore winked, taking another puff of his cigar. "First of all, it bought me the acquaintance of Harris Smith, the waterfront commissioner. After I'd picked up enough bar chits, he became quite friendly and talkative. He even offered to open up the port to me. The deal was that I'd pay Chang to bring in the coolies, and pay a small bribe to Moore for letting them slip into the city. How I was to get my slaves to Oregon was to be my problem."

"Wonderful!" Lewis enthused. "You see, Jessie? My plan in working! We can set up Moore's payment to Smith so that newspaper men can document it! The mayor will have to fire him!"

"Chang later approached me with the offer to ship the coolies directly to the Oregon coast, thereby cutting out Smith, and saving me—and my daddy—some money," Moore scowled. "Old Chang wanted to get his steel claw into the lumber business, I could see it in his eyes, which were as cold as those of the fish he used to butcher..."

"Chang has clippers of his own?" Ki asked.

"Some," Moore replied. "But these days he likes using iron-hulled three-masters and the new waterfront steam donkeys for unloading heavy cargo that belongs to a European-based business cartel. In order to reassure me that he could indeed deliver the coolies, he introduced me to the representative of this cartel."

"He was also a frequent guest of the bordello, I take it?" Jessie asked dryly.

"I never knew that about old Burkhardt," Lewis chuckled in response to Moore's nod. "So the old devil had his flings, eh?"

"Burkhardt and I became quite good drinking cronies," Moore boasted. "He'd get soused and then bitterly complain about how this cartel he worked for was replacing him—"

"That *I* could have told you," Lewis interrupted. "Let's get back to my plan to expose Smith's corruption."

"No," Jessie said, her voice polite, but steel-firm, so that there was no question as to who was in charge. "Smith is small fry. What we've got to do is disrupt the partnership between the cartel and the Tong. Smith will fall when they do. Only then will the Starbuck enterprises be able to thrive peacefully."

"Jessie," Lewis sighed, "you must not let the past influence your judgement. We cannot exterminate either the Tong or the cartel. Smith ought to be our main concern."

"Arthur, I disagree," Jessie declared flatly, but the warning look in Ki's eyes made her pause, think, and then soften her tone. "Dear Uncle," she smiled. "Up until now, the one constant mistake the Starbucks have made is in letting the cartel have the first strike. My father made that mistake, and it cost my mother's life. Years later he made it again, and that time it cost him his life. The cartel has started this skirmish by disrupting our commerce. Soon they will resort to violence. This time, I mean to strike the first blow!" Turning to Moore, she asked, "Did you, by any chance, discover the identity of the Prussian who will take over from Burkhardt?"

"I did," Moore replied.

After a moment's silence, Jessie demanded, "Well? What is his name?"

Moore looked apologetically at Lewis, and then confronted Jessie. "I don't think I'm going to tell you."

"But Jordan!" Lewis gasped, clearly astounded. "Why not?"

"I think I know," Jessie sighed. "You want more money, Mr. Moore, am I correct?"

"No, Miss Starbuck, you are *not* correct," Moore shot back, his temper rising. "You may have trouble understanding this, lady, but there are some things in my job I won't do. For instance, I won't compromise or in any way contribute to harming an innocent person, just because the folks who are paying me harbor some grudge."

"But you were willing to help me bring down Commissioner Smith," Lewis began.

"That's different." Moore shrugged, lowering his eyes to inspect the glowing tip of his cheroot. "Smith is a crook, and that makes him fair game. As far as I know, the person coming in to head up this Prussian cartel is innocent of everything but wanting to do a good job. Sure, this cartel made a deal with the Tong, but that's no reason for Miss Starbuck here wanting to—as she puts it—strike the first blow against the representative."

"I have good reason for wanting to battle the cartel," Jessie said.

Moore nodded noncommittally. "If you say so. I never argue with a lady."

"But I do!" she cried in exasperation.

"So go battle them," Moore said lazily. "But I don't intend to help."

"Jordan," Lewis interrupted, "I do think we've already paid for this last bit of information Miss Starbuck wants . . ."

"Then I'll refund that part of your advance, minus my expenses, of course, Arthur," Moore offered. "And we can call it quits." Moore set his cigar down in the ashtray and sat forward, his expression intensely serious, as he continued, "You all have to understand that I often work outside the law. That means I have to formulate my own rules of conduct. I don't want anything to do with some mysterious grudge—"

Ki got to his feet. "Perhaps Mr. Moore would tell *me* what you wish to know, Jessie," he growled, advancing on the seated private detective.

Quick as a flash, Moore reached beneath the left side of his coat, bringing out a pistol. The harsh *click!* of the gun's hammer being cocked echoed in the now-silent room.

"You're a lot stronger than I am, Ki," Moore smiled. "And from the look of you, you've probably spent a lot of years training yourself. Now, I know a little bit about Oriental fighting techniques. I've even studied a bit of Chinese boxing with a willing teacher in Chinatown." He hefted his pistol. "I'd hate to see all your years of effort disappear in a cloud of smoke."

"If you fire, you will miss," Ki warned.

"And that's what's called betting your life, friend," Moore said evenly, but his smile had faded.

"Ki, please sit down," Jessie said. "And you, Mr. Moore, please put away your gun." She tilted her head to get a better look at the weapon. "Unless I miss my guess, that's a double-action Colt Model T. The Thunderer, it's called. A .44-caliber."

"Good Lord," Moore laughed. "How did you come by *that* sort of expertise?"

"You mean because I'm a woman?" Jessie smiled back. "Perhaps someday I'll tell *you* something." She winked. "I see you've modified your pistol."

Moore held the gun in profile. "I've sawed off all but two inches of its original six-inch barrel," he explained. "I really have little call for distance shooting." He uncocked the pistol and slipped it back into the shoulder holster beneath his coat.

"What would you have done if you had not had your firearm?" Ki asked.

"I have it almost all the time, actually," Moore said good-naturedly. "I do apologize for pointing it at you, but I really did not want you to rip my head off."

Ki chuckled. "In that case..." He waved away their confrontation.

"Gentlemen, please!" Lewis moaned in exasperation. "We seem to be at an impasse. Jordan, if Jessie were to tell you why we need to know the new representative's identity? Might that change your mind?"

Moore nodded slowly. "It might."

"Arthur, it's really private business—" Jessie began.

"Excuse me," Ki interrupted, "but we need the information, and if we do not get it from Mr. Moore, we must seek it out ourselves. That would be both time-consuming and dangerous."

After a few seconds' hesitation, Jessie had to agree. "Very well. Mr. Moore, I ask you to keep this in strictest confidence."

Moore nodded, picking up his cheroot and relighting it. "I will if I can, but I have a partner, and if he needs to know some or all of this, I will tell him. Fair enough?"

"Agreed," Jessie said, impressed, in spite of herself, with Moore's straightforwardness. "At the time of my father's murder, he ran our enterprises from our cattle ranch in Texas."

"That's the Starbuck ranch," Moore said. "I've heard of it. It's supposed to be huge. It's where you really grew up, eh? And, I suppose, where you learned about guns?"

"And about roping and riding and a lot of other things, as well. Anyway, my father was shot dead in an ambush staged on our own land by agents of the Prussian cartel."

Moore frowned. "Arthur?"

"It's all true," Lewis assured him. "It's been substantiated by the federal government's own investigators. Jessie and Ki, along with a deputy United States marshal named Long, brought the actual killers to justice, at the same time foiling the cartel's plot to take over the Texas cattle industry."

"I'm impressed," Moore said with unfeigned sincerity.

"The murder of my father was not the beginning of the violence between the Starbuck empire and the Prussians," Jessie continued. "But they hoped it would be the final blow in their campaign to illegally take control of America's political and business establishment. The war actually began long before my birth, when my father first confronted these villains in the Japans. During a series of bloody trade wars between the two

31

business concerns, the Prussian cartel was responsible for the murder of my mother." Jessie paused. "I was only a child, then."

Moore watched the play of passions and memories drift across Jessie's lovely face, the way dark storm clouds will slowly fill a lovely summer sky. Her large green eyes grew shiny, and for one awful moment he was worried that she was going to cry. But no. Moore saw that she was made of sterner stuff than that. "Were your mother's murderers ever caught?" he asked.

"No, but my father retaliated by personally killing the only son of his chief Prussian adversary, the man responsible for issuing the orders to have my mother killed." The look of steely determination was back on Jessie's face. "That awful exchange of familial violence capped the bloodshed for some years."

"An eye for an eye," Moore observed.

"Until my father was struck down." This time it was Jessie who leaned forward in her chair in order to lock Moore's eyes with her own. "Ki and I travel the country in order to thwart the schemes sponsored by the cartel. I've got the resources of Starbuck Enterprises, and the guidance of a diary of leads that my father compiled down through the years. He'd hired private detectives, you see. Men like yourself. They told him of the various representatives of the cartel—crooked politicians, lawmen, businessmen, and outlaws—who are attempting to entrench these foreign powers in our nation."

Moore pondered what he'd been told. "I had no idea. I mean, I thought it was—"

"Will you help us, Mr. Moore?" Jessie asked softly.

"Wild horses couldn't keep me out of something like this, and please call me Jordan." He looked at Ki. "Both of you."

Ki nodded. "I would be honored. Now, the name of the Prussian representative? Who is he?"

Moore laughed. "What makes you think it has to be a man?"

Ki, Jessie, and Lewis looked at each other, obviously taken aback. Ki's face began to redden noticeably, and Jessie said, "Ki, what's wrong?"

"Nothing," Ki replied hastily, but a dreadful thought had occurred to him. He looked steadily at Moore. "What is *her* name, then?" he asked, though he was sure he already knew the answer.

"Greta Kahr," Moore said.

Jessie was still staring curiously at Ki. He felt the pressure of her gaze, and turned to face her.

"I met her this morning," he said. "When I went back to fetch our luggage, there was an attempted purse-snatching. This woman was the intended victim. I, uh, foiled the thieves."

Moore took out his little notebook and a pencil stub. "Do you think you can describe her for me?" he asked.

Ki's face reddened to an even deeper shade, and Jessie had to conceal a smile as she remembered Ki's tardiness in arriving at their hotel. "Go on, Ki," she said. "Tell Mr. Moore what the lady—to give her the benefit of the doubt—looked like. I'm sure you got quite a good look at her . . ."

★

Chapter 3

The morning after their meeting with Jordan Moore in Arthur
Lewis's office, Jessie and Ki went down to the waterfront.
Lewis had offhandedly mentioned that a Starbuck clipper was
scheduled for unloading today. Jessie did not want to miss this
opportunity to witness this first, vital link in the chain that
made up the Starbuck fortune.

The day had begun gray and cloudy, with a wind-driven,
slanting drizzle that made the cobblestone streets glisten. But
by the time Jessie and Ki had paid their five-cent fares to ride
the Market Street cable car back to the Ferry Building, and had
strolled north along the Embarcadero, the sun had broken
through the woolly gray of the overcast sky.

A strong, hot sun had soon dried the last drops of rain off
the smooth, stone-surfaced Embarcadero, the huge, manmade
esplanade that had taken decades to build and had added dozens
of blocks to downtown San Francisco. Before it was built,
deep-water ships usually ended up scuttled in the mud flats that
had reached to what was now the very fashionable and completely dry Montgomery Street.

But now the big three-masters could come directly to shore.
Jessie and Ki wandered past the ships, staring up with awe at
the spiderweb rigging of the cargo vessles, and trying to stay
out of the way of the swarms of denim- and canvas-garbed
longshoremen. Like ants swarming over the carcass of a dead
grasshopper, the longshoremen would disappear into the hold
of a ship, to reappear, each man lugging a wooden crate or
rag-wrapped bale of goods. Workhorses, their big, blunt heads

35

drooping patiently, stood still except for their fly-whisking tails as the rough-paneled carts they were hitched to were filled with, or emptied of goods. Jessie's and Ki's ears were filled with the squawking of gulls, the cries and shouts of the dock workers, and the hissing and clanking of the steam donkeys that were more and more replacing both animal and human muscle power for lifting and lowering heavy loads.

As they walked, Jessie and Ki spotted the flags of a score of companies flying from the masts of the docked clippers. The larger concerns, sensitive to public opinion, used longshore teams comprised of Caucasians, while the smaller, less established companies hired Chinese, who were supervised by white foremen. Nowhere during their walk did Jessie and Ki see a team where the two races were working side by side.

At last they reached the Starbuck ship. Flying from the mainmast of the docked clipper, and from a flagpole atop the cargo shed on the dock, were the Stars and Stripes and, just below it, the yellow pennant on which was emblazoned in red the Circle Star, the insignia of the Starbuck empire. The emblem, a five-pointed star enclosed in a circle, was branded on Starbuck cattle; it was stenciled on the crates of Starbuck goods that crisscrossed the country and the oceans; it was carved into the ivory grips of the derringer pressing so snugly against Jessie's thigh; it was even embroidered into a corner of her lace hankies!

A dock foreman, holding a clipboard, watched over the longshoremen who were tossing from man to man the crates of tea and spices and bolts of silk that made up this particular consignment. Finally they were stacked in Starbuck-marked dray wagons. Jessie and Ki stood well away from the action, and no one noticed them.

"I shall introduce you to the foreman," Ki said.

"No." Jessie took hold of his arm. "I'd rather they didn't know I'm here. I just want to see how it's done, Ki. I just want to watch it all happen, the way it happened when I was a little girl and my father was still alive."

Ki nodded, and left her to her memories. His own thoughts drifted back to his homeland, to the stern chain of islands that made up *Nippon*, the Land of the Rising Sun. His memories were nostalgic, but they were not happy. In *Nippon*, Ki had been considered a barbarian's offspring, a half-breed, a mongrel not fit for society.

He glanced at Jessie, so lovely in profile, her eyes half closed, dreamy with fond memories. What was she thinking of? Her blond-haired, blue-eyed father who smelled of the cherry pipe tobacco he smoked, and fragrant green tea and spices he imported? Of his worn leather jacket that—when she was little—smelled of the salty sea, and when she was an adult, carried the honest scent of clean, healthy horseflesh?

"Yes," Ki said, so abruptly that Jessie was startled. "Yes, your father's *kami* is here," he continued. "He watches over the men working, and he is proud to see that his daughter does the same."

Jessie, beaming, rose up on her toes to plant a soft kiss on Ki's cheek. "Then let's leave," she said. "All's well."

His cheek still tingling where her lips had touched, Ki took her arm to lead her away from this place so filled with bittersweet memories for both of them. Suddenly he stopped and raised a hand to point at a pennant snapping in the breeze above a nearby ship. The flag bore the insignia of one of the shipping companies that either belonged directly to the cartel or paid the organization a percentage of their profits for the privilege of being allowed to remain in business.

"The cartel's shipping dock!" Jessie exclaimed. "Let's see what's going on there!"

The dock and cargo shed were much the same, but the loading crews were not at all like those manning the Starbuck slip. Here, a rough-looking, unshaven dockmaster holding a billy club sauntered back and forth along the planking, goading his men to work ever faster. The workers were all Chinese, but unlike the other Oriental crews working the waterfront, these men wore the garb of coolies. They had no shoes to protect their feet, nor gloves for their hands as they scampered past the club-wielding foreman. The Chinese were thin and sickly. Some looked as if they would not last out the day's hard labor.

"These men are being used as slaves," Ki seethed. "It is clear that they receive only pennies—if that much—for their work."

"I'd love to know what contraband they're being forced to unload," Jessie replied. "Come on, let's go see—"

"Just what do you folks want?" came a voice from behind them.

Ki and Jessie turned to confront a large, corduroy-suited

figure holding a mean-looking, snarling dog on a short length of braided leather leash.

"We're just tourists out to see the sights!" Jessie remarked innocently, batting her eyes at the guard while Ki nonchalantly tugged lower the brim of his Stetson. From past experience he knew that his height, his garb, and his Caucasian features allowed him to pass as a non-Oriental as long as he kept his eyes shaded. He did not want this man to report back to his superiors that Jessica Starbuck had been spotted snooping about. A man and a woman could pass as just another tourist couple, but a woman of Jessie's beauty, accompanied by a half-Japanese, was another matter entirely! It was just his good luck that his encounter with Greta Kahr yesterday morning had ended as well as it did. Obviously she had just arrived—as had Jessie and Ki—and had not yet received a briefing on her enemies. Today she doubtless realized, as Ki now did, that she had made love with an arch-rival.

"You two go do your sightseeing somewhere else," the guard warned gruffly. "This here's private property."

The dog, a big, ugly brute, dull yellow in color, with a squashed-in face, drooled spittle from its loose black jowls as it shifted its attention back and forth between Jessie and Ki. All the while, a low, constant snarl vibrated from its throat, and the short fur along its spine stood stiff.

"Easy, boy," the guard muttered. As he bent to pat the dog, his corduroy jacket gaped open, revealing the worn wooden butt of a revolver shoved into his belt.

"Come, dear," Ki urged, before Jessie could say anything else. "We'd best be getting back to the hotel."

"You just do that," the guard guffawed, his eyes on Jessie's bouncing bottom as Ki hurriedly pulled her along.

Jessie waited until they were out of sight, as well as earshot, before digging in her heels. "I wish we could have gotten a glimpse of what it was those poor men were unloading," she sighed. "That sort of information would have been very useful in building a case against Commissioner Smith."

"Oh, we will find that out, all right," Ki remarked. "I pulled you away like that because I did not want the guard to take special notice of us."

"We do sort of stand out," Jessie admitted. "You're going back on your own, I take it?"

"I would like to," Ki said slowly. "But I am concerned about your safety."

"Don't be," Jessie reassured him. "I have my derringer with me, you know. What I'll do is take a cable car back, and do some of that shopping I'm so looking forward to. I'll meet you back at the hotel lobby. We're to meet Moore there at two."

Ki nodded. Moore had suggested that his partner, a man named Shanks, take over the job of concentrating on getting evidence against the corrupt waterfront commissioner. Moore, after first offering to act as Jessie's bodyguard, a gesture that Ki found immensely amusing, was going to build upon his tentative relationship with the Tong leader Chang to see if he could infiltrate the cartel.

After seeing Jessie safely off the docks and onto a cable car, Ki returned to the cartel's ship. The guard and his dog were nowhere to be seen, but there was still the billy-club-wielding foreman to get past.

Ki slipped beneath the stiff, salt-encrusted ropes barricading the actual loading area from the esplanade, and sauntered up to the foreman, whose attention was focused on the coolies. As the foreman turned, Ki pressed his stiffened fingers against the man's neck. The clipboard and club fell to the planking as the men slumped first to his knees, and then over on his side, out cold.

Ki grabbed the man's legs and pulled him flush alongside a stack of crates protected with a canvas tarp. He pulled the tarp lower to cover the unconscious body, and then stood back to survey his camouflage attempt. He doubted that the other guard would connect an extra bump in the lumpy canvas with the missing man. As for the coolies, they were all studiously avoiding Ki's eyes and simply continuing on with their work, as if nothing had happened. He doubted that any of them knew enough English to inform the guard, even assuming they felt they had a reason to . . .

Right now, time was Ki's only worry. The *atemi* technique he had used against the foreman, the sudden sharp pressure against a vital nerve center, was much more silent and faster than any hand or foot strike. But whereas Ki could, from long experience, gauge how long an adversary would remain unconscious after one of his more violent strikes, there was no way to know how long the effects of an *atemi* technique would

39

last on any given opponent. That the foreman would soon wake up wondering what had happened to him was a certainty, but *how* soon was the question.

Ki kicked the billy club into the water, picked up the fallen clipboard, and strolled up the gangplank, past the scurrying coolies who now kowtowed to him as if he were their new foreman.

On board the ship, using the pencil attached by a string to the clipboard to scribble nonsense, Ki began to make his way toward the cargo hold. He came across three men in long-shoremen's canvas garb, lounging on the deck. These men were white, and content to merely watch the coolies work as they passed a bottle of rum among themselves. Ki stopped short, hoping to back off and come around another way before he was noticed, but it was too late.

"Who the hell are you?" one of the men spat. "Where's Willie?"

Keeping his Stetson's brim low, Ki approached them. "Willie's busy. I've been sent down to take a special tally of the goods."

"We don't know nothing about that," another of the men muttered. "You just shove off before you get hurt."

Ki quickly scanned the clipboard. At the top was a printed form a half-sheet of paper long. In the space marked "Foreman" was scrawled the first name, Willie, and in the three spaces designated "Crew Supervisors" were written the names Tom, Matty, and George.

"You get off this ship, hear?" one of the trio now warned, rising to his feet and unbuttoning his coat. On the deck beside him was a baling hook. The man bent down and picked it up, all the time keeping his menacing scowl on Ki. As he straightened up, Ki noticed that the man's belt buckle was an oval plate that framed a raised, nickel-plated *M*.

"Take it easy, Matty," he said, turning back the way he'd come.

"Wait a minute!" the man ordered. "How'd you know my name?"

"See you around," Ki said matter-of-factly. He made a vague gesture toward the other two. "And Tom and George. I've seen you all around. No need to get so hot under the collar. I'm leaving. I'll just tell *her* that it was you three who—"

"Just hold on now!" Matty interrupted hastily. *"Who* are you going to tell?"

"Miss Kahr, of course."

"Oh, Christ!" one of the other two—either George or Tom—piped up. "Don't do that, man! She'll skin us for sure!"

"Don't I wish old man Burkhardt was still running things," Matty winced, shaking his head. "He was all right, he was."

"But Miss Kahr is certainly prettier," Ki bantered. "What with those big, violet eyes of hers..."

"You talk like you know her pretty good," Matty said thoughtfully. "Look, I'm sorry about before, but we was just doing our job, right?" He looked down to see the grappling hook still clutched in his hand, and hastily dropped it. "You go right ahead with whatever it is you're doing, sir," he continued, his voice now meek and mild.

"Right, then," Ki said crisply. "See you later, boys." He sauntered past them, smiling to himself. *Sir!* But of course. At this point none of them would dare admit that they'd forgotten his name!

Ki climbed down the narrow ladder, into the main cargo hold. There were two coolies waiting to climb up, and one whose bare feet were on the rungs just above his head.

"Matty!" Ki shouted up toward the square patch of blue sky framed by the hold's open bay.

"Yessir?" came Matty's faint reply.

"Keep these men out of the hold until I'm done with my tally!"

"Yessir!"

Ki continued on down the ladder, all the way to the bottom. The two coolies, who had respectfully stood aside, now climbed up. When they were gone, Ki was totally alone in the bowels of the cartel's ship.

A long, dark corridor, lit only by the shaft of light beaming down through the open bay, led to the cargo area. Ki's shoulders brushed either side of the corridor's mildewed walls as he hurried down it, breathing through his mouth so as not to smell the filthy stench of the ill-ventilated place. As he walked, he listened to the high-pitched squeaks and dry scrabbling of the rats that thrived in the hold.

By the time he'd reached the cargo area itself, it was completely dark. Ki wondered how the coolies knew what they were hoisting onto their backs. He struck a match, and in its

41

flickering circle of light he spied a kerosene lamp hanging from a nail hammered into a splintery crossbeam. The lamp's wick sputtered, but finally lit. The lamp hissed softly, its light driving back the shadows—and the rats—to the hold's farthest corners.

Stacked ten feet high were row upon row of wooden crates. Ki went to a case lying where one of the coolies had left it. Its lid was nailed tight. Ki formed the fingers of his right hand into a one-knuckle fist, focused his mind, and struck straight down, driving his knuckle into the wood. There was the hiss and rasp of Ki's sharp exhalation, and the crack of the lid splintering. Ki tossed the shards of wood aside.

He had to tear through several layers of oily brown paper before he reached the crate's contents, but long before that, the sweet, pungent smell rising up told him what he needed to know.

Opium. The rough-hewn bricks of the narcotic looked almost black in the kerosene lamp's illumination. Ki pinched off a bit and rubbed it between his finger and thumb. It was sticky and malleable, potent with the juice of the opium poppy. Ki quickly examined the rest of the crates; all were the same, and most likely, all were filled with blocks of opium. He hefted the crate he'd opened. It weighed about seventy-five pounds.

Rows upon rows of crates, stacked ten feet high . . .

Seventy-five pounds of potent narcotic, multiplied by so many rows, each ten feet high . . .

He thought about the barefoot, frightened, sickly coolies on board this one vessel, and how they would soon join their fifty thousand brothers in the fetid squalor of Chinatown. No wonder the countless opium dens of the area were filled to capacity! Homesick and hopeless, the Chinese flocked to the dark havens where they could escape into their sweet dreams of home, and fantasies of the future, while the opium further weakened their already ravaged bodies.

Behind him, Ki heard a thud, and the scratching of claws too large for any rat scrabbling for purchase on the smooth wooden planking. There came the sound of wet panting, and then a deep-throated growl.

Ki saw the silhouette of the guard dog as it stood at the head of the corridor, just out of the soft light coming down from the open bay.

The dog, all shoulders and massive head, began padding

down the corridor, straight toward Ki. From its throat there came that low, constant growl, rising to a snarl as Ki stepped into the corridor to meet the big animal.

Ki felt his body flood with adrenaline. The hold seemed to fill with odor as the animal lifted its hind leg in order to piss against the corridor wall. The canine was establishing its mastery of the hold. It was issuing its challenge to battle.

Beneath his jacket, Ki's shirt was sticking to his back. He felt fear crawling through him, but fought it. If the dog sensed it, all would be lost.

The dog was a problem. The corridor was too low and narrow for Ki to feint and dodge the dog's attack. He would have to stand his ground, meeting the brute head on, in order to kill it.

That he could kill the lumbering brute, Ki had no doubt. But he would have to do it with his hands. The narrow corridor would not allow him to get a shot at the dog's side with his *shuriken* blades, and the canine's low-hanging head protected its chest. Ki doubted that a *shuriken* tossed from this short distance away would be able to penetrate the dog's massive skull.

Ki would have to kill the dog with his hands. But the animal's powerful jaws could easily rip his arm from its socket.

It would be little comfort for Ki to know the dog was dead, if it had his severed arm in its lifeless jaws. He himself would end up helpless, and in the cartel's cruel clutches.

No, battling this four-footed killer on its own ground could lead only to his own defeat...

Ki could not fight the dog. So he would have to *charm* it.

It was called *ninpō inubue*—the ancient *ninja* technique of training animals such as monkeys, wolves, birds of prey, and dogs against an enemy. More than one hapless samurai had lost his eyes to the *ninpō inubue*-trained crow of an adversary, as the bird swooped down like some angry *shura*, or fighting demon, to pluck out his precious orbs. Huge, bearlike *akita* watchdogs often prowled the nighttime halls of Japanese nobles' castles, so that the guards could sleep, and in that way be refreshed for the next day's battle.

But every technique had a counter-technique. It was possible for the prepared samurai to distract the attacking crow by throwing bright coins into the air. It was possible for the infiltrating, black-clad *ninja* to ally himself with his enemy's watchdogs...

43

Ki began to breath in a deep and regular rhythm, focusing his *ki*—the physical and spiritual energy-substance that pervades the universe, and from which Ki had taken his chosen name—so that it flowed outward toward the now confused, but still wary beast.

Ki began to move toward the dog. He was careful to keep his steps feather-light, to allow no vibrations to travel through the wooden floor to the dog, thereby breaking the fragile spell. During Ki's years of training in the *bugei,* or martial arts, he had learned to walk on fragile, eggshell-thin, porcelain teacups without breaking them. This was how he now walked. An insect would not have been crushed beneath the leather soles of his Wellington boots.

The beast's growl still sounded. It stretched its neck out and up, angling its blunt head to peer at Ki's face. Not trusting its weak eyes, the dog's wet black nostrils widened as it sniffed this thing's scent, so manlike, yet so unlike any man it had ever confronted.

Ki did not look directly at the dog, but kept his eyes averted, watching the animal with his peripheral vision. To lock eyes with a beast was to challenge it, and Ki had no intention of doing so. Let the dog challenge *him;* it was always the challenger who was in the less secure position.

Ki began to speak to the dog, not in English, but in Japanese. He did not want to take the chance of inadvertently blurting some trick phrase—"good fellow," "nice dog"—that the animal's trainers might have drummed into its brain as the signal to instantly attack whoever uttered it. In any event, except for such training phrases, it was the tone of a man's voice that mattered with animals, not what was being said.

Now he was less than six feet away from the dog. Once again the low growl became a warning snarl. Ki knew that from the dog's point of view, he was now taller than the space separating them was long. This was the moment of truth. The dog had to decide whether it wanted to fight or capitulate.

Its hackles rose as its instincts took command. The ruffling of its fur was to make it seem larger to Ki, and in that way, help to intimidate him.

Ki rose up on his own toes, and now stared directly down at the dog. He gripped the two sides of his suit jacket and held them wide, like bat's wings, to further increase his mass, the

44

way certain birds will fluff their feathers and stretch their wings to frighten foes.

The dog's pointed ears flattened against its skull, and its lips pulled back to show still more yellowed fangs as its eyes narrowed. Its snarl rose in pitch as the animal became more and more tightly wound.

"Hi!" Ki sounded his *kiai,* the sharp, sudden shout delivered with the breath's exhalation, intended to shock the enemy and help focus one's *ki.* At the same time he raised his knee to deliver a front snap-kick, square on the dog's wet, sensitive nose. The kick was soundly executed, but Ki doubted that it would register as much more than a cuff. It did not matter. Ki had not meant to injure the dog, but to startle it and establish his mastery over it.

The animal leapt back, at the same time issuing a surprised yelp. Then it lowered its head and shoved its broad snout between Ki's knees.

Firmly, Ki patted the animal's side—soft touches excited animals, while firm touches calmed them—and scratched its ears.

The hard muscles beneath the dog's skin quivered with pleasure. It licked Ki's hand.

He stepped past the dog, into the patch of light coming down from the open cargo bay. He began to climb up the ladder.

"Yes sir, Commissioner Smith!"

It was the voice of the one named Matty. Ki climbed silently up the last few rungs of the ladder and peeked out over the rim of the open cargo bay. He saw the three crew supervisors, the guard he and Jessie had confronted earlier, and a short, fat fellow, nattily dressed in a three-piece suit of crushed red velvet. The man's black derby was in his hand. His reddish-brown, thinning hair was worn slicked back, and his mustache was neatly clipped.

"As soon as Willie gets back, I'll see that he gets this, Commissioner," Matty was saying. He tapped a blunt forefinger against the sheet of paper in his hand. "This is slick! 'Tea,' it says here. A ton of tea."

"That's what the official record will read," Smith agreed, his hoarse, gravelly voice suggesting that he'd spent more than this one day in the damp, salty air of the waterfront. "I wanted

45

to sign the duty sheet on this load of goods myself," the commissioner continued. "No one will dare question it now."

Ki shook his head sadly. The cartel would pay the trifling duty imposed on tea, and then would have a perfect cover for their crates of opium. No wonder the profits shared by the cartel and the Tong were so huge!

"You make sure Willie gets that when he returns," Smith instructed Matty as Ki climbed the rest of the way out of the hold and came toward them.

"I forgot *you* was here, sir!" Matty beamed.

"Not you again!" the guard exploded angrily. "Where's Bart? Bart! Here, boy!"

The dog bounded up the ladder and onto the deck. On its way to its master, it paused to nuzzle Ki's hand.

"What the hell?" the guard muttered in consternation. "What'd you do to my dog, you son of a bitch?"

"Christ, Terry," Matty hissed out of the side of his mouth, while still smiling at Ki. "Don't you know who he *is?*"

"No," the guard named Terry snorted.

"You don't?" Matty asked, turning his face toward the guard.

Ki took the opportunity to drive his fist into Matty's stomach. The crew supervisor dropped like a stone.

"Bart! Sic 'em!" Terry the guard screamed. The dog took a tentative step toward Ki, and then looked inquiringly at its master.

"*Somebody* sic him!" Commissioner Smith groaned as he hurried away toward the gangplank.

Ki stooped to snatch up and stuff in his pocket the duty sheet lying crumpled between the fallen Matty's limply curled fingers. The other two crew supervisors were now closing in. One was armed with a baling hook, while the other flashed a glittering stiletto. The guard, Terry, was clawing for the revolver in his belt.

The gun had to be disposed of first, Ki decided. Still facing the two crew supervisors, so as to slow them down, Ki crabbed sideways, toward the guard. The man's outstretched arm was just bringing the pistol to bear on Ki when the samurai executed a *yoko-geri-keage,* or sideways foot strike. Ki had never even looked at Terry, but his foot still hit the guard's wrist perfectly. The revolver went flying end over end, over the ship's side, to land in the water with a satisfying splash.

The gawking coolies who'd been watching all the action now laughed and applauded Ki's prowess. Ki gave them a smile.

"Shut up! Shut up!" Terry screamed at the coolies in frustration. He circled around to charge Ki's back as the other two—the crew supervisors—went for the samurai from the front, awkwardly waving their weapons.

The barking dog darted to and fro in excitment. The animal gave Ki an idea. He had no wish to kill. The very clumsiness with which they handled their weapons revealed that they were not professional warriors. No, he would not kill them...

"Bart!" Ki commanded in clear, firm tones, at the same time driving his elbow straight back in a devastating *empi-uchi* strike, catching Terry in the chest. The dog's head instantly snapped upward in attention as its previous master crumpled, moaning, to the deck. "Bart!" Ki repeated, and pointed at the hook-wielding man. "Sic him!"

"No!" the man wailed. In utter panic, he dropped his hook and turned to run. The dog covered the space between them in one bound, to clamp its snarling jaws on the baggy seat of the longshoreman's overalls. Screaming either in pain or fear— Ki wasn't sure which—the man ran for the far side of the clipper, the dog right with him, its jaws chewing and mauling while a deep growl hummed from its throat. The unlucky crew supervisor threw himself overboard. The dog braced its front paws against the gunwale and held on.

The man dangled for a moment before the suspenders of his overalls gave way. There was a sharp tearing sound, and then the man's long, high-pitched wail as he plummeted the fifteen feet into the chilled waters of the bay. The dog turned and pranced back toward Ki, proudly displaying the torn and tattered overalls that it still held in its mouth.

The stiletto man was so mesmerized by what had happened to his comrade that Ki was able to simply reach out and twist the man's wrist. The stiletto fell, point-first, to stick into the wooden planking of the deck. The crew supervisor, his wrist still held by Ki, attempted a clumsy, roundhouse left at the samurai. Ki caught that wrist as well, and then bent both of the man's wrists backward. The howling crew supervisor had no choice but to fall down in order to ease the excruciating agony in his wrists.

Matty, the man Ki had earlier dropped with a stomach

47

punch, was just now on his hands and knees, attempting to push himself into an upright position. Ki took a running start and leaped, to land with both feet on Matty's back, pile-driving the fellow right back down onto his belly and chin. Ki used the man like a trampoline, to rise high into the air and somersault over the clipper's side, landing on his feet, safely on the dock.

Another scattering of applause came from the coolies. They were clearly happy to see their cruel taskmasters get their long-overdue comeuppance.

Commissioner Smith was busy untangling the now semiconscious foreman from beneath the canvas tarp where Ki had stashed him. As Ki ran past, his eyes locked with those of the commissioner.

Smith reached into the watch pocket of his vest and pulled out a derringer. But Ki had never stopped running. Within seconds he was around the corner, and well out of range of the miniature firearm.

Back near the Starbuck dock, Ki took the duty sheet out of his pocket to examine it. At the top of the sheet was inked the designation, *Shipment #8452*. At the sheet's bottom was Smith's signature. Ki next removed the splinter of wood he had cached away in the deep breast pocket of his suit coat. Stenciled upon it was the number 8452. Completing his souvenirs of the encounter was a small chunk of opium, pinched off from a larger block of the stuff, and now safely wrapped in a scrap of brown paper.

In all, it was not enough to get Smith convicted, but it was a start in the right direction. Ki thought Jessie would be pleased.

★

Chapter 4

Jessie spent several hours going from shop to shop along the Line, San Francisco's six blocks of renowned stores that began at the Baldwin Hotel, paraded down Market to Kearney Street, and then wound its way around Kearney to Bush Street. She bought a wide selection of fabrics to be shipped back to the Starbuck Ranch, for herself and for her housekeeper, Myobu. The glittering window of a cutlery shop next caught her eye. Inside, she bought a matched set of Sheffield steel throwing knives. They were imported from England, and came handsomely displayed in a velvet-lined wooden case. The bone handles of the knives were suitable for engraving. Jessie arranged for the etching of the Circle Star insignia, a message of endearment from herself to Ki, and the date. This gift, as well, would be delivered to the Starbuck office, and then shipped to the Texas ranch.

At a florist's shop she ordered bouquets of orchids sent to both her own and Ki's rooms. The stern, stoic samurai was also a Japanese; he would appreciate the beauty and grace of the floral arrangement even more than she did.

As Jessie walked, she dodged the colorfully frocked shop and office girls who flooded the lunchtime streets. She modestly returned the smiles and nods of the dapper gentlemen strolling along in their fine suits and derbies. How delightful it was to encounter men armed not with Colts and Winchesters, but with walking sticks and umbrellas!

The bay windows that were the most distinctive feature of San Francisco's architecture greatly amused her. The jutting windows were designed to catch every glimmer of available light in this often gloomy city of gray skies and tall, shadow-casting buildings.

Several times, Jessie dashed out into the center of the street, avoiding the dense traffic of horsedrawn cabs, private gigs, delivery wagons, and cable cars, in order to stare up at the stacked windows of the four-and five-storied buildings in this part of town. She had to remind herself that there were entire unexplored worlds above the ground-level shops. Not only watchmaking schools, painless dentists, and attorneys-at-law, but furriers, bootmakers, and fine jewelers.

But the dresses, shoes, hats and parasols displayed in the picture windows along Market Street gave Jessie plenty of window-shopping. Although she could afford just about anything in the world she wanted, she found it more fun to look than to buy. Somehow, knowing that she could have anything made Jessie feel as if she needed less. But it was certainly fun to look!

It was while she was standing beneath the awning of an exclusive silver and chinaware shop, evaluating the tea sets artfully arranged behind the store's plate glass window, that she first noticed him. She'd been thinking about how her own silver serving sets, crafted in Mexico, were nicer than the ones being offered here, when she caught his reflection. He was across the street behind her, but he was staring at her, and Jessie's instincts told her that this man was not just another admiring gentleman.

He was a very large man, dressed in an ill-fitting suit of blue wool. The derby perched on his head looked about three sizes too small. It tottered on the man's head. Jessie waited for a wind gust to send it sailing back to the little fellow this man had filched it from.

Jessie casually strolled past several doorways on Market Street, and then stopped to peer into the window of a haber-dashery. The storekeeper inside saw her looking, and enthu-siastically waved at her, beckoning her in.

Jessie paid no attention to the clerk, but positioned herself so that this window too acted as a mirror. The man across the way had kept her pace. He was still staring at her. Suddenly he turned his back to Jessie, perhaps sensing that she was really looking at him and not at the men's woollen scarves, silk ascots, and leather gloves behind the window. Jessie saw that the man was now staring into the window of a dress salon.

She smiled, fleetingly. *Too bad we can't trade windows,* she thought. The idea made her chuckle, but at the same time she felt herself sadden. For a little while this morning she had been able to forget her troubles and lose herself in the wonders of the city. Now it all flooded back up on her: the bitter rivalry that had cost her parents their lives, the crooked waterfront scheme that now endangered her business, the ever-present knowledge that her own life would never cease to be in danger.

Jessie continued walking. She turned the corner at Kearney, and headed north. Here there were more stores and shops, but now Jessie paid no attention to the fine merchandise displayed in their windows. Past Geary Street, Post Street, Sutter, and then Bush, she walked, all the time watching out of the corners of her eyes. Her shadow was staying right with her.

Years ago, Ki had taught her that there were several ways to handle a situation like this. If she was in a busy area, surrounded by people, the best thing to do was to simply turn and wave at the tail. Once he knew that he'd been spotted, he often gave up and went away. The thing was, Ki had cautioned her, that you then had to make sure there wasn't another tail somewhere about. Very often, the first tail had been *meant* to be spotted, and in that way lull you into a false sense of security.

But Jessie did not want to scare this shadow off. She wanted to *catch* him. The cartel thought they could find something out about her, did they? Well, she was going to find out a thing or two about *them!*

Just to make sure she wasn't imagining the whole thing, Jessie did an about-face at Pine Street, and then headed back toward Bush. The fellow on her tail paralleled her actions from across the street. Jessie felt a moment's panic, but banished it. The cartel wanted her to be afraid, but she was damned if she was going to let them have their way...

She headed east on Bush, looking for a quieter thoroughfare, one where she could set and then spring her trap. She found what she was looking for between Kearney and Montgomery. It was an alleyway which stretched for two blocks. It was not used for trash, but for the businesses of shopkeepers of more modest means: cobblers, tailors, and the like. The pastel-painted doorways were clean, but their windows were dark and narrow, most of them wire-grated against burglars and vandals. Jessie doubted that any clerks could see through their bar-

51

ricades and out into the alley. It was perfect.

She ducked into the alleyway, went several doors down the thoroughfare, and then stood in a deep doorway. She quickly lifted the hem of her skirt up past her gartered thigh, and drew the ivory-gripped derringer. It held two .38-caliber rounds. She palmed the little gun and waited.

And waited.

Evidently the man following her had sensed that something was up. Jessie strained her ears for the sound of his footsteps on the cobblestones of the quiet alleyway. When she finally heard the slap of shoe leather, she had to remind herself to wait at least until the man was directly abreast of her, so that she could be sure it was her tail. How embarrassing it would be if she ended up accosting some innocent gentleman on his way to his tobacconist!

But it was not some innocent gentleman. It was the man in the blue wool suit. He looked even bigger to Jessie, now that he was so close. She took a quick step out of her doorway and jammed her gun into the spot on the man's neck just below his ear. He was so tall she had to stand on tiptoe to do it.

"You don't move a muscle, mister!" she hissed. "Now put your hands up!"

"How can I, if I don't move a muscle, lady?" he said contemptuously.

Jessie snapped back the hammer on the derringer. "Just do it! I've killed more than one man who didn't take me seriously," she warned, pushing hard to grind the derringer's snout into his neck.

"Okay! Take it easy with that thing!" the man winced. He slowly raised his big, hamlike hands. "A woman gets the drop on me . . . I don't believe it!" he scolded himself. He so shook with anger that his too-small derby toppled off his head and into a puddle. "That's a new hat, dammit!"

"Hope it doesn't shrink," Jessie said. She carefully came around to face the man, all the while keeping her gun tight against his neck. He had a flat, broken nose, and a lantern jaw. His full head of wiry, salt-and-pepper hair was cut short. There were deep creases around the fellow's gray eyes, and more of them around his mouth. He was clean-shaven. Jessie figured him to be around fifty.

"I could tell you that you're making a big mistake, Miss Starbuck," the man began wearily.

"That's what you *could* tell me," Jessie said scornfully. She unbuttoned his suit jacket and reached inside on his left, finding and extracting from its shoulder holster a nickel-plated Smith & Wesson .38-caliber Detective Special. "But what I'd rather hear from you is who you are, and how you know my name!" She dropped the man's gun to the cobblestones.

"Hey!" he cried. "You'll nick the finish!"

From his right breast pocket she took his wallet. She flipped it open and extracted a business card from one of its folds. The pasteboard rectangle read:

ANDREW SHANKS, PRIVATE INVESTIGATOR

Inquiries Discreetly Conducted

When Jessie looked back at her prisoner, he was smiling. "Can I put my hands down now, Miss Starbuck?"

"Oh, yes, of course, Mr. Shanks," Jessie said, quite flustered.

"Would you take your gun out of my ear?"

Jessie lowered and uncocked her derringer, slipping it into the pocket of her skirt. "I'm very sorry, but how could I know it was you following me? I told Mr. Moore that his services as a bodyguard were not necessary."

"Yes, ma'am," Shanks said. "But Jordan was worried about you, so he asked me to keep an eye on you whenever I wasn't busy tailing Smith." He grinned sheepishly. "I guess I can tell him that you can take care of yourself, Miss Starbuck. You sure got the drop on me!" He stooped to gather up his gun and hat.

Jessie handed him back his wallet. She was too polite to tell Shanks that a blind man could have spotted the big, badly dressed private eye. "I'm afraid all this has taken so much time that I'm going to be late for my appointment with Mr. Moore."

"You just continue on down this alley until you get to Sutter," Shanks instructed her. "It'll be easy for you to hail a cab. Or you can walk, since you'll only be a couple of blocks from the Palace. I've got to go back the way I came, to take care of some other business . . ." he trailed off.

Jessie, not wanting to pry, thanked the detective, apologized again for accosting him, and turned to hurry off.

"Miss Starbuck!" Shanks called.

Jessie turned to see the man staring down at his feet, his silly little hat in his hands. "If you don't mind—" Shanks glanced up bashfully. "Please don't tell Jordan what happened."

"Oh, Mr. Shanks, I can't believe Jordan is the sort who might *fire* you for something like this—"

"No, ma'am," Shanks agreed quickly. "Anyway, he *can't* fire me, as we're equal partners in the agency. It's just that I'd never hear the end of it."

"I understand, Mr. Shanks." Jessie smiled. "It'll remain our secret. But next time be more careful," she pretended to scold. "We *are* supposed to be the more deadly of the species."

"Certainly the more charming," Shanks muttered thickly, his big face turning pink.

"Good afternoon, Mr. Shanks," Jessie laughed, and went off down the alley. When she turned, she saw Shank's broad, blue-suited back disappearing into the traffic coursing along Pine Street.

Jessie walked quickly. She was half a block away from Sutter Street when she heard fast footsteps coming up behind her. She turned, expecting to see Shanks hurrying toward her with some message he'd forgotten to deliver. Instead, she saw a young, good-looking fellow dressed in dark wool trousers and a short leather jacket.

"Miss Starbuck!" the young fellow called.

Jessie slowed and waited for him to reach her. The man's hair was black and curly. He had what seemed to be an apologetic smile on his handsome, open face.

"I won't keep you too long," he huffed as he reached her.

Jessie smiled and nodded. She remembered once again what Ki had taught her about tails. Obviously, Shanks was the decoy. This man must be an apprentice of the two older detectives. She wondered if what he had to tell her concerned her meeting with Moore—

The leather-jacketed man brought up his arm and hit Jessie across the face with the back of his hand. She went down hard, to stare up at a crazily spinning sky. The left side of her face felt numb.

Above her, seeming to tower over her like a giant, the man flicked open a straight razor. He still had that open, friendly smile on his handsome, hawk-nosed face as he crouched to grab her foot with his left hand.

The derringer was in her skirt pocket. She'd managed to get

it out by the time he'd pulled her to him, bouncing and scraping her spine along the cobblestones.

Jessie aimed carefully, and shot him in the left shoulder. He shouted and let go of her foot as though it were a red-hot poker. His shoulder was bloody, and his left arm hung limp, but the razor was still in his right hand.

He went to swing the razor at her, and Jessie shot him in the face. A black-rimmed, red hole appeared between his eyebrows, and his eyes rolled up as if to look at the spot where the bullet had entered. Then, giving a little sigh, he folded to the pavement.

As Jessie's heartbeat returned to normal, she turned and looked toward Sutter Street, half a block away. Business seemed to be going on as usual. No one seemed to have noticed the life-and-death battle that had just occurred in the midst of this crowded city on a sun-drenched afternoon.

Her face was no longer numb, but was painfully throbbing. She carefully moved her jaw from side to side, her fingers gingerly exploring the line of bone. Nothing seemed to be broken.

Her derringer had sounded like a firecracker, the twin, sharp reports echoing weakly against the thick walls enclosing the alley. Nobody had heard or seen a thing.

Get his wallet, Jessie ordered herself. *Find out who he is— if he works for the cartel . . .*

Jessie heard two shrill blasts of a whistle. Was it a policeman? She did not want to become involved with the police. She wanted to go back to the hotel, to clean herself . . .

Before her, the dead man's body twitched in some muscular contraction. The razor, still clenched in his right hand, *moved*—

Jessie turned and ran from the alley.

★

Chapter 5

Ki was about to leave the Embarcadero, but the clock tower atop the Ferry Building told him he had a lot of time to spare before he was to meet Jessie and the detective back at the Palace Hotel. He'd watched behind him, but it was obvious that there was no one at the cartel's dock who was willing— or able—to follow him. He wasn't worried about the cartel's employees summoning the police. That was not likely while they had a hold full of opium.

He'd gotten away clean, and had been able to inflict some damage upon Starbuck enemies as well. Ki was pleased. It had all been excellent and honorable.

It was lunchtime. Several food vendors were pushing their carts along the Embarcadero in order to serve the longshoremen their midday meal. As Ki watched, laughing, hungry men— their baling hooks dangling from their shoulders, their work gloves tucked into pockets and belts—hurried to queue up in front of the food cart of their choice. Ki saw vendors selling sandwiches and fruit, milk and coffee. Several carts manned by Italians from nearby North Beach were doing a thriving business selling wine, food, and strong *espresso* coffee to those of their countrymen who had found their livings on the waterfront.

Ki felt hungry himself. He approached a cart being thronged by the few Chinese dock workers fortunate enough to be paid a wage that allowed them to purchase food. The cart was operated by an old Chinese man and a girl. The old man's long pigtail hung down the back of his frayed, blue cotton tunic.

His wide-brimmed bamboo hat looked like an inverted tray upon which the food he was peddling might be served. His pants were cut wide, and stopped just past his knees. Cork-soled, braided cotton slippers coverd his feet. A white apron protected his garb.

A charcoal brazier kept several pots steaming. The black-board hanging from the cart's side gave the menu and prices, but as the menu was in Chinese, Ki could not read it. He watched several workers being served. The aromas escaping as each pot's lid was lifted, combined with the appetizing appearance of the food, told him all he needed to know. Being offered was a clear broth loaded with vegetables, noodles, black mushrooms, and chunks of seafood. The fish had most likely been purchased on this very dock during the dawn hours, while the dried mushrooms had come from the far side of the world.

Ki kept the brim of his Stetson low on his forehead as he stepped up to the cart and asked for some of the soup. The old man scowled and shook his head; clearly he did not understand English.

"I apologize most humbly for my grandfather," the girl said in a lilting, lightly accented voice. "He has not learned the language of our new homeland." She quickly took a sparkingly clean, white bowl from a shelf beneath the cart's counter, and ladled into it a portion of soup. This she handed to Ki, along with a soup spoon made of white porcelain.

Now that Ki had noticed the girl, he could not stop gazing at her. She was exquisitely lovely. Her chin was small, so that the bottom of her face was full, but her cheekbones were high and pronounced, saving her face from the apple-roundness so common to those of her race. She wore no makeup, but there was no need for cosmetics. Her creamy skin was flawless. Her large black eyes sparkled and shone as if they had never seen misery. Indeed, what impressed and enthralled Ki most of all was the way this girl seemed untouched by the world around her. She glowed with serenity, with purity; this girl's heart and mind seemed to be joined together in quiet enlightenment.

"Please!" she twittered. "Eat your soup before it grows cold. Do not watch me so!"

"I must turn my back if I would eat. And I cannot turn my back." He watched her blush. Her lips—like pink cherry blos-som buds—parted in laughter to reveal her tiny, pearl-white teeth. She pressed her long, thin fingers to her mouth to hide her amusement, but not before her stern, scowling grandfather noticed, and chittered a reprimand. The old fellow may not have understood his words, Ki surmised, but he certainly understood their intent.

Like many Chinese people of her generation, the girl, unlike her grandfather, seemed willing to embrace her new homeland. Her English was good, and she did not bend and shuffle, but was ready to look an American in the eye and speak directly to him. Her clothing was well worn, but it was clean. She wore an ancient blue silk tunic, skillfully repaired many times, that could have belonged to her mother or even her grandmother, and beneath it a pair of ankle-length black cotton pantaloons; rope-soled cotton slippers covered her tiny feet. Her ebony hair fell in two long pigtails on either side of her head. By some wizardry, Ki noted, this plain clothing she wore only seemed to enhance her radiant beauty.

"If you will not eat your soup, please sample our other food," the girl asked, spooning pork and vegetables into a bowl. She began to hand the food to Ki, but then stopped, her expression perplexed. "But we have no fork for you, sir! Only chopsticks!"

Ki had to smile. The irony of the situation was too much. They clearly took him for an American, a Caucasian. And he could not correct their assumption, not if he wanted to continue talking to this delightful female . . .

"There you are, old man! You go 'way! But we find you!"

Ki watched as two stocky Chinese men swaggered up. The other Chinese around the cart backed out of the path of the two. Whoever these men were, Ki thought, they certainly cut a wide swath through their own people.

"Please," the girl hissed at Ki. "No charge for the soup. You go now. Quickly!"

The scowl had meanwhile left her grandfather's face, to be replaced by an expression that was one part servility and several parts real terror. He began to speak to the two men in Chinese, but they cut him off abruptly.

"You!" one of them pointed at the girl. "Tell him we will no longer speak Chinese, but only the English language of our new country!"

The girl, as well, seemed frozen by fear. She said nothing, but only stared at the two men.

"Tell him!" the first man barked. Ki noticed that he had a long, thin, cinnamon-colored scar running from the upper left-hand corner of his forehead, down across the bridge of his nose, to the lower right corner of his snarling mouth.

"Quickly, girl. We have not got all day to spend with you," the other Chinese said. His wispy, drooping mustache twitched whenever he talked.

The girl pressed her lips against her grandfather's ear and whispered what had been said. Ki took the time to further examine the two newcomers. They were dressed in snug-fitting, dark-hued suits of identical cut and fabric. On their heads they wore identical derbies. Beneath their tight clothes, their arm and chest muscles bulged.

"Tell your grandfather that he not paid us for a long time," the scarred one demanded. "We leave your restaurant alone. We make sure nobody else bother you. Where's our money? You pay or you get much trouble. Where's our money?"

The man had said all of this in a singsong voice, applying the vocal rhythms of his own tongue to his newly acquired English skills. The girl had seemed mesmerized by the rise and sway of his softly hissed threats. She was like some pretty little bird, grounded with a broken wing, forlornly waiting for the coiled serpent to strike.

"Tell him!" the scarred man suddenly shouted. Once again the girl jumped to do his bidding, desperately whispering to the deathly pale old man.

"And tell him that unless he pay us, Leno Alley lose one fine restaurant. Tell him unless he pay us, Gold Coin restaurant have bad fire. Be no more. His family go work in cigar factory. His grandaughter be a whore—"

"That is enough," Ki said.

The scarred one, startled, turned to glare. He gave Ki a quick once-over, taking in his shiny black boots and fine suit, and the Stetson, which still shielded Ki's face. The anger in the Chinese's narrow eyes turned to amused contempt.

"He Mr. Smith," he smirked to his mustached friend. "Mr. Smith, this no concern you," he told Ki condescendingly. "This Chinese matter. Why you interfere in Chinese matter, eh?"

"You are offending the girl," Ki said quietly.

"Ha! Ha!" Scarface's laughter sounded like the shrill braying of a donkey. Each 'ha' was given equal, painstakingly careful emphasis, as if the man had studied how to laugh in English, as well as speak. "You like girl, eh? Ah so, Mr. Smith? Ha! Ha!" he nudged his friend. "She not for you, Mr. Smith. Ha! Ha . . ." His laughter trailed off. "You go 'way now. This now for Chinese only, understand?"

"I think it is you who had better be on your way," Ki warned. He pointed around and behind the two men. The Italians, Irishmen, and other dock workers had heard the scarred man's loud taunts to "Mr. Smith." There was no love lost between these groups and the Orientals during the best of times. Now the dock workers were forming a rough circle around the old man's cart. They held their baling hooks pressed against their legs as they stared hard at these two Chinamen who had the audacity to dress in such finery.

"We go now," the one with the mustache whispered to his companion. "We all alone here . . ."

"All right, we go," Scarface agreed, his tone surly. "But first we teach old man—and Mr. Smith—a lesson." He turned to face the cart, bent his knees, and sprang up into the air, rising about four feet off the ground. At the apex of his hop, he kicked out with first his right and then his left foot, the steel-capped tips of his boots crashing into the wood paneling. The cart lurched, spilling red-hot coals and boiling food across the cement. There was the clatter of porcelain shattering as the shelves of bowls and spoons fell. The entire wooden side was stove in; the old man's vending cart was ruined.

"We go now," the scarred man said, smug and satisfied as he surveyed the slack-jawed, astonished looks of the surrounding dock workers. "And you, Mr. Smith," he addressed Ki icily, "maybe we see you in Chinatown sometime. We show you a good time then, okay?"

The two sauntered on their way, leaving Ki to stand with his teeth gritted and his temper flaring white hot. How he'd longed to thrash those two bullies! But there was no way he could have done so without losing all hope of knowing this girl. If he had revealed his martial-arts ability, both she and her grandfather would have demanded to know how a Caucasian had come by such skills. They would have realized that Ki was partly Japanese, and then all would have been lost. Long, long ago, the Japanese had conquered the surrounding nations of Okinawa and China, demanding crippling tribute, and showing no mercy as they inflicted cruel humiliations on the vanquished. Ki knew that the girl's grandfather would have

61

preferred that she die rather than associate with a Japanese.

She was gathering up the toppled pots and their lids now, doing her best to smile bravely through her tears. "You were most brave to speak up for us," she told Ki, her voice quavering. "But I wonder if you know how much you risked?"

"Who were they?" Ki demanded gently.

"They work for a bad man. A man named Chang. He is the head of a Tong." Her large, dark eyes, still brimming with the tears she was too strong to let flow, gazed questioningly at Ki. "Do you know what a Tong is?"

"Yes," Ki nodded.

"It is a sad thing," she continued. "We left China to escape such things, and now we find that all the old sorrows have followed us here." She shook her head. "Those men demand protection money from my family, or else we shall not be allowed to run our restaurant. You see how he smashed our cart? He and his friend are adept at Chinese boxing."

Wu-shu, Ki thought to himself. He knew better than to reveal his knowledge to the girl. In all, he didn't think much of Scarface's skill, but Ki was objective enough to know that two *wu-shu* adepts *could* give him a hard time.

"All of Chang's men are so skilled," she sighed. "They rule Chinatown."

"What is your name?" Ki asked.

"Ah, sir, I cannot . . ." She trailed off, glancing at where her grandfather was picking through the shards of porcelain, muttering to himself, clearly hoping against hope that some-where in the ruins he might find an unbroken bowl, or at least a spoon.

"I must know your name!" Ki persisted.

"It would just be more sadness. I could not bear it," she whispered. "You are American. I am Chinese . . ."

Ki could see how she was trying to catch a glimpse of his eyes, so carefully shielded beneath the brim of his hat. *If you could see me truly, how your beautiful face would curl with contempt and hatred,* he mourned silently. "But *you* are an American *too*—" Ki stopped, realizing that what he was ex-pressing was really his own heartfelt wish: that both of them could be together as Americans, and not as two lost and lonely foreigners, barred from each other by their nations' histories.

The grandfather had finished picking through his ruined possessions. He muttered something in Chinese at the girl, who turned quickly to him, nodding and answering respectfully in their own tongue.

"I am a good girl," she now told Ki, her voice even, but clearly wanting him to understand that she was saying all this on her elder's orders, and not because she had misinterpreted Ki's advances. "I am a virgin, and wish an honorable wedding to a Chinese man. I—" Suddenly her tiny hand darted out to grasp Ki's. Her grandfather's agonized voice reprimanded her sharply.

This time the girl showed her true spirit. She turned—still holding Ki's hand—to confront her watchful guardian. Whatever she shrilly told him, it made the old fellow lower his glaring eyes and nod resignedly. When he next spoke, his voice had lost its harshness.

She turned back to Ki. "My grandfather apologizes for his thoughtless rudeness. That a man of...your position should intercede on our behalf is a miraculous thing."

Ki understood what was being inferred by the phrase *a man of your position*. The miracle, as they saw it, was in a white man helping Chinese.

"Tell your grandfather this," Ki began. "A man must refuse the friendship of all who are not like him..." He waited for the girl to translate for her elder, then went on, "But if he finds he has made a mistake, then he must not be afraid of admitting the fact and amending his way."

First the girl's, and then the old man's eyes flew open wide. Ki had somewhat paraphrased this particular quotation from the philosopher Confucius, but of course, both Chinese had recognized it at once.

The old man murmured something. The girl nodded, and then smiled at Ki. "My grandfather says he has witnessed two miracles today. He says that the honored sir has given an old man much to think about. Now I must help him take our belongings home."

Ki watched them push their ruined cart along, beginning their arduous walk back to Chinatown. Once, the girl looked back at him, but no more words were exchanged. He'd longed to coax her to reveal her name, but he now knew that she was a virtuous young woman, brought up in such a way that a gentleman's persistence concerning such a matter could only cause her painful embarrassment.

The far-off chime of the Ferry Building's big clock reminded

Ki of his appointment back at the Palace Hotel. He would be late after all, but he thought he could temper Jessie's and Jordan Moore's displeasure at his tardiness by revealing the evidence he had gathered at the cartel's dock.

As Ki hurried, he reminded himself that he had overheard one of the Tong hatchet men mention the name and address of the girl's family's restaurant: the Gold Coin, in Chinatown's Leno Alley. When he could, Ki would visit. There was no doubt about it in his mind. He had to see that girl again.

Chapter 6

The girl occupied Ki's thoughts all the way back to the Palace Hotel. He avoided the main entrance, on the New Montgomery Street side of the block-square building, for it was always jammed by carriages waiting to drive right into the hotel's massive central lobby, dubbed the Grand Court.

The Palace was seven stories high, and contained eight hundred rooms. The Grand Court atrium soared for the entire seven stories, was ringed with the bannistered galleries of each floor, and was crowned by a roof of frosted glass. At one end of the Grand Court was a renowned restaurant, and at the other end was the carriage park. In the middle area were tables, leather chairs, and potted palms. Uniformed waiters hovered, ready to fetch drinks from the hotel's bar.

This was where Jessie, Ki, and Jordan Moore had arranged to meet. Ki saw Moore sitting in an armchair, almost lost behind the lush green fronds of a palm tree. As usual, Moore's suit was impeccably tailored, and of a somber shade of black, but this time his silk tie was bright red. On the table beside him was a drink, and one of his long, slender cigars was smoldering in the ashtray.

"I am sorry to be late," Ki began, but then froze. He stared at Moore's grim expression, at his white-knuckled grip upon the arm of his chair. The investigator's normally sparkling green eyes were now deep, dark pieces of jade.

Just then, Moore noticed Ki. "Now don't get excited," he cautioned.

"What has happened to her?" Ki rushed forward.

The slight detective jumped to his feet, raising his hands before him as if to deflect Ki's charge. "She's all right! Now take it easy, friend. *I* didn't do anything!"

Ki made a huge effort not to reach out and shake the man. Instead, he clenched his teeth and asked once again, "What has happened to Jessie?"

"First off, she's upstairs in her room, changing her clothes, all right?" When Ki nodded and seemed to relax, Moore breathed a sigh of relief. "Good! I always have the feeling you're about to punch a hole through something, and I never want it to be me."

"Tell me everything," Ki demanded.

"Certainly," Moore agreed. He pointed to the chair next to his own. "Sit down, order a drink, and I'll start from the beginning." Signaling the waiter, he asked Ki, "What will you have?"

"Scotch, neat," Ki told the waiter, who glided off to fill the order.

"Straight Scotch?" Moore couldn't suppress his mischievous smile. "What happened to green tea?"

"I am only half Japanese," Ki said evenly. "Anyway, Scotch became very popular in Japan, once the British began importing it. I myself developed a taste for it after I'd come to this country."

"Not very spiritual," Moore teased.

"Ah, but I regret that I am *not* very spiritual, friend Jordan." Ki showed his teeth. "I get impatient with chatter. I punch holes through things. Tell me what has happened!"

Moore told him. Ki kept silent through most of the detective's narrative, interrupting only when Moore mentioned that the razor-wielding assailant had knocked Jessie down.

"You'd said she was not hurt!" Ki snarled.

"She's not," Moore said quickly. "When she came in here, I was already waiting. Her clothes were soiled, but there wasn't a mark on her." He finished telling Ki the rest of it, and then paused. "Look, he's dead. You can't kill him again. It's over, and Jessie is all right."

"It is my sworn duty to protect her," Ki said.

Moore nodded. "As a samurai. Yes, I know that, Ki. You see, I took the liberty of asking Arthur Lewis a few questions yesterday, just after I'd met you and Jessie." Moore's expression was sincere. "I hope I have not offended you."

Ki pondered it a moment, and then shook his head. "Given our situation, it is appropriate that you would want to know more about me. There is nothing Arthur could have told you that could compromise my privacy. I take no offense."

Moore nodded. He said nothing, and kept his expression neutral.

"We must find out who hired this assassin," Ki mused. "Was it the cartel, or the Tong?"

Moore shrugged. "What difference does it make?"

"It matters to *me*," Ki said intensely. "Someone has sent a death to dog Jessie's footsteps. I will discover who has done this, and send a death to them."

Moore shivered. "We'll do what we can," he said placatingly. "And Jessie wants to know, as well, but we'll just have to see. She did the right thing in not waiting around for the police to arrive."

"The authorities might have given her trouble?" Ki asked.

"This *is* San Francisco, my friend," Moore scolded humorously. "We're not in some territorial cow town. We don't just plop our dead *banditos* into Boot Hill. There's also the question of publicity. A police officer arriving on the scene would have tipped off whatever city desk is paying the most these days. There would have been reporters flocking to the scene. Somebody of Jessica Starbuck's stature becoming involved in a shooting—well, you can imagine the headlines. "Beautiful Heiress Kills Would-Be Robber"—all that publicity would certainly hamper our cause."

"Is there nothing we can do to discover the identity of the assassin's employer?" Ki asked.

Just then, Jessie joined them at their table. Ki peered anxiously at her while Moore busied himself rounding up a third chair. She was wearing a different dress from the one she'd had on that morning, and was carrying a small leather case under her arm. Ki was greatly relieved to see that she was smiling.

He stood up to meet her approach. His voice was thick with the emotion he usually claimed to disdain. "It is a great dishonor to me."

Jessie took several quick steps forward, to rest her head against his chest. "You can't be everywhere at once," she murmured, trying to comfort him.

Ki smiled down at her upturned face. His arms were dangling at his sides. He could feel Jessie's warmth where she touched him, at his knees and stomach and chest. He could smell the fragrance of her hair.

It would be so simple to kiss her now, Ki thought. *So natural to embrace her.* Gently, firmly, Ki moved Jessie back a bit, so that they were no longer touching. He made a pretense of carefully tilting her head this way and that, examining her face to see if she'd been injured, so that his maneuver would not seem so awkward.

"No damage done," Jessie chuckled. "None that you can see, at any rate." Actually, she'd suffered a slight bruise on her cheek where the man had hit her, but she'd thought to cover it with face powder, more out of consideration for Ki's feelings than from her own vanity. That's what made them a team. "Now then, if one of you gentlemen would order me a rather unladylike amount of brandy, I'd be very appreciative."

After they were seated, and her drink had been served, Jessie asked, "Tell me what I've missed."

"Like you, Ki wants to know who the dead man worked for," Moore began. He pulled out his notebook and began to jot reminders to himself. "I'll ask Arthur Lewis to use his contacts to keep your involvement out of the papers. As the head of Starbuck operations in this area, he ought to have a few favors he can call in. I have some connections with the police department. I can get some information on the dead man that way."

Ki shook his head. "If he is a professional, he will not have evidence upon his body implicating his employer."

Moore nodded, sighing. "That's true. Look, both of you, you've got to face the fact that he's dead, so he can't tell anything."

"I didn't want to kill him," Jessie said dejectedly.

Moore was amused. "Could have fooled me," he smirked.

"I'm serious," Jessie scolded. "Honestly, Mr. Moore—"

"Jordan," Moore corrected her.

"Jordan, then..." Jessie rolled her eyes in exasperation. "You are the most infuriating man! You refuse to view me as anything but a woman—"

"A beautiful woman," Moore admonished.

Jessie chose to ignore that last remark with everything but her smile. "I only had two rounds in my derringer. After wounding him with the first, I tried to get him to surrender, but he was still full of fight, and so close to me with that razor of his . . . I only had that one shot left, I couldn't risk not shooting to kill."

"It does sound like you know how to use a gun," Moore said in obvious admiration.

"I do, and if anybody else tries what that fellow tried, I don't intend to depend on my little derringer," Jessie declared adamantly. She picked up the leather case she'd brought and unclasped it, to show both men what was inside.

"My word!" Moore laughed. He reached into the case and pulled out Jessie's revolver. It was a double-action Colt, finished in slate gray, with grips of polished peachwood.

"My father taught me how to shoot," Jessie explained. "He used a double-action Colt .44, just like yours, Jordan, but his didn't have a sawed-off barrel, of course."

"Of course," Moore mimicked teasingly, but he was genuinely impressed.

"Anyway," Jessie continued. "A .44's recoil is too much for my hand, so my father had the Colt factories in Connecticut modify this pistol for me. The cylinder is chambered for .38 shells, but mounted on a .44 frame, so the recoil's been reduced considerably, and it's fast and accurate."

A passing waiter frowned at Moore, who realized that waving a gun around the lobby of the Palace was probably going to get him a stern talking-to from the house detective. "Here," he said, handing the pistol back to Jessie. "You'd better put that back where I found it."

Jessie carefully tucked her Colt back into its case. "My point is that if I'd had this, I could have taken that man alive."

"I believe you," Moore said, his expression sympathetic. "But *my* point is that the man's dead. In a city the size of San Francisco, it is not at all uncommon for thugs like that to lie in wait for passersby. It happens all the time in the seamier sections of the city, and even here, in the better parts, an alley can be a tricky place."

"But how would just *any* thief know my name?" Jessie asked.

"He may have heard Shanks address you," Moore offered. "That's my guess. In any event we can't expect the police to dig too far into this. It happens too often, I'm sorry to say. You've heard of the Barbary Coast, right? That's the honkytonk section of town, where the sailors go to frolic. The whiskey sold on the Barbary Coast will make you blind. Knife fights there are so common that the police themselves carry blades, because they can get them out faster than they can their revolvers. We may never know if the man who attacked Jessie was an assassin, as Ki calls him, or just a thug looking for a bankroll or jewelry to pawn, and willing to kill to get it."

"But you will try to find something out?" Jessie urged.

"I will." Moore smiled. "I might even have something by tonight."

"You'll get in touch with me immediately, of course?" Jessie asked.

Moore shrugged, the smile still on his face. "I just don't know if I'll be able to remember," he teased. "You know, the safest thing for you to do, Jessie, is to have dinner with me this evening. That way—"

Jessie's laughter drowned out the rest. "Please stop! I'd be delighted to have dinner with you. Your company is reason enough . . ."

"I've got something of interest on Commissioner Smith," Ki said pointedly. He hauled out the duty sheet, the matching crate duty number stenciled onto the splinter of wood, and the sample of opium, telling them both how he'd come by the evidence.

Moore was impressed. "If you don't mind, Ki, I'd feel better if this stuff were locked up in Arthur Lewis's safe in the Starbuck Building." When Ki agreed, Moore promised to hand-deliver the items to Lewis. "Arthur is going to be anxious to get moving on his plan to discredit Smith," Moore confided to Jessie. "This sort of evidence is what he's been waiting for. The newspapers would love to get hold of dynamite like this."

"Tell Arthur not to do anything until he hears from me," Jessie said. "We're not yet ready to move against the cartel, and that's the root of our problem. If we act against Smith now, the cartel will simply put a new man in his place. Nothing would be solved."

"I agree," Moore said. "And so will Arthur, when he hears your reasoning." The detective paused, to glance at Ki. "There's one last thing troubling me. The men on the cartel's clipper got a good look at you, Ki, as did Commissioner Smith. They're sure to report their setback to their boss, Greta Kahr. I think that it's a safe bet you've made yourself some real enemies. They'll try and retaliate. Now Jessie's armed, and

70

she'll be with me tonight, but that'll leave you all alone. If you're intending to go out, I think my partner, Shanks, should tag along."

Ki held up his hand. "I appreciate your concern, Jordan, but I'm afraid that Shanks would be more of a hindrance than a help."

"Well, then," Moore sighed in resignation, "suit yourself..." He placed some money on the table to cover the cost of their drinks, bowed to Jessie, and said, "I'll call for you at eight?"

Jessie smiled, watching as Moore gathered up Ki's evidence on Smith. The detective tipped his derby a final time, and went on his way.

"What a fascinating man!" Jessie breathed.

"Skinny," Ki muttered.

Jessie turned toward him. "What?"

"Nothing."

"I hope you won't mind dining alone?" she asked.

"No." It startled Ki, but the dishonorable jealousy he always felt concerning Jessie and other men seemed somewhat less than usual. "Not at all," he promised her now, his mind on the girl he was going to see in Chinatown.

Chapter 7

Jessie's dinner with Jordan Moore went marvelously well. The smartly dressed private investigator had called for her at eight, as he'd promised. Jessie had decided to wear her copper-kissed blond tresses up, to expose her long, graceful neck. Instead of a string of pearls or a gold necklace, Jessie had fastened around her neck a snug black ribbon. Where another woman might have affixed a cameo or brooch to the band of black satin, Jessie had pinned at her throat a small ivory *netsuke*.

Netsuke were carved decorations used by the Japanese as fasteners for the wide sashes, or *obis* they habitually wore. The one Jessie had chosen to wear this evening was of a tiny figure of a kneeling woman bringing a long, thin, flutelike instrument to her lips. The carving was just minutely raised off the oval of ivory that formed the background. One had to look closely at the small *netsuke* to make out the figures, but any Japanese who did so would have instantly recognized it.

The significance of the carving was very special, and only very special women could wear it, as a badge of merit. The *netsuke* had been given to Jessie by her housekeeper, Myobu, years ago. Jessie, while still an adolescent, had spent arduous hours under Myobu's tutelage, learning the arts of the geisha.

Jessie had laughed to herself when she'd decided to wear her *netsuke*, thinking that if the detective was really good at his profession, he'd notice, and ask her about her throat decoration . . .

Long ago, Myobu had taught her that a man's "size" could be discerned by the size of his hands and feet. Jordan Moore,

73

a slender man of middling height, had rather small, delicate-looking hands and feet...

Well, Jessie had decided, should Jordan be clever and curious enough to ask her what the *netsuke* signified, he would find out, and get more than he'd bargained for!

And in that way, Jessie could satisfy *her* curiosity, as well.

Her blue velvet evening gown was cut daringly low, to reveal the tops of her alabaster breasts. She'd daubed perfume in her cleavage. It had made her smile to think how wicked all this would seem to the folks back in Texas. Here in San Francisco, it was just the sophisticated thing to do. A brocaded shawl of matching velvet, lined and collared with mink, would protect her from the evening's chill. She carried a larger-than-normal evening purse to hold her Colt.

By the look on Jordan's face when she'd entered the lobby, Jessie had known that the detective was pleased with her appearance. He'd eyed suspiciously the odd bulge in her purse.

"Is that what I think it is?" he'd asked.

"Yes, just in case," Jessie replied.

"Well," Moore sighed, "as beautiful as you look tonight, I suppose I'd have needed *something* to remind me not to be too forward."

Jessie had been surprised to see that the driver of the cab Jordan had waiting for them was Thaddeus Simpson, the elderly cabbie Arthur Lewis kept on call. Moore explained that Lewis had offered Simpson's services that afternoon, when Moore had deposited with the Starbuck executive the evidence Ki had gathered at the waterfront.

Moore proved himself a man who knew his way around his city. He first entertained Jessie with his anecdotes concerning the variety and quality of the food served in San Francisco's restaurants, as Simpson's cab made its slow way along the cobblestone-paved streets.

"San Francisco was settled by the natives of many different countries," Moore told her as the hack swayed down the bright, gaslit avenues. "All of them kept the customs of their homelands, including their native cookery. Also, you must remember that San Francisco was a gold, and then a silver town. Until recently, there weren't many females around. The lone-wolf miners had all their meals in restaurants, and had the gold and silver to pay handsomely for the exotic foods they craved."

74

"Where are we dining this evening?" Jessie asked, as excited as a little girl.

Moore grinned. "We're going to the finest French restaurant in the city, the Poulet d'Or. There are dozens of French establishments, but the Poulet has been around since 1850, starting out as a shack on Dupont Street. The miners back then liked the food fine, but they couldn't handle the French. They dubbed the place the Poodle Dog, and that's been the restaurant's unofficial society name ever since. Of course, it's no longer a shack, but a big, fancy place on Bush Street, just a stone's throw from its original location."

The Poodle Dog featured snow-white linen, sparkling crystal, and a clientele dressed for the most part in expensive suits and gowns. More than a few men wore formal evening attire. Jessie confessed that it was difficult to imagine a bearded hard-rock miner clomping across the plush carpet in his muddy boots, setting his pickax and Winchester across the linened table, and snapping his grimy, callused fingers to summon a liveried waiter.

"It might be difficult to imagine, all right," Moore replied. "But if that miner came in, he'd be given a table. Men like that built this place, and this city, as well. And for all its veneer of sophistication, San Francisco is still a rough-and-ready, violent town." He paused to taste the wine proffered by the steward, and after pronouncing it satisfactory, he waited for the man to pour them each a glass, and take his leave, before continuing on. "As far as your miner's Winchester, consider what you've got stashed in your purse. I'm armed, as well, and nine out of ten of the gentlemen here have a gun somewhere about their persons."

Jessie looked about the room. Ki had instructed her in what to look for to spot concealed weapons, and now that she was doing so, she could indeed see here and there, the telltale bulge of a shoulder holster or the gleam of leather showing between the tails of a gentleman's evening jacket.

Their meal lasted for hours, but Jessie was having such a fine time that it only seemed like moments. Moore handled their ordering with aplomb. Jessie, who had learned to speak several languages at college, knew that his French was fluent, as were his poise and self-confidence in greeting those people who stopped by their table. Moore, it turned out, was well

75

known. He did not introduce Jessie to any of his well-wishers, despite the fact that they were plainly curious.

"I hope you don't mind," he apologized to her, "but I'd rather it didn't get around that Jessica Starbuck is in town. Your name is well known, as is the fact that you are your father's sole heir, but nobody knows what you look like, or anything else about you. For example, even though I'd been working for the Starbuck organization, until Arthur Lewis said you were actually his employer, I had no idea you directly controlled the empire."

"But what about *your* identity getting around?" Jessie asked, changing the subject. "Aren't you concerned that being so well known will spoil your ruse of being a rich wastrel from Oregon? What if Smith and the others—"

Moore shook his head. "It *is* a rather large city, Jessie. The odds of our running into Smith are slim, and if we do, I'll simply take on my guise. My being with the loveliest woman in town would only add to it. The only person who might recognize you is Greta Kahr. But, again, the city is large and there are many night spots. Unless we want to keep you cooped up in your hotel room, it's a risk we have to take."

"What about Chang, the leader of the Tong?" Jessie persisted.

"Stop worrying!" Moore commanded. "Let me handle things. Tonight we are not employee and employer, but just a man and a woman." He winked. "To prove it, I'm not even going to charge this dinner to expenses when I submit my bill."

"Oh, thank you!" Jessie laughed. "I'm *so* grateful!"

"You will be, when you get my bill," Moore told her merrily.

Jessie smiled and kept silent, but she couldn't help worrying. She respected and trusted Moore's expertise, but her instincts told her that this time the brash detective was being overconfident.

After dinner, Moore instructed Simpson to drive them to Russian Hill. During the ride, he told Jessie how the hill had come by its name: during the 1820s, a Russian crew of seal hunters had buried their dead on that spot. Once, only the richest people were able to live on the hill, for horses were required to negotiate the steep grade and act as pack animals to keep a home supplied with necessities and luxuries. But all that changed with the advent of the cable car.

They stopped at a stone balustrade located in a peaceful cul-de-sac just beneath the hill's summit. Simpson waited with his carriage a discreet distance away, while Jessie leaned against the stone railing to gaze down at the sparkling, moonlit bay. Cypress and sycamore trees rustled in the night breeze, and the air was filled with the scent of daffodils.

Moore was standing close by her, so close that just by shifting a little, Jessie found herself pressed against him. A moment later his arm was around her. She turned to face him.

"I wish this night would never end," she breathed.

"It hasn't yet," Moore chuckled. "What we need now is champagne."

"But it's so late!" Jessie protested.

Moore kissed her lightly on the lips. Jessie felt weak in the knees as his hands caressed her back, vulnerable and bare, due to the low cut of her gown. "There's no such thing as 'too late' in San Francisco," he said, his jade-green eyes pinning hers, heating her to her very center. "Before anything *else* happens," he continued, his voice husky, "we can take our time, and have our champagne."

They went to what Moore described as a "private sort of club," hidden away on a dark and dismal street on the outer fringe of the notorious Barbary Coast. The place was called the Pink Slipper, according to Moore, but when they arrived at the address he'd given Simpson, Jessie saw no sign to tell them that they'd reached their destination.

"This sort of place doesn't advertise," the detective grinned as he escorted Jessie to the stout-looking, plain wooden door of the windowless building. She shivered, feeling awfully deserted as Simpson's cab rolled away. Moore had dismissed the cabbie for the night, confiding to Jessie that this was not the sort of area for the elderly cabbie to wait in, all by himself. The management would provide a cab for them when they were ready to leave.

Moore extracted from his wallet and showed to Jessie a pink calling card, upon which there was no writing, but simply the likeness of a ballet slipper gracing the meticulously drawn and detailed, shapely contours of a bare female leg. The detective rapped on the door and held the card up for inspection by the pair of eyes that appeared in the quickly opened peep-hole.

Once they were inside the dark and smoky place, a husky, bearded man who looked ludicrous in his too-tight, formal dinner jacket, led them to an intimate booth for two.

"Dis is one of our 'love nooks,'" he grumbled. "Would it be satisfactory?"

Moore assured him that it would be, and tipped the man a dollar for his trouble, asking that champagne be sent over as soon as possible.

"'Love nooks'?" Jessie giggled as soon as they were alone.

"Actually, this place stole the term from the Poodle Dog," Moore explained. "Before the Poodle got so fancy, it used to have an upstairs for drinking. The married pillars of society and the business world would take their mistresses and courtesans there, so the little booths came to be known as 'love nooks.'"

"Why all the secrecy about getting in?" she asked.

"Well, a few years ago, the more staid segments of society decided that San Francisco needed a little taming." Moore paused. "Say, do you mind if I smoke?"

"Not if you let me have a puff now and then," Jessie bargained. "Someday it'll be all right for women to smoke."

"Propriety doesn't stop Greta Kahr from smoking," Moore observed as he fired up one of his slender cheroots.

"Let's not bring *her* up," Jessie scolded. "Finish what you were saying about these after-hours clubs."

"Those staid church and civic groups lobbied their representatives to set closing hours for the bars. They did, and the police enforced the rules and, of course, turned a blind eye to the clubs that promptly sprouted, so they'd have a place to get a drink when they went off duty."

Jessie sipped at her champagne. It was icy cold, and tasted of strawberries. Its bubbles tickled her nose. "It's all so complicated," she marveled. "Police and politicians flouting the law. Aren't they afraid of getting caught?"

Moore shrugged. "There's no one to catch them, Jessie. Here, corruption is considered the norm."

"Well, I consider it just plain dishonest!"

Moore burst out laughing. "Shanks would hate to hear you say that. He's an ex-policeman. He has quite a crush on you."

"Oh, dear," Jessie giggled, taking another sip of her champagne. "I hope you didn't tease him about my getting the drop on him?" she warned. "He'd asked me not to tell you about it, and I wouldn't have, but then that man came after me, and I had to tell you what happened—"

"Hush," Moore said. "I never let on that I was informed of what had happened between the two of you." He shook his head. "Not that the big oaf doesn't deserve to be kidded . . ."

Jessie nodded in agreement. "He's not very good."

"Actually, he's better than you think," Moore argued. "Don't forget, most people are not as as alert as you are." He smiled. "Often it helps our interests for Shanks to be so obvious. It panics the subject he's following, and sometimes makes him or her do foolish things. Shanks, as I said, is an ex-policeman. He forgets that he's no longer on the force, and that he has to be careful for his own safety, as well as discreet. The police in this town are pretty much all-powerful. I hope Shanks's swagger doesn't get him into trouble one day."

And I hope that your overconfidence doesn't get you into the same kind of trouble, Jessie worried silently. "Lord! I've been having such a good time that I forgot to ask you about that man who tried to kill me. Did you ever find out anything?"

"Only what I knew we'd find out," Moore sighed. "I asked Shanks to talk to one of his old cronies in the department. It's true that your thug had an assault record, but there is nothing to connect him with either the cartel or the Tong. Shanks had a good point to make about it all, by the way. He pointed out to me that it's unknown for the Tong to use a Caucasian for their dirty work. They sometimes use whites as front men in their business dealings, but never to do anything underhanded. They only trust their own kind for that."

"That doesn't clear the cartel!" Jessie, sitting with her back to the door, heard some commotion behind her, but did not bother to turn around.

"It *could* have been them, Jessie, but we'll never know—" Moore froze in midsentence. His face blanched, and when he next spoke, it was in a hoarse whisper. "It's them! What rotten luck!"

Jessie, totally mystified, glanced over her shoulder, toward the entrance. A single, ceiling-suspended gas lamp lit the foyer area. She saw in that flickering light a rather full-figured, but extremely attractive middle-aged woman, dressed in a tightly fitted gown of gold lamé. Around her shoulders was a mink stole. Its shading matched the auburn color of her mass of curly hair. She wore no hat, but carred, despite there being no prediction of rain, a tightly furled umbrella.

"That's her!" Moore hissed. "That is Greta Kahr!"

"Oh, no!" Jessie groaned softly. "We've got to get out of here! I'm sure she knows what I look like. The cartel must have supplied her with my description before sending her to San Francisco."

"Jessie!" Moore admonished, his tone quiet, but commandingly sharp. "Just stay where you are. They can't see us, we're hidden by the shadows. Once they're settled in at their table, we'll slip out. For now, take the opportunity to see who your enemies are. The gentleman escorting Madam Kahr happens to be Chang Fong, leader of the Steel Claw Tong."

Jessie scrutinized the man with Kahr. He was short, about five feet, five inches in height, a small, barrel-chested, bandy-legged Chinese fellow, his middle-aged face clean-shaven, and his glistening, ivory-colored pate hairless. His expensive, pin-striped suit did nothing to hide the length and thickness of his shoulders and arms. "He looks so strong..."

"He got those muscles lifting and hauling tuna and sword-fish, back when he was a fishmonger," Moore told her.

"He doesn't look that special—" Jessie began, and then gasped. Chang had been standing with his left side toward her, in a three-quarters profile. Now he stood facing Jessie. "His hand!" she whispered, recoiling into the dark protection of their shadowy nook.

"They call him Steel Claw," Moore reminded her.

Where Chang's right hand should have been was not a metal hook, but a *claw*. It was as if there were a small, gleaming rake protruding from his sleeve, and each of that rake's five talons glistened needle-sharp in the flickering light.

"They say that he uses that thing to gouge the eyes of those Tong members who have displeased him," Moore whispered. "I, for one, believe it."

Jessie stared at Chang's eyes, like two pieces of black onyx set in the ivory-yellow folds of his Chinese face. Those twin, glittering spots of blackness were totally without expression. They reminded Jessie of the eyes of a Gila monster, the big poisonous lizard found in the Southwest. A Gila monster would bite down on you to chew its venom into your flesh, and once that demon's jaws clamped, there wasn't a thing you could do to make it turn you loose. *And all the time it chewed on you, its black, expressionless eyes would glitter like onyx. You could lop the lizard's head clear off with a pair of wire-cutters, but*

*it didn't matter, didn't change a thing; those black, shiny eyes
never changed, not at all . . .*

"Jessie?" Moore reached out, placing his hand on hers.

Jessie started. She almost jerked away her fingers.

"What were you thinking about?" Moore asked.

"About monsters." Jessie shuddered. "About *him!*"

She gestured toward Chang as he escorted Greta Kahr to
their table. Flanking the couple were a pair of stern-faced
Chinese bodyguards dressed in the traditional Chinese garb
of long, dark blue tunics and pajama pants. Their inky black
hair was plaited into queues that dangled down their backs.

"Chang's guards don't seem to be armed," she mused.

"They don't need weapons," Moore grimaced. "All of
Chang's hatchet men are Chinese boxing masters."

"*Wu-shu?*"

"Why, yes," Moore said, surprised. "What *don't* you
know?"

"What those two are going to be planning over *their* champagne," Jessie replied. "Whatever it is, it'll mean trouble for
me."

"For *us*," Moore gently corrected her. "You're not up
against them alone, remember?"

Jessie squeezed Moore's hand. "Yes, I *do* remember," she
murmured, her eyes sparkling.

"And right now, I'm much more interested in what *we* were
planning over *our* champagne." Moore put some money on the
table and stood up. "Come on, they're settled in. We can leave
without being noticed."

"Don't we need to call a carriage?" Jessie asked.

"I'd rather not hang around here waiting for it to arrive,"
Moore said slowly. "We're not so far from the Barbary Coast.
We'll walk a bit. We'll see a vacant hack soon enough."

As they left the club, Moore said. "Let's say hello to Shanks.
I know he'd love to see *you* again."

"What would he be doing around here?" Jessie asked, startled.

"I forgot to tell you," Moore grinned. "I've had him tailing
Kahr. I thought it might put some pressure on her to have a
man on her tail—if you'll excuse my poor choice of words."

"Hmmm," Jessie slipped her arm through his, to snuggle
close to the detective.

• "Perhaps I should have put Ki on her tail," he said slyly, as they strolled down the dark avenue.

"Just make sure you don't tease *him* like that," Jessie laughed.

"Don't worry about that." Moore's expression grew distant. "Uh, I'm not sure how to bring this up, but I'd like to know ... there's nothing between you and Ki, is there?" he asked tentatively. "I mean, as a man and a woman," he fumbled.

"No," Jessie said, smiling to herself. "It really would never occur to him to make love to me."

Moore wondered about that as he recalled the scene earlier today in the hotel lobby, when Jessie had hugged Ki. Moore had watched the look in the man's eyes. Ki was clearly head over heels in love with Jessie, who, most likely, had been just too close to the stoic samurai for too long to ever really see how the man felt. *Well, that's just my good luck,* Moore told himself.

"Jordan?" Jessie suddenly asked. "Where *is* Shanks?"

Moore stopped walking. "You're right, we should have run into him by now." The detective looked over his shoulder. "Let's walk down the block the other way for a bit."

"You mean past the club again?" Jessie nervously replied.

"Don't worry," Moore took her arm to lead her along. "Our two nasty friends inside won't be out for a while."

They were halfway down the block, on the other side of the Pink Slipper, when they heard faint moans coming from out of the darkness of an abandoned building's hallway.

Jessie's grip on Moore's arm stiffened. "Somebody's hurt in there!" she whispered.

"Stay here," Moore commanded. In one smooth move he drew his Colt .44 from its shoulder rig.

"Be careful," Jessie said.

"That's a great idea," Moore mumbled absently as he cautiously entered the pitch-black interior of the gutted structure. He struck a match against the side of a timber.

Jessie unclasped her purse to draw her own Colt. She watched the faint glow of Moore's match waver and fade as he went deeper into the building's hallway. "What is it?" she called out in exasperated fear. Moore's match went out. She heard the scrape of another against wood, as the weak, flickering light reappeared.

Moore's cry, when it came, was full of pain. "Oh, Christ!"

"What?" Jessie pleaded. When there was no answer, she swore under her breath and rushed into the building, her gun at the ready.

Deep inside she saw a small but steady light. Moore had found an inch of candle stuck into one of the many empty whiskey bottles strewn about the place. Some vagrant had evidently used the abandoned building as a temporary home.

Moore was kneeling over a moaning, ashen-faced Shanks, who was sitting sprawled on the floor, his back propped up against the wall. Shanks was clutching his belly. Blood seeped from between his tightly interlaced fingers.

"He's been stabbed," Moore muttered, his face grim. "Who did it?" he asked his partner. "Hurry! Tell me."

"Miss Starbuck, you there?" Shanks gasped.

"Yes, I'm here," Jessie said, looking down at the man.

"H-hate for you to see me like this, ma'am," Shanks said sorrowfully.

"Christ! He's been run clear through!" Moore exclaimed. "He wasn't stabbed with a knife, but with a sword." He pried apart Shanks's clutching fingers to examine the wet, bubbling wound. He shrugged helplessly. "There's nothing for it, old friend," he said. "Please, you must tell me who did it!"

"You was right, Miss Starbuck," Shanks mumbled. "You . . . told me . . . more deadly . . ." His eyelids fluttered as his big lantern jaw slumped to rest upon his chest.

Moore turned to stare up at Jessie. His green eyes were wet with emotion. "He's dead!" Moore snarled. "My partner's dead!"

Chapter 8

Ki walked the distance between the Palace Hotel and China-town. It was just dusk when he began his trek. As the sun sank into the bay and the purple shadows lengthened, the samurai found himself on the enclave's outskirts.

All around me is darkness, Ki thought to himself. *Yes, it is fitting that the light of the sun should fail as I leave behind the world of San Francisco for the world of Chinatown.*

As the darkness had increased, so had the narrowness of the streets. Here the clapboard buildings had no bay windows, for trying to catch a ray of light was futile. Little sun could penetrate past the crooked eaves and slooping roofs of the packed-together tenements, themselves like so many stoop-shouldered, gaunt Chinese men, each wearing a broad-brimmed hat.

Ki kept his own hat brim pulled low over his distinctly Nipponese eyes. A Japanese would find no friends in this place. Ki had to smile sadly; he had more in common with these downtrodden people than with his own race.

Truth did indeed have many facets. To Dennis Kearney and his Workingmen's Party followers, the Chinese undercut the white man's wage and happily accepted their exploitation. To the Chinese, the problem was that no one would pay them a decent wage, and that their children could not learn to better themselves because they were not allowed in the whites' school system. A silent, bitter banding-together was the price these proud people had to pay in order to survive in a land that despised and feared them.

Ki found that he had to walk in the muddy streets. The

warped, rotted wooden sidewalks were completely taken over by whole families, some of whom were trying to make a living by rolling cigars upon wooden crates. The cigars would later be sold by tobacconists for prices the Chinese could not even dream of getting. There were groups shrilly hawking fruits and nuts to any passing fellow resident who might have the meager purchase price jingling in the pockets of his cotton tunic.

Above the streets, and framed by brightly colored banners painted with Chinese characters, people were literally hanging out of their tenement windows. Most of them were working at various occupations by the weak light of candles inside wire-strung paper lanterns. On one widened window ledge, a cobbler perched like a pigeon in order to repair shoes. From one window there wafted clouds of steam. In that room a family not only lived, but ran a laundry as well.

Ki knew that in the summer the weakest of these people would suffocate. There simply was not enough oxygen in the air for so many to breathe. What air there was grew swiftly spoiled by the blanket of smoke rising from the thousands of charcoal cookfires. In the winter the Chinese were forced to interlace their thin bodies, for warmth against the cold, like barnyard animals.

Deeper into Chinatown, Ki passed fish stores displaying mounds of gunmetal-gray squid with eyes of glinting gold. He saw a store that offered bottles of preserved chickens, snakes, and seahorses to eat for rejuvenation, and jars of leathery deer testicles and fuzzy antlers to eat for virility. A butcher shop was lined with shelves of live rabbits, ducks, and chickens, all penned in wire cages, all patiently awaiting their slaughter. Beneath the cages, his head drooping toward his crimson-spotted apron, the shop's proprietor sat dozing upon his stool.

What were the butcher's dreams, Ki wondered as he walked on. Was he musing on his similarity to the doomed animals he sold? Who—rabbit or man—had the brighter fate? Who—man or rabbit—was locked into the less cruel cage?

Ki stopped to watch four young boys, none of them more than five or six years old, hurrying on their way in the darkness. Each had a pigtail almost as long as he was tall, and each held on to the pigtail of the child in front of him. The little boys had no shoes, and their clothes were tattered and torn, but the weather was mild, and being children, they as yet felt no shame concerning their poverty. They disappeared around the corner, their bright, chirping laughter trailing behind them.

So many *kami,* Ki thought. So many ghosts and spirits...

He stared after the children, seeing himself in their forms. He remembered his own past...

An old woman, hidden somewhere in the shadows, began to wail an ancient Cantonese lament. It startled Ki out of his reverie. He hurried on, deeper and deeper into the heart of Chinatown, searching for Leno alley, the location of the girl's family's restaurant. Fortunately, the street signs were in English as well as Chinese, for the benefit of the many police officers who made extra money by guiding groups of tourists around the area.

When Ki finally found the right alley, he had to follow its twists and turns for some distance before coming to a group of restaurants lining both sides of the narrow throughfare. Each establishment's sign was written in Chinese, but each had an accompanying painted illustration to tell Ki what he could not read. There was the Green Dragon, the White Lotus, and the Kite. Ki paused before a restaurant that featured above its door the carefully painted likeness of a gold coin.

Ki's entrance attracted several quickly averted stares and much hushed whispering among the few Chinese families seated around the large round tables to the rear of the restaurant. No tourists had ever ventured this far into Chinatown to dine, Ki thought. He took a small table in a shadowy corner. There was barely room enough for him to sit, but the nook allowed him a clear line of sight while partially protecting him from the attentions of the overly curious.

The interior of the small restaurant was modest but clean. The rough walls were painted yellow, the floors were sprinkled with sawdust. Large cardboard placards, covered with Chinese writing, hung everywhere. Ki assumed they were menus. He had no idea what was on the bill of fare, but he did not care. He could not eat; his heart was pounding much too hard with anticipation. Where was she, he wondered. Tending the tables were a traditionally dressed middle-aged man and woman, and a boy of ten or so. The girl's parents and little brother, he surmised, but where was she? Bitter disappointment began to well up inside of him. She was not here...

Ki stared down at the worn, scarred surface of the table. Perhaps she was even now being courted by a suiter, possibly an elderly but wealthy Chinese merchant. It was common for widowers to purchase a marriage to the young and lovely daughter of a poor family . . .

She came out of the kitchen, passing through the oilcloth-curtained doorway with a tray of food in her arms. She was dressed as before, in the same old blue silk tunic and black cotton pantaloons, now protected by a white apron. Her long hair was bundled on her head and fastened in place with several plain wooden combs, so as not to get in the way as she worked.

She almost dropped her tray when she saw him. For one brief moment her large black eyes seemed to be filled with joy, but then she shook her head sorrowfully—whether to him or to herself, Ki could not tell.

He could think of nothing but the gleam of her hair and the lovely sway of her walk as she carefully served her waiting customers. She was starting toward him when one of the diners intercepted her, demanding something that forced her back to the kitchen. Ki waited in maddening frustration until she reappeared holding a pot of tea, which she quickly placed on the customer's table.

She was on her way to Ki when the doors of the restaurant were loudly slammed open. She stopped, to stand trembling as four Tong bullies strode in.

Ki recognized the first two as the pair who had earlier terrorized the girl and her grandfather on the waterfront. They were still wearing the cheap, American-style suits. The two men behind them were traditionally dressed. They had long, plaited queues dangling down their backs. The sleeves of their tunics were rolled up to reveal their thick forearms. Garish tattoos of dragons and tigers wound their way around the backs of the men's hands, all the way up to their elbows. Ki understood the tattoos' significance. These *wu-shu* men were fighters trained in one of the ancient schools of China, and were more skilled than the two who had earlier demonstrated their ability.

The tattooed men stood guarding the restaurant's door while the other two barged on into the kitchen. All of the customers had stopped eating, but continued to stare morosely at their plates. Not one lifted his head for so much as a glimpse toward the silent, scowling Tong men.

The girl had sidled closer to Ki. "Do nothing!" she whispered anxiously. "If they should notice you, they will kill you. There is no one here who could come to your aid."

The little boy, the girl's parents, and even her grandfather were herded out of the kitchen. As before, the man with the mustache did little. He left it to the scarfaced one to gather up the front of the father's tunic and slam him against the wall.

"I tol' the old man that we come for Chang's money," he spat into the father's face. "You pay us money now!"

"I not have it," the father protested feebly, in an accent made even harsher by his fear. "Please! Maybe tomorrow—"

"Now!" Scarface hissed. "Or we burn you down!"

Ki was shocked by the brazen threat, until he realized that it was highly unlikely that any of the cowering customers could understand English.

"I beg you!" the girl's mother cried in panic. She was blocked from rushing to her husband's aid by the mustached Tong man. "Please let him go!" she whined. "He is telling the truth. We cannot pay!"

"Then we burn you down," the scarred one said, letting the husband slump to the floor. His tone was bored. "It make no difference to me."

"If you do that, then we can never pay," the father reasoned quickly, still sprawled on the floor, afraid to try and get to his feet while Scarface loomed over him.

"That true," the hatchet man laughed. "Maybe we punish you some other way." He glanced about the restaurant, his cruel eyes settling upon the man's daughter.

"You!" he called. "Girl! Come here to me!" He reached into his suit pocket and pulled out a gravity knife. There was a crisp *click!* as the blade snapped open.

The girl, mesmerized by the knife, shook her head in terror, even as her feet were carrying her toward him. "No, no, no," she repeated hopelessly.

Scarface reached out to yank her the last few paces. The girl stood with her eyes tightly clenched as he pressed the flat of his knife blade against her cheek.

"How 'bout I do this?" the Tong man began reasonably. "I give her scar on face, like mine . . ."

"Oh, please, cut *me*—" the mother began.

"Silence, foolish woman!" the Tong man bellowed. "Why I cut you? You already ugly! You already married! I cut girl, no more chance of profitable wedding. Cost you much money. But you still have restaurant, so you can still pay my master, Chang, what you owe."

The girl began to cry. Scarface laughed. "I think you will do much crying before the night is over," he cackled.

Ki stood up. *"I* think it is *you* who will be doing the crying."

Scarface craned his neck to squint into the shadows. "Who?" he demanded. Then his eyes widened. "Mr. Smith, again!" He threw back his head and laughed.

"Laugh now," Ki said evenly. "Soon you will be howling with your dog ancestors."

There was a shocked intake of breath on the part of the girl and her parents. Even the little boy stared, awestruck. The scar on the bully's face seemed to thicken and pulse in his fury.

"You talk very big, Mr. Smith," he rasped harshly.

"Maybe he got a gun," the mustached man suggested. He had begun to move sideways, widening the space between himself and his companion.

Ki watched him out of the corner of his eye. "I have no gun," he announced matter-of-factly. He was watching the two men by the door, as well. They looked only mildly interested in what was going on. Ki didn't think they could understand English.

"You don't got a gun, that's too bad," Scarface chuckled, his good humor seemingly restored.

"Maybe he could go buy one, and then come back," Mustache joked. He'd placed himself next to the curtained kitchen doorway, almost out of the periphery of Ki's vision.

"No, I think the stores are closed now," Scarface answered. "I think it too late for Mr. Smith to get a gun." He spat on the floor in front of Ki. "I do think it's too late." He stared at Ki, and licked his lips.

Ki said nothing. Throughout their exchange, he'd been patiently waiting for his opportunity to attack. It would come, he knew, when the scarred one looked away. He was the leader of the group, and he was the one with a weapon in his hand. Ki would kill Scarface first; that would throw the rest of these vermin into confusion.

They were four, and he was one, but his great advantage lay in the fact that they thought he was a Caucasian. Ki smiled. Chang would lose four men tonight . . .

"What you smiling for?" Scarface shouted. "You like this girl?" He stretched out his arm, to use his knife like a pointer against the shivering girl's cheek. "Then you will choose which side of her face I cut."

Ki crossed his arms. Strapped to both wrists, but hidden beneath his sleeves, were two leather sheaths. Each held a razor-sharp *shuriken* throwing blade.

"Which side, Mr. Smith?" Scarface snarled. "Choose!" The man glanced away from Ki in order to glide his knife across the bridge of the girl's nose, almost, but not quite cutting her.

At that moment, all eyes in the room were on the scarred man's knifeblade. Ki saw his chance.

He slid his arms apart so that the inner sides of his forearms and palms rubbed together. The smooth motion forced the two throwing blades out of their sheaths. His hands rose up, the blades—four-inch knives without hilt or handle—glinting in the light as they left his fingers.

Scarface's gravity knife fell to the floor. The Tong man's eyes screwed up, and his mouth opened wide as he began to squall like a newborn babe. His right limb was still stretched out and pointing toward the girl, but now his fingers could only flutter uselessly as his trembling arm spurted blood. The first of Ki's blades had transfixed the man's elbow joint, slicing through the tendons and bone to act as a steel pin, locking the man's arm in its extended position.

One of the Tong men by the door began to charge forward, but he paused momentarily when he realized his partner was not with him. He watched, amazed, as his companion slowly crumpled to the sawdust, his ornately tattooed fingers clutching at the second of Ki's blades, now embedded in his chest.

The man's hesitation gave Ki the extra time he needed to reach into his coat and extract another *shuriken*, this one a disc in the shape of a six-pointed star. The disc looked like a spur-wheel, except that the *shuriken* was four inches across and forged of high-grade steel.

"Jibon-ren?" the pigtailed man uttered incredulously. *Japanese?* He rushed toward Ki, at the same time reaching a hand around to the small of his back. From a sheath hidden there he pulled a three-piece rod, similar in design to one of Ki's *nunchaku.* Each eight-inch segment of the rod was connected to the next by a short link of chain. The Tong man whirled this weapon in front of him as he advanced. Soon it was moving so fast that Ki would only see it as a blur.

Ki knew that even a glancing blow from the three-piece rod could shatter his skull.

He dodged and feinted before the attacking killer, looking

91

for an opening. His *shuriken* throwing star was ready in his hand, but he knew that the Tong man could easily deflect the star; the three-piece rod was now a whirling wall protecting the Chinese warrior.

Meanwhile, Ki reminded himself, there was still the mustached one to deal with. Ki glanced behind him in time to see the man disappear through the oilcloth-curtained doorway into the restaurant's kitchen.

It is not like a Tong man to run away, Ki thought, puzzled, but then the answer came to him. The mustached fellow had wisely decided that it was more important to ensure that his master knew of Ki's presence. Ki could not allow the man to escape. If Chang knew that a Japanese had challenged his men, he would come to the obvious conclusion that it was Ki, and that would implicate Jessie. If Ki did not kill all four of these henchmen, the entire mission against the cartel and the Tong would be jeopardized.

"Is there a back door?" he asked the girl, who was now huddled against a wall, along with her family and those customers who had not yet found an opportunity to flee the restaurant.

The girl shook her head. "There is no other door but that one," she said, pointing to the way Ki himself had come in.

That meant that the mustached man would be coming back this way, Ki thought. That meant he had to dispose very quickly of this Tong fellow whom he was now facing.

Scarface, meanwhile, had become quite oblivious to all that was taking place in the restaurant. He'd been hopping from one foot to the other, whimpering and moaning, desperately trying to get a grip on the slippery wedge of steel protruding from either side of his elbow.

Ki was embarrassed for the man, thinking he was carrying on rather too much for such a minor wound. Then it occurred to the samurai that his *shuriken* blade must be pressing against a nerve. Only that could explain the man's obvious agony.

The pigtailed Tong warrior chose that moment to lunge forward, whipping his weapon sideways, trying to catch Ki's ribs. The samurai bounded high into the air, drawing his knees up to his chest in order to escape the whistling rods, which skimmed across a table top, shattering plates and dishes. At the apex of his jump, Ki snapped his wrist to send the lethal star on its short journey to its target. There was a glitter of light and a high-pitched whine, like wailing wind, as the *shuriken* whizzed downward.

The Tong man tried frantically to twist out of the way, but Ki had taken into account the target's probable direction of escape when he'd figured the star's trajectory. As the Tong man lowered his head, the disc seemed to angle down accordingly.

There was a dull *thunk!* as the disc buried half of its diameter into the man's forehead. The Chinese toppled like a chopped tree, three points of the star jutting out from his brow like the silvery visor of a cap.

As the man twitched himself still, the last few remaining customers stepped over him in their anxious rush to the door. The girl's family seemed to be in a state of shock. They were standing huddled together, chittering in Chinese and vigorously shaking their heads, as if in denial of what had taken place in their restaurant. Only the girl seemed in control of her emotions.

She disengaged herself from her kin, to approach Ki. "Who *are* you?" she began.

"Hush," Ki said gently. Breathing lightly, his hands on his hips, he turned to face the curtained kitchen doorway. The mustached one had not come out. That meant he was lying in wait, for surely the man realized that Ki was not about to wander off, letting one of the Tong henchmen go free...

Ki stiffened as the curtain moved—but it was only a draft from the open front door. The mustached man now had the advantage, Ki knew. From his place of concealment he could strike at Ki as soon as the samurai barged through the curtain.

The scarred Tong man was now sitting on the floor, softly mewling. He'd given up trying to extract the solidly wedged *shuriken* blade from his elbow, and was now simply cradling the bleeding joint with his left arm.

Ki hurried over to the man, grabbed him by his lapels, and yanked him to his feet. He smacked off the caterwauling man's derby, and slammed him back against a wall.

"Who is crying now, dog?" Ki spat into the man's pale face. He removed his own Stetson and plopped it down on the Tong man's head.

"You are...*Jibon-ren*...samurai?" the man asked between his wheezes of pain.

Ki nodded, and began to drag the man toward the kitchen.

"Please," the Tong man whimpered. "Remove the blade!"

"Do not worry," Ki replied. "You will not feel it for much

longer." He shoved the man through the curtain, and crouched to somersault into the kitchen, right behind the moaning Chinese.

As Ki had hoped, the waiting mustached man had mistaken his friend for the samurai. There was a shot, ear-shatteringly loud within the close confines of the kitchen. The scarred man jerked against the impact of the bullet. He staggered for several more paces into the kitchen, to collapse across a table stacked with pots and pans. His dead weight upended it, sending his corpse, as well as the utensils, crashing to the floor.

The mustached man's momentary confusion allowed Ki to take cover behind a large chopping block.

"Now it is just the two of us," Ki called to the man, who fired twice more in reply. One of the bullets gouged a furrow along the top of the chopping block, while the other chewed a hole into the wall several inches above Ki's head.

"There is no way out of here, but past me," Ki reminded the man, who answered with another shot.

"That's four!" Ki taunted the Tong henchman. He could just see the fellow, hiding alongside one of the two large wood-burning cookstoves in the ten-foot-square room. Steaming cauldrons were on top of the two ranges, and overhead were hung cast-iron racks from which dangled still more pots and pans. Between Ki and the Chinese were one long table stacked with groceries, and the overturned table, beside which lay the dead body of the scarred man. On the other side of the doorway, on Ki's side of the room, was a large wooden tub. Ki assumed that was where the dishes got washed. He was thankful that the small room was so cluttered; the maze of objects kept the Tong man from merely advancing upon Ki, his pistol at the ready. The Chinese had seen Ki in action, and knew how fast he could move. The samurai doubted that the Tong man had the courage to test himself—even with his pistol—against Ki's agility and his flashing *shuriken* blades.

"Hey, *Jibon-ren*," the mustached man called. "You better give up to me. I think more of my men will soon come. This is Chinatown. *My* town, Japanese dog."

"Who will come to save you?" Ki asked, stalling. "None of your comrades escaped to summon help. There is only you, and soon you will be with your ancestors."

As he spoke, Ki crawled on his belly out from behind the chopping block. He was after one of the cast-iron skillets lying on the floor beside the scarred man's corpse. Exposing himself to the other's gun was risky, but Ki needed one of the heavy iron skillets. He still had *shuriken* blades, but they did not weigh enough for the plan he had in mind.

He'd just wrapped his fingers around the handle of the skillet nearest him, when his adversary squeezed off two more shots. One of them richocheted off the skillet, the impact almost tearing the utensil from his grasp.

Ki ducked back behind the chopping block. There were no more shots. The Tong man was reloading his revolver.

Ki leapt to his feet and threw the six-pound skillet as hard as he could toward the big, bubbling cauldron sitting on the stove just above the crouching man. The skillet whacked into the big pot with a satisfying *clang!* Boiling liquid sloshed over the rim of the cauldron, which tottered slowly, and then toppled off the stove's burner, spilling its contents upon the Chinese.

The Tong man screamed, rising up from his place of con-cealment like an apparition. The revolver fell forgotten from his fingers as he clasped his hands to his face. Steam was rising from his skin, which was already blistering from the oily, boiling hot stew that clung to his hair and coated his face, seeping into his eyes and running down his neck.

Blinded, the Chinese could only stagger forward, wailing for help. He tripped over the body of his partner, to sprawl facedown on the floor. His entire body seemed to convulse. He exhaled one long, drawn-out wheeze, and then, incredibly, seemed not to breathe at all . . .

Ki, disbelieving, prodded the still form with his foot. He crouched, suspicious and ready to strike, as he pressed one hand against the man's chest, and then felt his pulse.

It was no ruse. The man was dead. Perhaps his heart had stopped from the shock of being scalded; Ki did not know. What mattered was that it was over.

He retrieved his Stetson from the floor and, holding it in his hand, left the kitchen to reenter the restaurant area.

The girl gazed at him fearfully.

"It is done," Ki said. "They are dead."

"And so are we!" snarled the girl's father. "What do you think will become of us when Chang learns of this?"

"Father!" the girl pleaded.

"Silence, daughter!" he cried. "You can see his face now. You've seen what manner of weapons he uses. He is a Japanese, a samurai!" Turning toward Ki, the irate man demanded, "What say you, *Jibon-ren?* Will you return to defend us against the *rest* of the Tong? Will you fight again?"

Ki stood with his head slightly bowed, accepting the man's rebuke, for what the girl's father was saying was true. Ki had won this battle, but this helpless family might suffer the consequences of his victory. His reckless heart had motivated him to make this visit, but soon he would go on his way. As usual, his *karma* had led him to violence, and now these Chinese would reap the bitter harvest of his actions.

"Noble samurai," the father said sarcastically. "Proud conqueror of China—why *have* you graced this humble establishment?"

"To see your daughter," Ki mumbled. His throat seemed suddenly dry. Why were his words so thick? "To view her beauty, and to experience—to *savor*—her serenity..."

"Noble samurai," the father repeated. "You wish to make my daugher's acquaintance?"

Ki, his heart pounding, found he was unable to speak. He looked deep into the father's eyes, and slowly nodded. "Yes," he whispered. "Your daughter's acquaintance..."

"Noble samurai," the father spat, "I would rather her throat had been cut! Go now," he muttered, turning away from Ki. "We will clean up the filth you have left for us, just as we will suffer the retribution meant for you."

Ki stood stock-still. His eyes were closed, and yet beams of glittering light seemed to be piercing deep into his brain. His skin felt hot and flushed; was this the agony the scalded Tong man had felt just before he'd died of a ruptured heart? Ringing in Ki's ears was the cruel tittering of children. *"Mongrel!"* they were taunting. *"Dog fit only for the dung-filled streets..."*

How many men had he killed, Ki wondered? How many taunting, disrespectful men, and yet the children kept up their cruel laughter...

"I asked you to leave, *Jibon-ren*," the girl's father hissed.

Nodding, Ki began to walk toward the door. "My blades in the corpses of Chang's men prove that it was I who slew them," he said dully. "Tell Chang this: that a samurai was forced to chastise his unruly pets. Tell Chang that I came to Chinatown to see your daughter. Tell him that you rightly refused me this honor. Tell him that you believe I will come again, and that if I should, you will send your boy to fetch Tong men to capture or kill me."

"So far, I will have to tell no lies," the father said dryly.

"Then Chang will not harm you," Ki told him. "Chang will leave you as you are, hoping that *I* will be lured back."

"He cannot leave Chinatown alone," the daughter interrupted. "The news that a Japanese is here will have spread throughout the area. He will be set upon, should he walk the streets this night."

The father waved off his objection. "That is not our concern."

"I will guide him through the back alleys," the girl declared.

"No!" her mother moaned.

"Daughter!" her father roared. "I forbid this!"

"I wish to cause no further anguish here," Ki said. He hurried toward the door, but his way was blocked by the girl.

"Come," she whispered, ignoring her parents' pleas as she tugged at his hand. They took a few more steps, and then they were out of the restaurant, and wrapped in the blessedly peaceful darkness of the nighttime streets.

The girl was silent and grim until they were far enough from the restaurant so that her mother's piteous cries had faded. She led Ki around to the back of the building, indicating the narrow path they were to take.

"What is your name?" Ki asked as he followed her to a narrow, high-walled, trash-filled alley. The only light was that which weakly filtered through the back windows of the tenements on either side. "Please," he begged, "I must know."

"My name is Su-ling," the girl said reluctantly. Then she glanced up at him, smiling shyly. "Now tell me yours! I have not been able to stop thinking about you since this afternoon!"

"I am called Ki," he said, noticing that the girl's shortcut was allowing them to bypass many of the main streets of the area.

"But that could not be your true name?" the girl wondered, confused. "If you are a samurai, you must be of noble birth?"

"I was, but I no longer use my real name," Ki explained. He thought about how his aristocratic grandparents on both sides of the Pacific had rejected him when he was a helpless child. "I care nothing for my noble birth, and will not honor my families' names by using them. I took the name Ki when I became a samurai."

97

They left the alley to hurry across a deserted lumber yard. Ki lifted Su-ling up over a low wire fence, nimbly hopped it himself, and then went with her through a small park. With a start, Ki realized that they were no longer in Chinatown. At the top of a low hill, the girl paused. She gestured down toward the wide, gaslit streets below them.

"We are very close to the waterfront," Ki observed. "Very close to where we met, earlier this day."

"Yes," Su-ling sighed wistfully, turning to him. "Is it not sad? If I go any further, it will be I who am not safe." She shrugged. "You can not exist in my world. I cannot exist in yours."

"Su-ling," Ki began, looking into her large, dark eyes. "It is not my world, either. I have no place . . . to belong . . ." Ki looked away. How could he talk about this? He had never talked about his past to anyone.

"I understand what you mean," Su-ling coaxed gently. "You have no place to belong because you are of mixed parentage. You are unable to live in your homeland, for your blood is not pure. In America you are despised, called a foreigner, or worse, a 'Chinee'!" She laughed bitterly. "Oh, Ki, do you not see that it is the same for me?"

"You long to be accepted as an American," Ki said quietly. "But the Americans will not have you . . ."

Su-ling nodded, looking up at him. Ki watched the glistening tears escape her large eyes. They rolled down the perfect smoothness of her cheeks.

Ki reached out to scoop her up into his arms. She trembled like a tiny bird against his chest. Ki desperately hoped she understood that he wished only to comfort her, to protect her from the world.

"My parents do not approve of my wanting a life outside of Chinatown. They wish to arrange a marriage for me. They wish our lives to be as people live them in China." She tilted her head up toward Ki's. "They mistrust the outside world, the police, the government. They have made their wishes concerning my future clear to me. How can a daughter refute her parents' desires, and yet retain her honor?"

She tried to pull away from him, but Ki, worried that this chance might not come again, bent to kiss her. Her fragrant mouth yielded to his. Her arms wrapped tightly around him as her supple body pressed against him.

When their long kiss ended, she did not pull away, but kept her face close to his. Her eyes were halfshut, her mouth partly open. Ki ran his fingers through her shiny black hair, and then his hands moved gently over her body, caressing her firm, round bottom, tracing the curves of her hips and the swell of her warm breasts.

"Oh, noble samurai," she breathed, even as her lips nuzzled Ki's neck. "Twice today you have saved me from harm. Are you strong enough, true enough, to save my honor as well?" Her embrace tightened as her legs parted, then locked around Ki's thigh. "If you are so strong, please fight this battle for me! I fear that my body has betrayed me, and that my womanly honor hangs by only a few silken threads."

Ki knew she would willingly, totally, give herself to him this night. He had only to take her—and then leave her to regret and recrimination, leave her without her honor. And what would life be like without that most precious thing?

Ki kissed her one again. With his lips lingering against hers, he said, "Those silken threads shall not be torn by me this night, but one day I shall unravel them, slowly, carefully, one by one...

Once, very timidly, Su-ling brushed her fingers against Ki's erection. "I have never *touched* a man before," she murmured. "I—I wish you *could* be mine..."

She pulled away from him, and stood staring down at the brightly lit streets below.

"I will see you again," Ki began.

"No!" Su-ling said adamantly. "Once again, you must be strong for *both* of us. Ki, there is no *honor* in this. We could not be happy. I cannot go against my family's wishes. Should I do so, it would poison our union."

Silently she began to walk back the way they'd come.

"Will you be safe, going home alone?" Ki asked uncertainly.

She turned to smile at him. "Safer than I would be, traveling home with you, Japanese," she said wistfully. Then she blew him a kiss, and hurried back down the hill toward the small, tree-filled park.

"I *will* see you again!" Ki called after her. She did not answer. He watched until she'd disappeared among the trees.

She did not answer me, Ki thought as he walked down the opposite side of the hill, toward the gaslit streets and the nearby waterfront. *But then again, she did not say no...*

Ki decided he would walk for a while. There was much for him to ponder. All his adult life, he had secretly loved Jessie. His love for her would continue, but it would always remain chaste.

Su-ling...no woman had ever touched his heart the way she had. How he longed to make love to her! *All my life I have been homeless and alone,* Ki thought. *There is the Starbuck ranch, and Jessie, but they are not my own.*

Ki wandered slowly down the hill. Could it be, he wondered, that in Su-ling he would find his home?

Chapter 9

Jordan Moore did not want Jessie's name to appear in the papers. He escorted her to his well-kept, four-room apartment on Clay Street before returning to the site of the murder, to wait with Shanks's body until the police arrived.

Jessie made coffee in the small kitchen, and then, despite the only moderate coolness of the evening, stoked a fire in the living room's hearth. She wanted the light and cheerful crackling of the flames for companionship, not warmth.

She sat staring into the fire for about an hour before she heard Moore's key in the lock. The slightly built detective looked haggard and worn. His tie was loosened, and his shirt front was spotted with Shanks's blood.

"How did it all go?" Jessie asked him quietly.

"About as poorly as possible," Moore said, wincing. "They kept asking me what he—and I—had been doing there, and all I kept saying was that Shanks was there on his own time, and that I'd received a message that my partner was in trouble at that address."

"Did they believe you?" Jessie's tone was worried.

"Oh, sure." Moore laughed humorlessly. "And then I explained to them how if they were good, Saint Nick would bring them some clues for Christmas." He shrugged off his suit jacket. "Excuse me while I slip into something a little less blood-stained . . ."

Jessie watched the man trudge wearily into the bedroom. "The most ironic part," Moore called through the partly open bedroom door, "is that I really don't know for sure who killed him. I mean, obviously it was one of Chang's bodyguards, but Shanks was run clear through. Chang's men would have broken Shanks's neck, or chopped him with a hatchet. They don't have much use for swords."

"It wasn't Chang, or his men," Jessie said.

"What?" Moore came out wearing a thick velvet robe. "What do you mean? Of course it was. Shanks was following them and got careless—"

"Greta Kahr killed him." Jessie noticed that Moore's legs were bare between his slippers and the knee-length hem of the robe. Was the rest of him bare, as well? What a time to think about that! Jessie scolded herself, at the same time fingering the *netsuke* carving on the black ribbon around her neck.

"Now, why do you think it was Greta Kahr?" Moore asked her. "Wait, I'm going to fetch some of that coffee." He returned with a mug of the brew on a tray, along with two small glasses, and a bottle of sour-mash bourbon. "I have no brandy," he apologized. "Or rather, it's all gone. I had breakfast at home today, you see."

"Oh, stop," Jessie chided him, laughing. "You don't really drink all that much, do you?"

"I used to," Moore grinned, pouring them each a bourbon. "Before I left my old profession for this line of work."

"What did you do before?"

"I was a journalist, a police reporter, actually." Moore sat down next to Jessie on the couch, setting their whiskey on a small table nearby. "After a few years of scribbling accounts of crimes, I realized that what I hankered to do was to solve them. I thought of joining the force. Shanks was on the force then, and he advised me against signing up. Told me I wasn't the type to take orders, told me to open up a private agency, and that he'd throw some work my way." Moore shook his head sadly. "I sort of loved that man, Jessie. Big and dumb as he was . . . there was no question that he'd become my partner once he'd retired from the department . . ."

"I am so very sorry," Jessie murmured.

Moore nodded. He took a big swallow of his drink, and kicked off his slippers, to wiggle his bare toes before the warming flames. "My dear woman, I do hope I have not offended you?" he teased. "I mean, my feet being unclothed, or unshod, as it were . . ."

"I am scandalized," Jessie pretended to huff. "But as this

is 1880, and as we *are* in San Francisco, I suppose I will have to make allowances..." She burst into giggles, picked up her glass, and knocked back her dram of bourbon.

"Damn, woman! You keep drinking like that, and next time you can just bring your own bottle!" Moore said, and drained his own glass. "Just to stay even," he grimaced, and poured them both another. "Now tell me why you think Greta Kahr murdered Shanks," he said.

"This afternoon—or yesterday afternoon, I suppose it is now," Jessie said distractedly. "I mean, it must be after midnight..."

"The witching hour, but that can wait," Moore replied. "Go on with your story." He got up to walk over to the fireplace mantle, and extracted one of his cigars from a humidor.

"Well, I got the drop on Shanks, as I told you," Jessie continued. "I teased him about it, telling him to be more careful. I distinctly remember saying, 'Women are the more deadly of the species...'"

Moore stood at the mantle, his unlit cigar forgotten in his fingers. "That explains what Shanks's dying words were all about," he mused. "That stuff about how you were right, and that phrase, '...more deadly.'" He took a match from a canister next to the humidor, lit his smoke, and then returned to his place on the couch. "Greta Kahr..." he grumbled, puffing angrily upon his cigar. "Oh, I can just see Shanks falling for her line, letting her get close to him...too close..."

"One of the Tong bodyguards must have been carrying her weapon," Jessie mused.

"Sure!" Moore sneered. "A European-style rapier, it all makes sense. Poor Shanks!"

"That is a Prussian's sort of weapon," Jessie agreed. She glanced at Moore, who was glowering into his drink. "One thing I'd like to know," Jessie began tentatively. "Why didn't you tell the police of your suspicions concerning the Tong bodyguards? Was it because of me?" she softly added.

Moore looked at Jessie. Slowly his dark expression brightened into a smile. "You are so beautiful," he said. "I'm a fool for not lying to you, but you were only *partially* why I told the police nothing. You see, with no witnesses to the murder, it would be our word against Kahr's and Chang's. Both of them have enough contacts in the city government to be able to walk away from that kind of accusation. You would have revealed yourself to your enemies for nothing."

"So you *did* do it for me!"

"Only partially, as I said," Moore frowned. "You see, Jessie, *I* intend to *kill* both Kahr and Chang."

"Oh, no, Jordan," Jessie began.

"Quiet! You don't understand," the detective cut her off fiercely. "When a man's partner is killed, he's supposed to do something about it. That was the first thing Shanks taught me, Jessie."

"But what good can possibly come of risking your own life to avenge—" Moore's burst of laughter stopped her. "What's so funny?" she demanded, her green eyes flashing fire.

"Of all the people to lecture me about taking the law into my own hands," Moore gasped.

"Oh! Yes... I see..." Jessie blushed. "Well, just remember, you're not alone against them. You have Ki, and myself..." Once again she felt warmth suffusing her cheeks.

"My, what a pretty shade of pink you are," Moore teased.

"It's—the fire, of course," she stammered distractedly as Moore sidled closer to her end of the couch.

"I do compliment you on the way you pieced it together that it was Greta Kahr who did the killing," he murmured, sliding his arm around Jessie's shoulders. "Maybe"—he began to peck cool, light kisses upon her lips—"you... ought... to become... my new... partner..."

Jessie leaned back against the arm of the couch. She ran idle fingers through Moore's thick black hair. "Whatever kind of *partner* do you mean, Mr. Moore?" she asked wide-eyed.

Moore slipped the top of her low-cut gown down past her shoulders. He stopped, amazed at his good fortune as Jessie's lush, lovely breasts jiggled free. "My word!" he gasped. "You're not wearing any... underthings!"

"I don't always like them," she remarked shyly. "Sometimes—well, they get in the way."

"What a sensible woman," Moore remarked heartily. He watched the twin alabaster globes of Jessie's breasts rise as she reached up to remove the pins from her hair. Her coppery tresses fell about her shoulders like a shimmering curtain, reflecting the flickering glow of the hearth's flames.

Jessie leaned back and closed her eyes as Moore stretched out alongside her. She felt her nipples tighten and rise, as if to meet Moore's darting tongue.

104

"What a strange-looking cameo," Moore said, fingering the ornament at her throat.

Jessie's eyes flew open. "The *netsuke!*" she said distractedly, and then she laughed. She'd totally forgotten her amusing little vow to make Moore notice the emblem before they would make love ... or maybe she had only partly forgotten. *Something* had made her position herself so that Moore's nose was poking into it!

"It seems to be a carving of a kneeling woman, playing a flute," Moore said.

Jessie kissed the top of his head. "Do you know what a geisha is?" she asked him, at the same time settling her hands on his buttocks, tight and muscular beneath the plush velvet of his robe.

"It's getting a little hard to think," Moore began. "Actually, it's also getting a little hard to talk—"

"I think it's getting a little hard, period!" Jessie snickered, wiggling her gowned lap against what was fast thickening and beginning to peek between the two halves of Moore's loosely tied robe.

"Why don't you just explain to me what a geisha is while I take your dress off," Moore suggested brightly.

Jessie arched her back to allow the detective to begin unhooking her gown's buttons. "The word *geisha* best translates as 'artist,'" Jessie murmured. "A geisha is taught all through her childhood to be skilled in music, art, literature, the preparation and serving of fine food, and finally, when she is old enough, and if she had proven herself worthy, she is taught the skills and techniques of love—oh, God!" Jessie sighed, as Moore's nimble fingers danced the length of her now totally bare spine, coming to rest at the warm cleft of her gently undulating backside. "These techniques of lovemaking are the keys to a man's—and a woman's—soul ..."

Jessie lifted her legs to allow Moore to slide her gown off. Now she was completely nude before him. The detective stared down at her small waist, and the way it contrasted with the smooth flare and curve of her hips. Her firm, shapely legs were without flaw.

"Jessie," he said in awe. "You are the most beautiful woman—"

Jessie sighed with pleasure. "I am also a geisha, my love. That's a sort of priestess, as well as artist. It is said that through a geisha's body, a man can experience enlightenment. For the brief time a man spends with a geisha, they are both one with the universe."

"Is all of this symbolized by that likeness of the kneeling woman playing a flute?" Moore asked.

"It is," Jessie replied, and then moaned, as Moore began to slide his tongue down the slope of her flat belly. Downward, ever downward his tongue skated, until at last he had reached her first tendrils of fragrant golden softness. He paused to kiss and suck at the warm, downy fur, before his tongue flicked deep between her thighs, to lap at the moist sweetness cradled there.

Jessie's fingers caressed Moore's cheek. He looked up at her lovingly, his eyes bright.

"Jordan," she whispered. "Would you like me to play the flute for you?" Now it was *her* eyes that glinted with a mischievous sparkle.

Moore frowned. *"Now?"*

"Uh-huh . . ."

"Well . . ." Moore said, doing his best to remain polite. "But you didn't bring your flute!" he exclaimed with relief.

Jessie sat up, pushing Moore into an upright position along with her. "You silly man," she teased. "I *play* the flute, but *you* supply it!"

She plucked at the bow of his robe's sash. It quickly came undone. Her eyes widened in amazement as Moore's hardness bounded up toward her.

"Myobu was wrong, for once in her life!" Jessie laughed.

"Whatever are you talking about?" Moore sighed happily as Jessie's fingers tickled and played along the full length of his gently throbbing erection.

Jessie quickly related what her tutor had taught her concerning the supposed correspondence in size of the various parts of a man's body.

"I see," Moore chuckled. "And because I'm less than six feet tall, and rather thin, you thought that my—*ohhhh!*" Moore's mind blanked of everything but the marvelous feel of Jessie's lips upon him.

Now it was his turn to moan, as Jessie ran her lips up and down his shaft. She watched Moore's face; his head was thrown back, his eyes squeezed shut, his expression a grimace of ecstasy. After a few moments he twisted away. Jessie tried to hold him down, but she found that the slender detective was too strong for her. As a matter of fact, she found that he was as physically strong as any man she had ever been with.

Moore stood, to pick Jessie up and lightly stretch her out full length on the couch. Supporting himself on his hands and elbows, he pressed his muscle-ridged belly against her stomach, to blanket her with his warmth. He moved himself up, to slide his swollen erection into the sweat-damp cleavage of her breasts. Jessie used her hands to squeeze her breasts together, to caress and massage him between her satiny globes.

"I had so much more of my tune to play," Jessie whispered.

"I don't want you to play it." Moore smiled down at her. "Woman, I aim to make you sing it!"

With that, he nimbly slid his sinewy body down Jessie's silky length, until their tongues could intertwine, while his hardness teased and kissed the moist folds between her thighs. Jessie writhed beneath him. At the same time, her hands restlessly explored every inch of him. Her fingers stroked his erection, pressed and cradled his scrotum, and tickled their way along the crevice between his buttocks.

Moore's soft grunts of pleasure were muffled as he buried his face in the warm valley between Jessie's breasts. He inhaled her womanly fragrance as he licked, sucked, and then used his teeth to lightly rake her swollen nipples. Jessie's pleasured purr rose to a sob of joy.

Her legs parted then, almost of their own volition, to draw him greedily into her. Moore's initial stab downward seemed to reverberate within her. She whimpered and shuddered, and came at once, gyrating her bottom against the couch while her inner muscles squeezed his marble-like firmness.

Moore slowed his movements in order to give her time to recuperate. He pulled Jessie in tight against him, and slid his hand underneath her, to cup and stroke her trembling buttocks.

"Lord," Jessie breathed. *"That* one got started the day we met! Now let's start from scratch!"

She lifted her legs to lock them about his waist, and started her hips rolling and rising to meet his slow, deliberate thrusts. Moore kept her cradled in his arms as his hips swung up and down, each plunge taking them both deeper and deeper into the bottomless pit of sensation. It went on like this for long minutes. Neither of them felt any desire to hurry. Moore slowed his own movements each time he felt his orgasm near, until he heard those tiny whimpers again start to build in Jessie's throat. Then he clamped his hands on both of her hips, using them like handles to give him better purchase as he went faster for a few tremendous lunges.

"Sing to me, Jessie," Moore ordered, between lingering, wet kisses. "I want to hear that tune!"

Jessie, on fire with passion, could not help but oblige him. Her mouth opened wide, and her feline wails were music to Moore's ears. Growling, he bucked and kicked to drive himself into her, as Jessie licked and bit at his nipples. Her nails raked down his shoulders and back. They dug as deep as a rider's spurs into his buttocks.

Jessie knew they were both ready now. Her strong thighs lifted, to draw him in to the hilt. Clutched like that, Moore felt himself explode in a burst of blissful, molten sensation that left him sweat-drenched, breathless, and drained of energy.

"Jessie, you are wonderful," Moore huffed as his breathing returned to normal. "To think of all those fools throwing away their money in that bordello run by the cartel, while there are women like you in the world..."

"But I bet you'll still go back there," Jessie teasingly chided him.

"Well, I go there for business, not pleasure." Moore grinned. "After all, that's where I've been getting our information on the enemy. For instance, I found out that the cartel and the Tong are expecting a big shipment to arrive in port sometime during the next few days."

"A big shipment?" Jessie repeated. "Of what, I wonder?"

Moore shrugged. "Opium, probably."

Jessie nodded. "Maybe that shipment was tonight's topic of discussion between Greta Kahr and Chang..."

"Right after they'd killed Shanks," Moore agreed gruffly. "Well, once I learn the shipment's arrival time, I can intercept it, and begin to avenge his death."

"What are you planning?" Jessie asked in concern. "You know, it won't help matters to go and get yourself killed."

"Don't worry about me," Moore assured her. "I know how to handle myself."

"Oh, you've proved *that!*" Jessie said languidly. Her fingers burrowed into his groin, to rouse his flagging erection. "But why handle *yourself* when I'm around?"

Jessie scampered across Moore's lap, facing him. Slowly,

ever so agonizingly slowly, she lowered herself onto his strain-ing shaft. With her hands on his shoulders and her straddling legs firmly planted upon the cushions of the couch, she began to bounce up and down, her moistness lubricating him, pre-paring them both for a series of rapid, slippery strokes.

Moore gave himself up to the pleasure of being engulfed. As Jessie rose and fell, he wiggled and lunged, wanting to touch every velvety bit of her. He didn't want to stop any more than she did, but this time Moore felt even less hurried.

"Slow down. I want to make love to you nonstop, for the rest of the night," he confided.

Jessie kissed him. "That's fine," she laughed, "but first I want to ask you a favor."

"Well?"

"I want you to take Ki along with you when you try to stop that shipment from reaching the cartel and the Tong."

Moore winked. "I was planning to ask him if he'd accom-pany me. I've no desire to go up against the cartel and the Tong, all by my lonesome. I may be conceited, but I'm not stupid!" He locked his hands on the cheeks of Jessie's backside to hold her in place, and stood up, without breaking the bond of flesh that joined them. Jessie's legs swung up, her knees grazing his armpits. Moore gazed into her ever-widening eyes as he slowly sank his entire length into her. The new angle of penetration sent dizzying jolts of sensation along Jessie's spine.

"Oh, don't wait!" she now pleaded as Moore stood as still as a statue. "Give it to me hard!"

Moore obliged, slamming into her, and at the same time spinning her around and around the room, until Jessie was as weak as a kitten, helpless in his twirling embrace. She threw back her head and sobbed her pleasure as her copper-gold tresses whipped along behind her head like the tail of a comet.

She came for a third time, in a tangled mix of little screams, a series of jerking quivers. Moore's own spasm buckled his knees so that he fell back upon the couch and Jessie, her legs still clamped around his middle, fell with him, to wring the last drops of his passion out of him. Moore's convulsions made him shudder and shake, but Jessie stayed firmly around him, as if her sweet love juices were a special sort of glue locking their bodies together.

Sighing contentedly, Jessie asked him, "Am I really as good as the girls in the bordello?"

Moore, his eyes still screwed shut, moaned, "Compared to you, they barely qualify as girls!"

"Then it's only logical!" Jessie said triumphantly. "I'm going to go there tomorrow and get a job!"

Moore nodded, without really paying attention to anything but the delicious shivers of feeling in his loins. Then his eyes flew open. "You're going to *what?*"

"Well, not for real," Jessie rushed to reassure him. "I mean, I'm going to go undercover, like you did."

"Undercover is *right,*" Moore growled. "And under the covers is where you'll land. What do you think those girls *do* to make their living?"

"I know very well what they do!" Jessie admonished. "But I only intend to be there a couple of days, and there are ways a woman can avoid lovemaking for that length of time without arousing suspicion."

"It's much too dangerous—" Moore began.

Jessie cut him off, pressing her finger to his lips. "Jordan, I've never let danger stop me. Our lovemaking is wonderful, but you mustn't let it put any silly ideas in your head. I can handle *myself* too, you know."

"But Jessie—"

"Hush now, don't argue with me. You have to admit that my being on the inside will help us. Why, just think about all the useful information you got by just spending a few *hours* in the bordello as a paying customer. If I can spend a few *days* in there, I'm sure to hear something about that shipment you want to intercept—"

"All right!" Moore laughed, shaking his head. "You've convinced me. Besides, there really isn't anything I could do to talk you out of it, is there?"

Jessie said nothing, but arched her back to stretch and yawn. Then, grinning like a cat, she began to plant kisses across Moore's chest.

"You'll—you'll take your gun?"

"Uh-huh." Jessie slipped off the couch to get down on her knees between Moore's spread legs.

"We'll inform Arthur Lewis of what you're planning—"

"Um-hmmmm . . . mmmmmm . . ." Jessie delicately lifted Moore's tender, swollen, sensitized member, and slipped it into her mouth.

Moore felt his spine turn to jelly as Jessie's lips locked

110

around him. His head rolled on his shoulders, so that his wide eyes fell upon the *netsuke* that had fallen from Jessie's neck during their first bout of lovemaking. The ornament had lodged itself into the corner of the couch. Moore's trembling hand found it, to lift it to view. In delight, he looked first at the carved image of the kneeling woman playing the flute, and then at the real-life version, playing *his* flute . . .

And, as it turned out, Jessie knew how to play it for a very long time, indeed. Before she was finished, sometime toward dawn, she had managed to coax out of Moore some very flute-like songs.

Chapter 10

Jessie and Moore managed to snatch a few hours' sleep bundled together in Moore's big double bed, but it was still very early in the morning when they sat down to eat the bacon-and-eggs breakfast the detective had prepared. Now that he'd been won over to Jessie's scheme, Moore turned out to be very knowledgeable concerning the way she had to go about landing her "job" at the bordello. He'd explained that Jessie couldn't just waltz up to the front door and present herself for hire. Foxy Muscat, the madam of the bordello, had her own method of recruiting what she considered the right sort of girls. Any overt, brazen approach on Jessie's part, and Foxy would smell a rat. Jessie had to be like all the other girls, which meant that she had to make the bordello's madam think that she had been swept up in her trawling net...

Jessie returned to the Palace Hotel in order to bathe, change her clothes, and gather up the props Moore had said she would need to put her ruse into effect. She asked Ki to fetch her several threadbare dresses from a secondhand clothing store Moore had told her about, and to purchase for her a shabby valise at a nearby pawn shop.

She donned one of the cotton dresses, pulled her hair back into a braid, and kept her face free of makeup. She packed the rest of the dresses into her "new" valise, along with her hairbrush, comb, and a few other odds and ends. Buried deep in the bottom of the bag was her Colt revolver, with extra ammunition. Jessie hefted her valise and examined herself in the mirror. With her clean-scrubbed face, girlish hairstyle, and modest dress, she looked to be no older than a girl in her teens.

Ki knocked on the door to her suite, and then came in. He stared at her for a moment, and then his face broke into one of his rare smiles.

"You are very beautiful," he said, "but appear to be unaware of it. Like a diamond in the rough."

"Let's hope so," Jessie replied in uncertain tones. "According to Jordan, I've got to look good enough to attract attention from the most exclusive house of ill repute in San Francisco, but not so good that I might turn and shout for the police at the recruiter's approach."

"Do you have your gun packed?" Ki asked.

"Yes." Jessie shrugged. "I almost decided not to take it."

"Jessie, you must have it!" Ki exclaimed. "I will watch over you for a time, but once you go into that place, you will be on your own."

"I know that." Jessie gave herself a final once-over, and then turned from the mirror. "The danger is that they might decide to go through my belongings, looking for something of value to steal. If they find my revolver, my goose will be cooked."

"What you must do," Ki advised, "is find a place to hide the weapon."

"Somewhere in the bordello where they won't find it, but where I can easily get to it, should I need it," Jessie muttered. "Well! That sounds easy enough."

"Jessie, deciding to do this was your own idea," Ki gently chided.

Jessie smiled at him. "Yes, I know. And I think I'd better get started. I find that carrying out these crazy schemes of mine are never as scary as *thinking* about them."

"Shall we, then?" Ki laughed.

Jessie scrutinized her friend. "Ki, you seem *different* somehow . . ."

"Really? How so?" Ki winked at her.

"You seem . . ." Jessie hesitated, suddenly not at all sure whether it would be appropriate to tell Ki that he seemed different because he seemed *happy* . . . "Oh, never mind. Time for me to take my fall into the gutter."

"To *pretend* to take your fall," Ki sternly warned.

"Now you sound like the *old* Ki," Jessie chuckled.

They left the hotel, and made their way by cable car to the

Ferry Building, down by the waterfront. They'd timed their arrival to coincide with the docking of one of the Oakland ferries.

Jessie merged with the passengers disembarking. Ki kept well away from her, watching as she wandered uncertainly. She did indeed look like a girl fresh off the farm, and lost, now that she'd finally arrived in the big city. Ki smiled to himself. He watched with satisfaction as Jessie began to be stalked by a well-dressed, respectable-looking matron. As the gray-haired, middle-aged woman approached her, Ki turned to make his way back to the hotel. He had preparations of his own to make. Jessie had informed him of Jordan Moore's plans.

Ki was a man of action. He relished the idea of going up against the cartel under the cover of darkness, of disrupting their schemes and perhaps even destroying their clipper ship's cargo of damned opium.

And yet, striking at the cartel was only a part of it. Ki hoped that combat would take his mind off Su-ling; it was quite remarkable how she had conquered his warrior's heart. Jessie had even noticed it, but then, that was not so unusual, the samurai thought. After all, Jessie was his closest friend, his soul-mate, in a way . . .

But so was Su-ling his soul-mate, and, unlike Jessie, she might one day truly be his mate.

Ki felt his heart lighten with a kind of joy that had been unknown to him for too long. He rejoiced in this odd sensation of pleasure that seemed to arise upon contemplating the face and form of a loved one.

Ki rejoiced in this feeling but did not totally give himself over to it. He still had his duty to consider. Jessie had asked him to assist Jordan Moore, and honor demanded that he acquiesce to her wishes. He knew that she had spent the night with the detective, but for once the jealousy that usually clawed at his insides now seemed bearable. It was Su-ling who had blunted his savage emotions, who turned his thoughts away from Jessie, replacing her as the object of his shameful jealousy. Woe to the man who should dare to touch Su-ling!

Grinning savagely, Ki hurried to where the hacks waited to be hired. He would return to the hotel and wait until Jordan Moore summoned him.

The joy of love was a strong joy indeed, but there were other kinds. The good, clean joy of combat was what he now needed, Ki realized. When a samurai's mind became befuddled, only the blood of his enemy could wash it clean...

Jessie's sixth sense had told her she was being watched. She did her best to remain relaxed, and wandered about the swiftly deserted exit ramp of the docked ferry. She'd noticed the middle-aged matron who was noticing *her*, and, most likely, hesitating in her approach in order to make sure that Jessie was not waiting for some tardy beau or parent to come fetch her. Sure of her audience, Jessie now went into her performance. She headed slowly toward the cable cars, but then stopped to open the valise and extract a small, beaded change purse. She opened the little purse, peered at what was inside, and then clicked it shut, shaking her head and daubing at her eyes with a worn linen handkerchief she'd had balled in the pocket of her dingy dress.

"Pardon me, young lady."

Jessie turned, startled, to face the kindly visage of the gray-haired matron who had been watching her all this time.

"Y-yes?" Jessie said timidly.

"I couldn't help noticing that you seem a bit lost, child," the woman smiled. "Are you new to our city?"

"Yes, ma'am."

"And have you no one to meet you?" the woman asked.

"No, ma'am."

"No one at all?" the woman persisted. "No family or friends in these parts?"

"I'm not from these parts, you see, ma'am," Jessie explained. "All of my family is in the Midwest. I'm from Chicago, you see..." Jessie stopped. She turned slightly away from the woman and began to cry, wiping her eyes with her hankie.

"Come, come now, child," the matron murmured comfortingly. "It can't be as bad as all that." The woman paused. "What did you say your name was, child?"

"Annabelle," Jessie sniffed. "Annabelle Willis. But you can call me Annie," she blurted, a trifle more brightly. "Everybody does. I mean, everybody *used* to..." Once more she began to sob quietly.

"Here now, Annie! No more tears," the woman chided her gently. "My name is Mrs. Fitzroy. I happen to have a few spare moments. You come along with me over to the café, and we'll have a nice, hot cup of tea."

"That would be lovely, Mrs. Fitzroy," Jessie gushed, "But—"

"But what?" Mrs. Fitzroy asked. "Come now, child, surely you're not afraid of an old woman like me, are you?"

"Oh, no, ma'am!" Jessie giggled. "I mean—" She put her fingers to her lips and opened her eyes wide.

"What lovely hazel eyes you have, Annie," the matron said admiringly. "And lovely hair." She paused. "Well, if you're not afraid of me, why won't you share a cup of tea?"

Jessie averted her eyes. "It is so embarrassing to admit," she whispered. "But—"

"Could it be that you don't have any money, child?" Mrs. Fitzroy coaxed gently.

Jessie nodded quickly, still not looking at the woman.

"Then you shall be my guest!" Mrs. Fitzroy said cheerfully. "What do you think of that?"

Jessie's hands flew to her breast. "I couldn't—" She glanced hopefully at Mrs. Fitzroy. "Could I?"

The matron's steely eyes had followed Jessie's hands. "You have a lovely figure, child," she mused aloud. "Tell you what. You have a cup of tea at my expense, and next time it'll be your turn to pay."

"Next time," Jessie said doubtfully. "That can't be until I find myself a job, you realize . . ."

Mrs. Fitzroy took her arm, steering Jessie along toward the cafe. "You're looking for a job, are you? Tell you what—a big, healthy girl like you could do with a nice blueberry muffin or two. Am I right? They make lovely muffins here." They entered the café and took a table for two. "Young girls do have hearty appetites, I've found," she prattled on. "By the way, how old did you say you were?"

"Why, I'm twenty-y-y-y . . ." Jessie purposely spun the figure out. ". . . three!" She ended adamantly, but with a slight uncertainness to her tone.

"Oh, really?" Mrs. Fitzroy appeared amused. "Then quickly! What year were you born?"

"1862!" Jessie blurted. "Oh, my!" she sighed.

"Just as I thought!" the matron chortled triumphantly. Jessie stared down into her lap as the waiter approached their table.

117

"Two cups of tea, please," Mrs. Fitzroy ordered. "And a plate of your blueberry muffins." After he'd left, she said, "So! You are really eighteen. I'd thought as much."

"I'm sorry I fibbed," Jessie said. "It's just that I'd heard that young girls have trouble finding work."

The waiter arrived with their tea and muffins. Jessie hurriedly snatched one up and bit into it.

"Hungry, are. you?" Mrs. Fitzroy chuckled. "Imagine! expecting me to believe that a young slip like you was twenty-three—"

"I *am* sorry," Jessie sighed.

"Well, see that you don't lie to me again, child, or I'll turn you over my knee and show you what hiding things from me will earn you!"

Jessie shivered. There was something very ominous in the woman's tone, despite the light-hearted nature of her threat. Jessie wondered what might happen to the poor girls already trapped into the bordello by Mrs. Fitzroy. What did this kindly-looking woman do to punish them for lying to her? *She'll be as sweet as can be until she's gotten you inside the bordello,* Moore had told Jessie over their breakfast that morning. *Old Fitzy's job is to lure the girls in. She's not the madam, but then, Foxy Muscat herself couldn't go out in broad daylight without attracting a crowd. Fitzy acts as the madam's assistant. She sees to the girls' needs—their health, linens, things like that . . .*

Jessie pondered Moore's final caution: *Don't let Fitzy's "grandmother" act fool you. Word has it she's slit the throat of more than one girl who didn't "fit in" at the bordello.*

Jessie thought about how helpless most young women would be, once they were ensnared in the web spun by this black widow spider. She herself was lucky. She was only pretending. But how many before her had had to live out their years locked into this little farce? How many unknowingly sold themselves for the price of a cup of tea and a blueberry muffin? This time, Jessie did not find it difficult to wring the tears from her eyes.

"And *now* why are you crying?" Mrs. Fitzroy asked. "Don't tell me that my rebuke has frightened you?"

"No. It's just that my own mother used to say that to me . . ." Jessie sniffled wetly into her hanky. "And not so very long ago."

"Why did you leave home, Annie?"

Mrs. Fitzroy had sounded only mildly curious, but Jessie had a glimpse of the matron's piercing gray eyes. Jessie's instincts told her that what she said next would influence the course of events. Her story had to convince Mrs. Fitzroy that she was vulnerable, but not so fragile as to be useless in the bordello. If the woman decided against her in the next few moments, Jessie would have lost her only chance of getting in to spy upon her enemies.

"My father worked for a warehouse in Chicago," Jessie began. "He and my mother were very happy together. Then one day we got a message..." Jessie lowered her eyes along with her voice for the next part. When she spoke, it was in a hushed, shamed whisper. "The police had gone to the warehouse, and many people had been shot. They said my father had tried to hurt a policeman. But I don't believe it! Not for one minute! Anyway... it turned out the warehouse was filled with stolen things. But if it had been, my father certainly didn't know about it!"

"Of course not, child..." Mrs. Fitzroy sipped at her tea. Her eyes, above the rim of her cup, looked thoughtful.

"I had a beau," Jessie said. "But things between us became strained after... after the incident. Mother was so ashamed that she refused to leave the house. I got a job as a laundress, but then Mother began to get sick, and I wasn't making enough money for us to live on, let alone pay for doctors. So she ... died..."

Mrs. Fitzroy was silent for a moment. "Well," she finally said, "I'm sure you did your best. So you decided to come to San Francisco to start anew?"

Jessie nodded. "None of my friends wanted anything to do with me after what had happened to Father. We had no other family, so that once Mother had ... passed on ... I found myself all alone. I sold our furniture and used that money to pay for my passage west. The bank took our house." Jessie looked up at Fitzroy, and then shrugged. "So here I am." She smiled tentatively.

"Yes, and almost too good to be true," Mrs. Fitzroy said softly.

Jessie froze. Had she come on too strong with her tale of woe? Well, all she could do now was wait.

"I must say, I'm quite impressed with your strength, Annie," Mrs. Fitzroy remarked. "Have another muffin, child. You

119

know, many girls would have crumbled after what you've been through. But you went out and found yourself a job, and tried to keep your home together. Yes, I'm very pleased."

"Thank you, ma'am," Jessie modestly lowered her eyes.

"And you say you're looking for work?"

"Oh, *yes*, ma'am!" Jessie said hopefully.

"I might know of something," the matron mused. "However, I'm afraid you've given me cause to be suspicious, to doubt your word . . ."

"I have?" Jessie's stomach did a sickening flip-flop.

"You lied to me about your age." Mrs. Fitzroy shrugged. "Before I could possibly recommend you for the position I have in mind for you, I'd have to see proof of your age and name."

Jessie smiled in relief. "Oh! That's *easy!* I have my birth certificate with me. It's the only identification I have. I do hope it is enough." She retrieved her change purse, and took from it a worn-looking document folded into quarters. This was the birth certificate Moore had supplied her with. It had turned out that the detective had a stack of blanks in his desk, along with other forms of bogus identification, including the carefully preserved and alphabetically filed business cards of the various individuals he met in his day-to-day activities. Moore would often use the cards to pretend to be those professionals. It was just amazing, he'd confided to Jessie, how often people would accept a proffered business card as gospel.

The detective had carefully inked the name Annabelle Willis onto one of his blank birth certificates. Next he'd sprinkled a mixture of water and lemon juice onto the fresh, crisp paper, in order to yellow it. He'd gently crumpled the damp sheet, and then set it by the hearth to dry. By the time their breakfast was over, the frayed document appeared at least as old as its new owner purported to be.

Jessie unfolded the certificate and handed it over to Mrs. Fitzroy. Now the thing to do was to try and figure out a way to distract the matron as much as possible from a close examination of the document. Moore had promised that the aging process would pass a cursory examination, but a too-careful inspection would reveal his handiwork. Her eyes fell upon the plate of muffins still on the table.

"Do you mind if I wrap these last two in a napkin, for later?" she asked bashfully.

Mrs. Fitzroy looked up from the certificate. "What?" she asked. "Oh, the muffins!" she chuckled. "Go right ahead, Annie." She did not hand the certificate back to Jessie, but left it on the table, beside her teacup.

Jessie wondered if it would be more in character to straightforwardly ask for the identification back, or to say nothing. She decided to say nothing, for the time being.

"Well then, I think you might do nicely for the job I have in mind," Mrs. Fitzroy beamed. She summoned the waiter, and asked for their check. "A very wealthy lady I know has need of a servant. I happen to be the lady's companion and business secretary, so if you should accept the job, it would mean seeing a lot of me." She smiled widely.

"That would be lovely!" Jessie exclaimed. "I'd be an excellent worker, Mrs. Fitzroy. I can cook and sew and clean—"

"Yes. Well. We shall see." Mrs. Fitzroy handed the waiter some money, took back her change, and slipped it into her purse—along with Jessie's "birth certificate."

"Um, excuse me," Jessie murmured, "but that's the only identification I have. May I have it back?"

"Come now, dear," Mrs. Fitzroy said brusquely. "I'll need to present this to my employer—and your *prospective* employer—if you're to get the job."

Jessie purposely looked doubtful. "Well . . . I . . ."

"It includes room and board, by the way," Mrs. Fitzroy added offhandedly.

"Really?"

"And if you like, you can come along with me right now for your interview."

"Yes, thank you!" Jessie cried happily.

She followed the woman toward the hacks waiting on the other side of the Ferry Building. The trap had been sprung, Jessie thought. But then she wondered: who had caught whom?

The carriage ride to the house on the corner of Dupont and Washington Streets, just on the outer fringe of Chinatown, did not take very long. Mrs. Fitzroy kept Jessie distracted by chattering on about what her duties would be, her hours, and so on. When the cab finally pulled up in front of the rambling, four-storied, ramshackle house, Jessie felt a wave of panic wash over her. She had to remind herself that she was not really Annabelle Willis, but Jessica Starbuck, and that she had a gun in her bag, and capable friends who knew of her whereabouts.

Jessie also had to remind herself that all of this had been her idea—and that, maybe, in the future, she ought to keep her bright ideas to herself.

Then Mrs. Fitzroy was herding her up the walk, up the front steps, and through the front door. Then Jessie was *in*.

The things Moore had told her about were nowhere in evidence. Jessie had expected to see loitering girls garbed in flimsy lingerie, a black man at the keyboard of a honkytonk piano, and a bar manned by a beefy bouncer. What she did see was a modestly decorated foyer, and a flight of wide, curving stairs that led to the upper floors. Perhaps the bordello part of the house was reached through another, more discreet side entrance, Jessie mused.

"Now, before you meet the lady of the house, why don't you let me show you upstairs, to what may well turn out to be your room," Mrs. Fitzroy said. "I'll have a bath drawn for you so that you can freshen yourself after your long journey."

Jessie was led upstairs to the second floor of the house. She was shown a small but tidy bedroom, complete with a single bed, a dresser, and a washstand. Jessie noticed the sturdy lock on the door, as well as the fact that the single window was barred with a decorative but strong iron grate.

Mrs. Fitzroy supplied her with a thick cotton robe and told her to get undressed, while she saw to the bath. Once Jessie was alone, she hurried to search the room for a place to hide her gun. She had no doubt that her belongings would be rifled while she was in the tub. There was no closet in the room, and in any case a closet, the dresser, even the space under the bed, would be searched as well. Jessie knew that she could not be the first girl brought to this room who had tried to conceal something—a piece of jewelry or a bit of cash—from the owners of the house.

Jessie heard footsteps coming down the hallway, and froze fearfully, thinking that she'd run out of time.

But the footsteps went past Jessie's door, to fade gradually into the distance. All was not yet lost, but she had to move fast!

Jessie eyed the narrow, single mattress on the bedframe. *Yes,* she thought. *That just might work. But I've got to hurry.*

She dug into her valise to find her sewing kit. With it in hand, she yanked the mattress off the bed, stripping away the blanket and sheets. She used the tiny scissors in her kit to cut a horizontal, five-inch slit into the edge of the mattress that had been against the wall. She jammed her gun and ammunition through this slit, and then used needle and thread from her kit to rapidly stitch the slit more or less closed. It was a ragged job, but it was all she had time for. Jessie hoped her sewing would keep telltale bits of mattress ticking from falling to the floor.

She quickly placed the mattress back into position, and then remade the bed. She'd shucked her dress and undergarments, and wrapped herself in the robe, just as Mrs. Fitzroy came knocking at her door.

Jessie was soaking in the steaming tub when she heard the door to the bathroom open. She turned in time to see a hand snake into the room and steal away the cotton robe.

She sat—as she assumed she was supposed to sit—in the fast-cooling water. Every now and then she called out plaintively, "Mrs. Fitzroy!" gradually increasing the need in her voice as she grew even colder.

Ki had long ago taught her meditation techniques that could help an individual to combat the ill effects of debilitating cold. These techniques Jessie now practiced, so that even though she was pretending to be thoroughly chilled and terribly uncomfortable, her mind was still clear and sharp. The effectiveness of what the bordello's proprietors were attempting to do was not lost to her, however.

Jessie knew that any other girl would very likely be close to hysteria by now. Bone-weary, undernourished, and now naked and cold in a strange house, in a strange city, with no one to turn to except Mrs. Fitzroy, a stranger, most girls would be at their wits' end. Such a girl might well agree to anything in exchange for a bit of warmth, food, and a chance to sleep . . .

They left Jessie alone like that for over three hours. Once she'd tried the door, only to find it locked from the outside. The window was nailed shut, as well. Its outer side was covered by another of those wrought-iron, decorative versions of prison bars.

Jessie sat cross-legged on the icy cold, tiled floor. She kept her back straight, her hands folded in her lap, and her eyes half closed, just as Ki has taught her. She pictured in her mind the radiant, sunlike energy pulsing up and down her spine, and the white, glowing ball of warmth that smoldered in her middle like coals inside a potbellied stove. Her ears, sharpened by the hours of meditation, picked up the sound of footsteps approaching the bathroom door. Jessie quickly came out of her trancelike state, and scampered on her hands and knees into a corner of the room.

Mrs. Fitzroy opened the door to see a huddled, shaking, and apparently very frightened girl. The matron was now wearing a plain gray skirt, a high-necked white blouse, and a workman's sort of blue cotton apron. Her gray hair was pulled back into a tight bun.

"On your feet," Mrs. Fitzroy said. She'd sounded bored. Jessie wondered how many times the woman had done this to other girls.

"W-why'd you leave m-me here like th-this?" Jessie cried. "S-somebody took my r-robe and—"

A look of annoyance twitched across Mrs. Fitzroy's seamed, pallid face. "Just shut up, girl. And *get* up."

"How d-dare you talk to me like th-that?" Jessie whined, still crouched in her corner. She laced her arms across her bare breasts. "G-give me b-back my c-clothes!"

Fitzroy strode over to Jessie, grabbed a handful of her hair, and yanked upward, hauling her to her feet. "I told you twice to get up!" the matron hissed as she got a better grip on Jessie's tresses, in order to twist and pull.

"Ow! Please! Stop!" Jessie screamed in agony. It felt like Mrs. Fitzroy was going to tear her scalp off.

"Go on," the matron chuckled, still pulling Jessie's hair. "Shout your lungs out. No one will come."

"Ow! *Please!*" Jessie stood still, trying her best to appear docile.

Mrs. Fitzroy stopped. "That's better, child," she smiled, her gray eyes glinting with pleasure. "Now stand straight. There's someone here who wants to see you."

The door to the bathroom swung open. In walked a woman who had to be Foxy Muscat, the madam of the bordello.

Moore had somewhat prepared Jessie for the sight, but still, Jessie could only stare, awestruck.

Foxy weighed at least two hundred pounds, and was a mere five feet tall. She was wrapped in a bright red kimono of sheer silk that gaped open to her barrel-thick waist. She wore her thin hair in a tightly coiled topknot, making her head look about two sizes too small for her gargantuan lump of a body. Her flapping breasts and pendulous belly were melded together in what looked like one huge mass of tallow. Her face was powdered a garish white; two silver-dollar-sized spots of rouge dotted her flabby cheeks, and her puffy lips were smeared with rouge of a darker shade, almost purple.

"Well, what do you think of her?" Fitzroy asked proudly. "Isn't she everything I told you?"

"And more, Fitzy, and more!" Foxy's little-girl voice was filled with admiration. "Make her stand up straighter," the madam ordered. "Arch her back."

Fitzroy gripped Jessie's arms and pulled backward. "You heard her!" she hissed into Jessie's ear.

Jessie felt as if her arms were about to be yanked out of their sockets, but she continued to feign helplessness.

"Her breasts are splendid!" Foxy chirped. Her sausage-like fingers reached out to pluck at Jessie's nipples, while her sour, whiskey-sodden breath thudded into Jessie's face.

It was too much for Jessie. Involuntarily, she shrank away from the grotesque woman.

"Fitzy?" the madam complained in her tiny voice. "Hold her still!" She stamped her slippered foot. "Fitzy!" she whined. "Make her behave!"

Jessie felt herself being spun around to face Mrs. Fitzroy. Without a word, the matron pulled back her arm and slapped Jessie hard across the face.

The sickening *splat!* of Fitzroy's palm across Jessie's cheek reverberated off the tiled walls of the bathroom. As her head rocked back and her eyes suddenly filled with sparks and stars, Jessie felt herself toppling off her feet. She would have fallen, to crack her skull against the hard floor, if Fitzroy hadn't caught her in time.

Far, far away, she heard Foxy Muscat say, "Take her back to her room. You've done well, Fitzy. Our client will be so pleased!"

Then a roaring built in Jessie's ears, until she could hear nothing at all.

She awoke to find herself lying atop the still-made bed in her room. Mrs. Fitzroy was sitting on the edge of the bed, just beside her. Jessie's jaw throbbed. Her fingers gingerly explored her tender cheek.

"You'll live," Mrs. Fitzroy said. "Sit up. And do it fast,

if you don't want another—"

Jessie sat up before the other woman could even finish her threat. She most certainly did not want another slap like that last one. She looked around. As she'd expected, her valise was gone, along with her clothes. She resisted the temptation to glance down at where she'd slit open the mattress.

"Why are you treating me this way?" Jessie asked meekly. "Please give me my clothes and let me go..."

"Not so soon," Mrs. Fitzroy laughed. "But if you'd like to wear something, you can put this on." She tossed Jessie a garment that had been lying across the foot of the bed.

"This is all I get to wear?" Jessie stared at the gauzy chemise, little more than a nightgown, really. "Why, I'll freeze!"

Mrs. Fitzroy smirked. "Not at all. Notice how warm this room is, for example. The entire house, with the exception of that bathroom, is steam-heated. Cost Foxy a pretty penny, it did, but then again, Foxy Muscat earns a pretty penny off of this place."

"Yes, it is warm in here," Jessie admitted slowly.

"Yep, and in the whole house. We've got too many females running about this place to ever let it get cold. The clientele doesn't much cotton to girl-flesh being all blue and goose-bumpy."

"What kind of place *is* this?" Jessie pleaded.

Mrs. Fitzroy looked skeptical. "You mean you don't know?" She grinned. "You really haven't figured it out yet?"

"Oh, please!" Jessie said in exasperation. "I just want to leave."

"You do, eh?" Mrs. Fitzroy laughed. "Well, first put that on."

"I want my own clothes!"

"They've all been burned," Mrs. Fitzroy gloated.

"Oh, no!" Jessie paled.

"So, you can put that on, or stay naked." The matron shrugged. "It's all the same to me, child."

Jessie grudgingly slipped the nightgown on over her head. No matter how hard she tugged at the see-through fabric, the gown barely reached past her crotch.

Mrs. Fitzroy tossed her a pair of high-heeled slippers, and watched, licking her thin lips, as Jessie put them on and tottered about the room.

"Excellent," the matron hissed. "Your nipples are poking

126

through the gauze in front, and in the rear, the way your bottom just peeks out from beneath the hem will drive the men wild."

"Men!" Jessie cried, aghast. "You mean to say that men shall see me like this?"

"Of course men shall see you, and do a good deal more than just look at you, I might add."

"Please let me go," Jessie begged. "I'll do anything!"

"I daresay you will," Mrs. Fitzroy drawled. "But why do you carry on so? You told me all about your beau, back in Chicago, remember? You don't mean to tell me you are still a virgin?"

Jessie thought fast. She could get away with a great many falsehoods, but claiming to be a virgin was not one of them. That kind of lie could very easily be checked by somebody like Mrs. Fitzroy!

"No . . ." she whimpered. "He and I did it. Once . . ."

Mrs. Fitzroy roared with laughter. "Once is all it takes! Lordy! You look good enough to eat, standing there half bare like that," the gray-haired woman leered. "It's a good thing for you—" and then she stopped.

"What?" Jessie asked fearfully. "What's a good thing—"

"Never mind!" Mrs. Fitzroy grumbled. "You'll find out, and soon enough!" She grabbed Jessie's arm and steered her out of the room. "Come with me, I'm going to show you what the situation is, around here."

She dragged Jessie down the corridor to an archway. Before, the archway had been open, but now, securely locked sliding doors had turned it into a dead end.

Mrs. Fitzroy rattled the locked doors. "Through here are the stairs that lead down to the front foyer, and the front door. That's how we came in, remember?"

Jessie nodded.

"Well, we keep that front entrance for the benefit of new arrivals like yourself," Fitzroy explained. "It wouldn't do to have brought you in through the entrance our patrons use."

The matron pulled Jessie back down the corridor, all the way to the other end, where there was another set of double doors, although these were unlocked.

"These doors lead to another staircase. On this floor and the floors above are rooms where the girls"—here Mrs. Fitzroy paused to tweak one of Jessie's nipples through the sheer fabric—"*entertain* their clients. Downstairs we have the sitting rooms, the piano, the bars, and the kitchen. *All* the way down-stairs, in the basement, are the opium dens."

"What about these rooms, in this hallway?" Jessie asked.

"We let the girls sleep in these rooms when they're not on duty," Fitzroy replied. "Or when it's that time of the month . . . The room you were in will be yours for the next couple of days, until you're used to things . . ."

"Did you really burn all of my clothes?" Jessie asked timidly.

"Yes, indeedy! Those tawdry dresses aren't suitable attire for one of Foxy Muscat's girls."

"But I'm not one of her girls!"

"Not yet, of course," Mrs. Fitzroy sniffed. "But you soon will be. Training you is my job, you see."

"B-but—"

"But nothing! Here's the facts, Annie. The door you came through is closed off to you forever. Downstairs you'll find plenty of other doors and windows, but those that aren't locked or barred are guarded by the men Foxy keeps about the place to keep order. And even if you do manage to escape, what good will it do you?"

Jessie shrugged. "I could go to the police."

Mrs. Fitzroy threw back her head and laughed. "Why bother? Most of the department's top brass are regulars at Foxy Muscat's," she said. "You've no money, Annie. And no clothes. You'd be wandering bare-naked on the street. The police would just pick you up and bring you right back here. Foxy would pay them for their trouble. And then I'd tan your hide." Mrs. Fitzroy's steely eyes narrowed. "You wouldn't want *that* to happen, would you?"

Jessie shuddered. "No, ma'am," she whispered.

"All right, then," the matron said, satisfied. "Remember one last thing. If you do try to escape, I have a special pun-ishment lined up for you. I have your birth certificate, remem-ber? I know your hometown, and the rather sordid circum-stances surrounding your father's death. Run away, and I'll send news of what's happened to you to the Chicago papers, along with your birth certificate to prove my story. I can just imagine how all your friends—and your ex-beau—would love to titter about your fate here in San Francisco."

Jessie hung her head, defeated. "I won't try to get away," she whispered.

"That's a good girl." Mrs. Fitzroy slipped her hand beneath the hem of Jessie's chemise, and patted her bare bottom. "It won't be so bad, you'll see," she confided. "Once you're broken in and can begin to earn your keep, you'll be paid a beginner's wage, just like all the other girls have been paid. You'll get more money as you become more accomplished. You'll shop at the finest stores for your clothes . . . You wanted to be a servant! Why, servants shall soon envy you, Annie . . ."

"Then . . . I *can* leave, for a little while, I mean?" Jessie asked plaintively, but only to stay within the confines of Annabelle's character. Moore had told her that even the new girls were allowed their liberty, once Fitzy had explained how foolish it would be to try and run away.

"Of course." Fitzroy nodded. "Eventually."

Jessie spun around. "What?" she demanded. "I mean, I—" The plan she'd made with Moore called for her to meet him at a prearranged spot tomorrow afternoon!

"We usually let our girls do what they wish with their free time," Fitzroy was saying. "But you're a special case. You'll be serving those clients who frequent the opium dens. Don't worry, those men aren't interested in anything but fondling a woman now and then."

"I don't understand," Jessie mumbled, her mind working furiously. She had to meet Moore—

"No man shall have you, dear," Fitzroy giggled, as if she'd been let in on some private joke. "Not right away, anyway. Your debut will be for the pleasure of a very special client. All of your free time will be spent with me. I've got to prepare you." The matron licked her lips. "This client has certain predilections, you see . . ."

Jessie stood silent. Her mind was blank. She felt helplessness sweep over her as Fitzroy opened the double doors that led to the bordello.

"Now you skedaddle downstairs," Fitzroy ordered, pushing her through the doorway. "One of the other girls will show you how to light the opium pipes. Get used to it, child. You're not leaving here for a while!"

★

Chapter 11

"She didn't meet me," Moore explained worriedly to Ki. "I waited for an hour, but she never arrived."

It was the early evening of the day after Jessie had entered the bordello. Jordan Moore and Ki were sitting in the Palace Hotel's lobby. The detective was anxiously puffing on a cigar and sipping a double bourbon. Ki was not drinking. A cup of tea, untouched, sat before him.

Keemun—a Chinese tea, Ki thought, as the trail of steam rising from the cup reached his nose. It seemed that all of his senses—and the consciousness that nested in his abdomen—had been sharpened and intensified by his long period of meditation.

"You seem awfully damn calm," Moore grumbled.

"I spent all day yesterday, and last night, in the hotel's garden," Ki replied.

"All night?" Moore stared dubiously. "A cold night like last night—"

"I was not cold," Ki interrupted. "The garden was serene."

"Didn't the night watchmen bother you?"

Ki smiled. "The night watchmen did not notice me, my friend."

Moore shook his head. "I can't believe they didn't see you."

"They may have *seen* me," Ki said. "But they did not *notice* me."

I'm in no mood for Japanese riddles, Moore thought, although what he *said* was, "Have it your own way, Ki. But I can't understand how you can sit there so cool and collected, when Jessie could be in danger."

131

"'Could be,' is correct, Jordan," Ki pointed out.

"Just the other day, her being attacked by that thug put you in a rage," Moore countered.

"True, but I'd blamed myself for leaving her alone to fall prey to that attack," Ki explained. "This situation is different. Jessie chose to enter the bordello. She is ultimately responsible for her own actions. She has her own *karma* to live out. I am just as concerned as you are, but I refuse to jump to conclusions."

"Well, I can't help myself. I'm worried," Moore confessed. "What if they've caught on to her somehow?" The detective's anxious, tired features suddenly contorted. "What if she's—"

"No," Ki whispered, his almond eyes boring into Moore's. "She is not dead."

"How do you know?"

"I would know," the samurai whispered. "I would feel such a thing." He patted his belly. "I would feel it, *inside.*"

Moore took a long pull of his drink. "All right." He heaved a deep sigh of relief. "I don't know why, but I believe you." He sat back in his chair to observe his companion. "You seem different, today. Your meditation could make that much difference?"

Ki shrugged. "Perhaps, my friend. However, I have met someone who has taught me the true meaning of serenity in the face of adversity. She is truly an enlightened being."

"If you're saying what I think you're saying, good for you," Moore smiled. "I'm kind of a changed man, myself." He hesitated, staring into his glass.

"I think I understand." Ki offered the detective a smile.

"Let me make sure you do," Moore hurried on. "I meant that I've also met a woman who has changed me, and it's Jessie. We were together, night before last . . ." He glanced at Ki, wondering how the samurai was taking his confession. He half expected the man to lunge for his throat.

"I do understand, Jordan," Ki replied softly. "And if you will permit me to say so, I believe that it was the lover who lost control of his emotions and panicked a few moments ago, not the professional private investigator."

Moore nodded slowly, and Ki went on, "But all of this is quite difficult for me to discuss. Let us get back to the matter at hand."

132

"Which is somehow getting Jessie out of that bordello," Moore said.

Ki shook his head. "I think not. I think the thing to do is for me to get *into* the bordello."

"I don't follow you."

"Then clear your mind of emotion!" Ki ordered. "Think logically! There is no need to compromise Jessie's cover merely because she missed her meeting with you. Perhaps there was some coincidental, random circumstance that has kept her inside the bordello."

"We don't know if that's true," Moore insisted hastily.

Ki was amused. "And we do not know for a fact that it is false," he softly countered. "In any event, the two of us charging in would only further jeopardize her safety."

That's true," Moore admitted sheepishly. "And I can't call in the police at this point."

"Will you ever be able to?" Ki asked. "I would think that the chain of bribery forged between the bordello and the police is quite strong."

Moore shrugged. "Something big enough, or *bad* enough, could sever that chain. Foxy Muscat's payoffs only buy her clemency for her petty sins. Something major would bust that joint wide open. The police would then have to act."

"But there is the cartel to consider," Ki answered. "They are the ultimate owners of the bordello, and they have now allied themselves with Chang's Tong. Surely their contacts within the city government are strong?"

"Sure they are," Moore said. "But even those hard-won connections would vanish if we could expose our enemies by pinning a headline-grabbing crime on them. Hell, they're vermin," the detective spat contemptuously. "They're insects. Shine a light on them, and they'll scatter."

Maybe so, and maybe not, Ki thought. He'd battled the cartel before, and considered Moore a bit rash in his estimation of their adversaries. "Jordan?" he asked. "Could you draw me a rough layout diagram of the bordello?"

Moore laughed. "Sure. I've spent enough time there!"

"Good," Ki said. "I would like to bring some things to your apartment that I will need to infiltrate the bordello. I will leave from there."

"Of course," Moore said. "But why? I mean, the hotel is closer to the bordello."

"You see, I shall be dressed in such a way that I could not just saunter through the lobby," Ki remarked. "I may climb down the outside of the hotel—"

"Never mind," Moore groaned, burying his face in his hands. "I'm sorry I asked." He glanced up at Ki, and winked.

"I will also bring to your apartment those things I will need if we are to intercept the cartel's opium shipment," Ki mused aloud. "The clipper may well be due in port this very night. Jessie might tell me so." The samurai regarded the detective. "Be prepared for *action* tonight, my friend."

"Annie!" Foxy Muscat chirped in her high, reed-thin voice. "Come here, girl! I want to introduce you to a very important man!"

Jessie stood wearily up from the pillow upon which she'd been kneeling. One of Foxy's rules required that a new girl, called an initiate, could only sit in a kneeling position while she was on duty in the bordello. As Foxy had put it, an initiate was the newest addition to the "harem," and as such, had to maintain a respectful posture at all times.

"Quickly, girl!" Foxy scolded. Tonight she'd exchanged her crimson kimono for one of a shocking pink. "He's in one of the opium dens!"

Oh, no! Jessie moaned silently. Here it was, just the start of her second evening in this damned place, and already it felt as if she'd been here for an eternity. Last night, after being whisked around on a bewildering tour of the labyrinthine four-story house, she'd been assigned to a few hours of duty in the opium dens—a series of rooms in the basement—before being allowed to return to her tiny bed-cell for a bit of much-needed rest.

Resignedly, Jessie followed the billowing, saillike form of Foxy Muscat out of the front parlor. The big, high-ceilinged chamber was where the clientele "got acquainted " with Foxy's courtesans. The parlor had wallpaper flocked with red velvet, and a long, polished mahogany bar manned by two bartenders who quickly and efficiently served drinks, hampered not at all by their shoulder holsters, which bulged beneath their steward's jackets.

Two long, black leather sofas met at a right angle beneath a dimly flickering, crystal chandelier. Here sat Foxy's girls, all of them scantily and seductively dressed in satins and lace,

134

but none of them in so humiliating and revealing a manner as Jessie herself. For example, several of the courtesans wore gowns that bared their breasts, but Jessie was the only female forced into the indignity of prancing about bare-bottomed.

True to their word, Foxy Muscat and Mrs. Fitzroy were saving Jessie for some special client, as yet to arrive. They would let no man have her, although several clients had already offered exorbitant sums for the privilege.

Jessie grimaced as she walked, for her rear felt very sore. She had the bad luck to be the only initiate presently in the bordello. Accordingly, she was the only one wearing the back-side-baring chemise. She'd spent close to twenty-four hours bending across aroused, semi-inebriated men in order to light their smokes or serve them their drinks, at the same time suffering their supposedly good-natured slaps and pinches upon her prominently displayed and quite vulnerable buttocks. Her bottom was spotted black and blue, and felt like she'd spent all this time on the back of a bucking horse, its saddle smacking her backside at every jump.

As Jessie left the room, she'd passed the piano player, a black man flailing away at his instrument's keyboard. He was a friendly soul, and the only male in the place who'd deigned to smile at her, to treat her like a human being, and not some sort of creature to be poked and prodded at will.

This place had sounded so exotic and racy, when Jordan had described it, that she had laughed then, but she wasn't laughing now. How different this place was from the geisha houses in Japan that Myobu had told her about. There, apprentices were allowed to blossom naturally. They did not ever come into contact with men until they were officially graduated.

In Foxy Muscat's bordello, even the other women treated the initiates cruelly. Jessie surmised that it was because they remembered with shame how they themselves had been roped into their present state of affairs. Perhaps it made these women feel better about themselves to look down upon the newest members of their dismal club.

Well, there was one benefit to being assigned to the opium dens, Jessie thought as she stumbled down the dark stone steps, precariously balanced upon her absurdly steep high heels. The men down there had little interest in fondling women. They had little interest in anything except where their next pipeful of wretched dope was coming from.

As Jessie descended behind the madam, the stale basement air began to reek from the sweet smell of opium smoke. Purplish clouds of the stuff fogged the basement landing.

Foxy nodded to the one burly armed guard standing sentry duty at the opium dens' entranceway. Jessie followed her in. One guard was all they needed down here; the dope made the men so docile that there were never any arguments or fights.

The clients paid handsomely for the privilege of indulging their vices in the bordello, so Foxy Muscat took great pains to offer them a much more pleasant environment than could be found in any of the Chinatown dens, where a man could smoke ten times the amount of opium for mere pennies. In Chinatown, the dens were damp, dirty, and rat-infested. They were filled with tiers of narrow wooden bunks that reached from floor to ceiling.

The bordello's opium dens were luxuriously appointed. Fantasmagoric murals lined the walls to inspire the dreams of the lazing smokers. The murals featured the nude forms of female water sprites cavorting in a pond, and ample-figured wood nymphs sunning themselves in sylvan glades. The smokers reclined on upholstered couches, or sprawled upon the large floor cushions scattered across the deep carpet. The dens were lit by the soft, lambent glow of candles, some of which were encased in pastel-colored glass lanterns. Beside each smoker's place was a small charcoal brazier and a lacquered tray that held a pipe, wooden tapers, and a carefully doled-out portion of the sticky brown opium.

The dope was kept under lock and key, behind a counter manned by a surly-looking Chinese fellow. Jessie took it for granted that the man worked for Chang, and was there to make sure that Foxy Muscat did not try to sell off any of the surplus opium supplied to her by the Tong. Both the Tong and the cartel took the lion's share of the profits generated by the huge shipments of opium. Foxy was really low man—or woman— on the totem pole. Of course, that was difficult for Jessie to remember while she was in the obese madam's power, and forced to cater to her every whim . . .

Foxy led Jessie through the first two dens, and into the third and last of the chambers. The rooms were connected railway-fashion. The last room had no back exit. To leave the dens, one had to retrace one's steps. A feeble current of air—a draft from the stairwell, perhaps—tended to push all the excess smoke into this last room. Here the still, sweet clouds seemed to hang the thickest. Jessie did her best to take shallow breaths, but the fumes still got to her. Her head began to spin, and her fingers began to feel thick and clumsy.

Foxy snickered as Jessie stumbled against her. "Easy, girl! You could sink into a nice little dream of your own if I left you down here and forgot to come fetch you."

The madam clamped her pudgy hand onto the back of Jessie's neck and steered her roughly into the far corner of the den. A short, fat man sat on the carpet with his knees drawn up, and his back propped against the wall. His shirt was unbuttoned, and his soiled tie was askew. His vest and suit jacket lay in a crumpled ball next to him. The man's thinning, reddish-brown hair dangled in greasy strands across his forehead. His eyes were closed, but he was not asleep. He kept stroking his clipped mustache, either out of nervous habit or to furtively sniff the scent of the opium that had stained his fingers.

"Commissioner!" Foxy Muscat impatiently nudged the man with the toe of her slipper. "Commissioner Smith, open your eyes!"

Commissioner Smith? Jessie thought, startled out of her own stupor. *The waterfront commissioner himself?*

The man opened his bleary, bloodshot eyes. "A woman?" he slurred. "Don't want a woman . . ."

Foxy scowled. "Come on! Snap out of it for a moment, you—" She stopped, catching herself in time. "Lucky for me he's too out of it to hear," she confided to Jessie. "Kneel down before him."

"Commissioner?" Foxy tried again. "What do you think of the girl?"

Smith shook his head adamantly. "Don't want a girl—"

"Not for *you!*" Foxy warbled. "Not for *you—*"

The commissioner stopped his spastic movements and peered first at the madam, and then at Jessie. He squinted his red eyes, doing his best to bring them into focus. *"Who,* then?"

Before Foxy could reply, the answer evidently dawned on him. He threw back his head and let loose a high, wheezing laugh. "Wonderful, Foxy. Wonderful!" He stared at Jessie, and stretched out his hand to chuck her under the chin, but he underestimated the distance and ended up tickling the thin air six inches in front of Jessie's nose. "Does this one know yet?"

Foxy shook her head gleefully. "Nope! And not a word from you about it, understand?"

Smith nodded, still laughing to himself. "Wonderful! Lots of money. For you, for me . . ." His eyes fell upon Jessie. "Poor little thing . . ." Once again his loon laugh echoed off the cellar walls.

Jessie fought to suppress her anger. No *wonder* this waterfront official who was making things so difficult for the Starbuck concern was accepting bribes to let opium enter the city. He himself was an addict!

Smith, meanwhile, was fumbling at his tray. He came up holding his empty pipe.

"Very well, this one here will bring you more," Foxy chuckled. "More and more, as much as you want, my dear Commissioner." To Jessie she hissed, "Get to your feet!"

"Yes, ma'am." Jessie did as she was told.

"This little fellow happens to be very important," Foxy whispered. "Never you mind why, for the time being. You'll see a lot of bigwigs in my house, but if you should ever blab to anyone about what you see, I promise to cut your tongue out! Understand, girl?"

"Yes, ma'am." Jessie couldn't believe her good fortune. She was being ordered to serve the one man who could supply her with the information Jordan Moore and Ki would need to intercept and destroy the expected opium shipment.

"I'll come back for you in a bit," Foxy was saying. "Nobody but these damn smokers can stand it down here for long," she wheezed, rubbing at her eyes. "Bring him what he wants. I'll clear it with Lee."

"More opium!" Smith muttered as Jessie knelt before him.

"Are you sure you don't want to rest a bit, Commissioner?" Jessie suggested as soon as Foxy was out of earshot. It wouldn't do for Smith to pass out before Jessie got the information out of him.

"I want it *now!*" Smith demanded.

"Yes, sir!" Jessie rose and hurried through the front dens to Lee, the Chinese man in charge of the drug supply. Several other smokers were patiently waiting for their ration, but Lee waved them aside to let Jessie come to the front.

"Lucky that Smith is an important fellow," Lee said, his sunken eyes greedily gazing at Jessie's proud, jutting breasts, naked beneath the sheer gauze of the chemise. He had the waxy yellow complexion and the brown-stained, rotting teeth of a long-time opium user. "You smoke with me later, okay?" the Chinese leered.

Jessie merely snatched up the penny-sized chunk of opium on its little plate, and hurried back toward Smith. Lee's lewd chortles followed her. Jessie thought the opium smoke must be getting to her. She could actually feel the man's eyes hotly devouring her body. Never had she felt so helpless!

"What took so long?" Smith whined when she'd reached him. "Hurry up!" His hand went into a tremor, tapping a staccato rhythm upon the lacquered tray.

Jessie did as she'd been taught the previous night. She squeezed the opium between her fingers in order to warm and soften it, and then pinched off a bit and packed it into the thimble-sized bowl of the pipe.

She held the pipe to his lips, the bowl pointing downward. He sucked at it the way an infant sucks at its mother's nipple. She took up one of the wooden tapers, held it to a glowing charcoal ember, and then held the flame beneath the bowl.

There was a wet, gurgling sound as the opium melted and began to bubble. Smith sucked in a lungful of smoke and held it until Jessie thought his eyes were going to pop out of his head. Then he exhaled, the smoke coming out of him in a hissing billow.

"Good!" the commissioner babbled, his red eyes half closed, his blissful smile stretching from ear to ear. He reached out tentatively, even a trifle shyly, to fondle one of Jessie's breasts.

No! she thought, as her spirit rebelled. It was too much! She was a person, she was not some pet to be slapped and fondled at any man's whim. Let Smith squawk to Foxy, or even Mrs. Fitzroy! Jessie no longer cared. She was fed up with being manhandled. She was not a whore! She was not! If necessary, she would go upstairs, tear out the gun she'd hidden in the mattress, and show them who she was: Jessica Starbuck!

She deflected Smith's hand, and then waited for the roof to cave in on her. But nothing happened. Smith was so deeply under the influence of the opium that he literally couldn't remember what he was doing from one moment to the next.

The realization calmed Jessie. It allowed her to regain control of her outraged sensibilities. She was locked into this demeaning role for a reason, and would only be here for a little while longer. Right now she had a chance to ferret out what she was seeking. Smith couldn't remember what he was doing. Maybe he wouldn't be able to remember what he said, either.

Jessie filled the pipe. "You do like this stuff, don't you, Commissioner?"

"Need it," the man replied. "Makes me happy, makes me dream..."

Once again he sucked greedily at the stem of the pipe as Jessie lit it. While he was inhaling, another tremor overcame him. Sparks flew from the bowl, to rain down upon the bare skin of his chest, where his shirt gaped open. Jessie quickly brushed away the burning ashes, marvelling at the man's obliviousness to pain. He'd felt nothing.

"Commissioner, the opium comes on ships, doesn't it?" Jessie asked quietly, at the same time glancing over her shoulder to make sure that she wasn't being overheard.

"Big ships!" Smith slurred dreamily. "I sign in every one. Nobody questions *me!*" he boasted happily. He started suddenly, giving an involuntary shiver. Slapping at himself, he muttered, "Bugs on me. Bugs down here."

"There are no bugs, Commissioner," Jessie promised. Her time was growing short. Smith could lapse into unconsciousness at any moment, and Foxy might return to fetch her.

"More!" the commissioner demanded.

"More opium is coming," Jessie whispered into his ear. *"When* is it coming?"

"More!" Smith moaned.

"There isn't any more here," Jessie told him. "When's the next shipment due in?"

"Week, maybe..." he mumbled, his head sinking down to his chest.

Jessie slapped him across the face. Then she slapped him twice again. They were short, light blows; she wanted to wake him up, not knock him out.

"Sooner," Jessie corrected Smith as his eyes fluttered open.

"More opium—" he began.

"Tell me when it's coming," Jessie hissed. "There's a shipment due any night. When?"

Smith stared stupidly into her eyes. "Tonight? But that's not opium, coming *tonight...*"

Jessie had the pipe loaded and ready. She jammed it between

140

his teeth and held the burning taper to the bowl. Smith sucked in reflex.

"Not opium," he said as he exhaled the smoke. "Slaves! Ol' Chang's bringin' in coolie slaves! Fella wants 'em for his daddy's lumber business in Oregon—"

"Smith!"

Jessie almost jumped out of her skin. The pipe fell from her fingers. She looked up to see the rage-flushed, garishly made-up face of Foxy Muscat. The fat woman was literally quivering with anger.

Foxy Muscat's glowering eyes were fixed not on Jessie, but on Smith. "Damn fool!" she spat. "What'd you babble about? Answer me, you damned addict!"

A loud, rasping snore escaped from Smith. The waterfront commissioner slowly slid down the wall, to end up with his chin coming to rest on his chest.

"Bah!" Foxy grumbled. "He'll be out for hours. First come the sweet dreams, then the nightmares." That last thought seemed to bring her some pleasure. The tension went out of her as she fixed her gaze on Jessie. "There's always the nightmares," she remarked jovially. "Terrible things, opium nightmares."

"Horrible!" Jessie gasped.

"Yeah, yeah..." the madam sighed wearily. "You'll see worse," she promised. "Now, on your feet with you!"

Jessie rose, only to begin to black out. "Got up too fast, I guess..." she mumbled as Foxy supported her.

"Too much of this damned opium smoke is what it is," the madam said. "Let's go upstairs."

They were out of the dens and halfway up the stairs when Foxy paused to give Jessie a shake. "What else did that fool babble to you about?" she demanded.

"He kept talking about slaves, and he did mention that he was in charge of getting you opium." Jessie innocently widened her eyes, and then shrugged. "Or something like that... it was awfully hard to understand him, ma'am," she finished.

"*He's* in charge of the opium!" Foxy laughed. "Oh, that's rich! That fool may just have hung himself this time. Wait until—" She stopped, realizing who she was talking to. "Well, you never mind, Annie."

"Yes, ma'am," Jessie replied with genuine relief.

141

"You can go upstairs to your room," the madam said. "Sleep off the effects of the opium for a bit."

As Jessie hurried past the madam, Foxy clamped her strong fingers about Jessie's wrist, jolting her around and almost yanking her back down the steps.

"And if you're smart," Foxy threatened, "you'll forget everything you heard. Understand?"

"I promise!" Jessie exclaimed.

"Go on, then." Satisfied, Foxy waved her off. As Jessie scooted upstairs, the gargantuan madam gruntingly made her own lumbering journey up to the first floor.

Once Jessie had reached the relative safety of her little bedroom, she breathed an exhausted sigh of relief. She flopped down on the narrow bed. Right now it felt ten times more comfortable than the big, soft, expensive bed that the Palace Hotel had so recently supplied her.

Well, she thought to herself. *She had the information she'd wanted. Now all she had to do was figure out a way to get it to Jordan and Ki.*

But first she had to sleep. Her eyelids felt as though somebody had attached lead weights to them.

She prodded the mattress until she felt the reassuring bump of her revolver, and then began to drift off. *Need clothes,* she mused. *Can't go dashing about San Francisco with nothing but a gun and a swatch of sheer gauze wrapped about me . . .*

The thought made her giggle. She nestled her head into the pillow, thinking that her wisp of a chemise was as insubstantial and useless as the wisps of purple opium smoke fogging the basement air . . .

She sank swiftly into a deep slumber. The residue of the opium swirled through her system, pulling her deeper, ever deeper, into darkness.

Chapter 12

It was just a bit after nine at night when Ki arrived at the bordello. He gave its front and side entrances a wide berth, jumping the high board fence that separated the house's backyard from a neighbor's property, then flitting like a phantom from tree to tree and shrub to shrub, until he'd reached the rear of the house.

Ki peered up through the darkness at the bordello's exterior. The architect who'd designed the place must have done his work while high on opium. The style was an ill-conceived mess of gingerbread: there were ornamental eaves, scroll-sawn window frames, and what appeared to be half-rotted-away, Italianate neo-classic balusters.

Ki shook his head, muttering in disgust. He'd take clean, tidy, clapboard anytime. It was true that the building's excesses offended his Japanese-born sense of simplicity, but his objections were more practical than esthetic.

What it looked like was beside the point. It was going to be very difficult to *climb*.

Ki was dressed in worn denim jeans, a collarless cotton twill shirt, and a loose, many-pocketed well-broken-in brown leather vest. He was barefoot, but the sharp-edged litter of the city's streets was no threat to him. His feet were callused, their soles tougher than any shoe leather.

He'd memorized the layout Moore had sketched. The detective had also told him that Jessie had most likely been assigned to a room somewhere on the second floor of the house. That was the procedure followed for all the other girls, so there

143

was no reason to think it had not been followed for Jessie.

Assuming that her cover has not been broken, Ki thought as he stared up at the row of narrow windows, each barred with a scrollwork grating. *And assuming that she is not somewhere else in the bordello.*

There were ten windows on the second floor, which meant that there were ten rooms. None of the windows were lit.

Where to start? Ki wondered. The logical thing to do would be to begin at either corner of the house, and then progress in an orderly fashion from one end to the other. But to climb at a corner would expose him to view from the sides of the house. That was too risky. He would have to start in the middle and work his way along to one end, hoping he'd see her through one of the windows on that side. If he didn't, he would have to retrace his steps, leaping from ledge to ledge until he could begin to peer through the windows making up the other half of the floor.

Throughout it all, he would have to avoid being seen by any other of the girls who might be resting, and, of course, if he didn't find Jessie in any of the rooms, he would have to enter the bordello, start at the top, and then work his way down until he did find her. Without being seen, of course.

Ki was slightly worried about that last part. It would be very nice to find Jessie in one of those second-floor rooms. Yes, that would be quite excellent . . .

If he had to enter the bordello, the chances of his being seen were greatly increased. There were armed guards inside; Moore had said so. If he was spotted, Ki knew that he would be forced to begin something of a rampage, killing his way through the house until he'd found Jessie, and then killing his way *out* of the place, with Jessie safely tucked under his arm.

It was not the killing that bothered the samurai. He would be merciful. Everybody who ran away from him would be spared. It was confronting Jessie's anger that concerned him. She would be distressed over the fact that his clumsiness in being spotted had spoiled her plan to infiltrate the enemy.

Oh, well, Ki thought. *One's karma is one's karma. One learns to live with it, and live it out . . .*

He remembered what his honored teacher, the master samurai Hirata, had drummed into his brain when he was only a youth: *A samurai never makes mistakes; other people do, when they cross his path at an inopportune moment . . .*

Ki felt himself smiling. Perhaps it was the hot Yankee blood of his father coursing through his veins, and most certainly his soul would pay for it in some future incarnation, but *oh!* how he preferred *action,* or even the thought of action, to thinking serene thoughts in a flower garden!

From one of the pockets in his vest, Ki removed a tightly wound spool of cord, similar in its thickness to fishing line, but many times stronger. Attached to one end of the cord were several razor-sharp hooks of tempered steel. Ki stepped back several paces, unwound a sufficient length of cord from the spool, and began to twirl it in an underhand motion until he'd built up enough centrifugal force to send the hook flying upward. It rose to land on the sloping, shingle-covered roof of the bordello. Ki tugged the hooks along until their barbs caught. He gave the line an experimental tug, to make sure that the anchor was a secure one.

Ki went into the position known as the "horse stance." His legs were bowed, as if he were straddling a horse, while his head, neck and back formed a straight line, even with the heels of his feet. He gazed at the dangling cord, just a foot in front of his face, and focused the energy of his body, in preparation . . .

Then he sprang up, not like the falcon, but like the locust taking wing. At the apex of his jump, many feet above the ground, his fingers locked about the cord as the soles of his bare feet soundlessly braced themselves against the side of the building.

Ki scuttled up the cord. He covered the remaining few feet to the level of the second floor's windows in an instant. He could have climbed the entire four stories in less than ten seconds. Early in his apprenticeship, he had learned to move vertically up walls and across ceilings, like a human fly.

Ki now began to leap from window ledge to window ledge. Once, the rotted wood gave way beneath his feet, but Ki did not fall. He darted onward to the next ledge, the way a bee darts to the next flower, and then the next. His trained eyes only needed a split second to penetrate the darkness of each room's interior.

The resemblance of Ki's movements to those of the locust, fly, and bee showed his good form, for the ancients had long ago devised this climbing technique by studying the ways of the insects. The technique's secret was a simple one: if a man

145

moved fast enough, there was no time to fall.

Ki hopped from the third window ledge, cartwheeling sideways through the void, his arms and legs extended straight like the points of a *shuriken* star spinning through the air on its deadly journey. He did not come to light at the fourth window, but only glanced through it—

There! Jessie, lying on the bed!

He touched down briefly on the fifth ledge, using that impact to hurtle himself back to the fourth window. He hooked his fingers and toes through the wrought-iron grating, and hung like a spider in the center of its web as he peered through the metal and glass at Jessie's sleeping form.

The samurai congratulated himself on his good fortune. It had turned out to be very easy, indeed!

Ki tapped upon the windowpane. Jessie, lying on her back, did not stir. He tapped louder, finally resorting to scratching one of his *shuriken* blades against the window.

Something was wrong. Ki had never known her to sleep so deeply.

He had a file that would make short work of these iron bars, and breaking the window itself was no problem, but then Jessie would have to explain the damage to the bordello's proprietors. No, it looked as though he was going to have to do this the hard way. He was going to have to make his way into the bordello after all.

The windows above the second floor were not barred. It would have saved a bit of time to have gone directly up the side of the building, but Ki did not trust the bordello's exterior walls. The hand and footholds available were simply too pitted with rot to support his weight. He made his way back to the cord dangling down from the roof, and scurried up to the third floor. Several of the rooms were occupied by women and their clients. In some, the lamps were lit, in others, only the shadowy forms of the figures entwined in copulation could be viewed. Ki finally came upon an empty room. He slid open the window and went in.

It took him a moment to get his bearings in the hallway. Moore's diagram showed a stairway at the far end of the corridor. It would take him down to the second floor.

Ki hurried along. He was not worried about being discovered at this point. There were no guards posted on the third floor, and the couples behind the closed doors on both sides of him were all making too much noise on their own to hear his swiftly passing bare feet upon the carpet.

Raucous laughter, and tiny strains banged out upon an out-of-tune piano floated up the stairwell as Ki made his way to the second floor. Just one flight below was the front parlor of the bordello, according to Moore's drawing. Curiosity impelled Ki to stick his head around the corner of the landing and catch a glimpse of the goings-on down there.

He had the chance to see several women dancing, and wearing some very interesting—and exciting—costumes, before another woman, leading a gentleman up the stairs by the front of his trousers, forced Ki to duck back around the corner. The woman's silvery giggle faded as he went through, and then slid shut behind him, the set of unlocked double doors that led to the second-floor hallway. Ki went to Jessie's closed door and swung it open, hurrying to her side. She was still sound asleep. Ki had not realized that she was so naked; the slip of clothing she was wearing covered nothing.

"Jessie!" he whispered, trying his best not to gaze at her lush, lovely form. It was not proper to stare. "Jessie! Come now! Wake up!" Ki said as loudly as he dared, more than a note of pleading in his voice.

Jessie stirred, but did not wake. She spread her legs languorously, while stretching her arms above her head, so that her breasts rose and tightened. Every inch of her was exposed . . .

"Jessie!" Ki fairly begged. It was awfully warm inside the bordello. Perhaps that explained the perspiration suddenly coursing down his body . . .

"Jessie . . ." Why wouldn't she wake up? Was she ill? Ki bent over her. He pressed his lips against her forehead, only, of course, to see if he could detect any trace of fever . . .

Jessie's eyes sprang open. "Ki!" she murmured through lips still thick with sleep. Her fingers brushed against his thigh, and then feathered along his groin in an instinctive movement. She'd only wanted to prove to herself that he was *real*, that he was truly *here*, and not just a remnant of a dream brought on by the opium.

Ki leapt back, quite flustered, and positively on fire where Jessie had touched him. He wished that his jeans were several sizes larger, and mourned the fact that there were some parts of the body over which even a samurai had no control . . .

147

"Uh, Jessica," Ki stuttered, blushing bright red, and looking everywhere in the room but at her. "You're . . . *nude!*"

Jessie laughed richly. "Well! This is no dream. That's *you* all right. And am I glad to see you! I've got a lot to tell . . ."

"You make it sound as if Jessie had been expecting you!" Moore laughed in astonishment. He poured Ki a large measure of brandy and set it down before the samurai, who was sitting by the hearth, warming his hands before the fire. Ever since Ki had arrived back at his apartment, the detective had been positively giddy with relief over the news that Jessie was alive and well. "Wasn't she surprised to see you?"

"Why should she have been?" Ki took a moment to savor the brandy's bouquet, and then took a sip, letting the mellow fire of the liquor warm his innards. "She knew I would find a way to get to her. And when I did," Ki added ruefully, "It was I who got the surprise. Should you come to know her for any length of time, my friend, you will find that it is usually Jessica Starbuck who does the surprising."

"I still don't understand why you didn't take her out of there," Moore grumbled. Ki had already filled him in on what Jessie had learned. "We can't strike against the cartel if their cargo hold is going to be filled with coolie slaves. Attacking the clipper would cost the slaves their lives. Burning a ship loaded with opium is one thing, but—"

"It can be done," Ki interrupted.

Moore looked at him questioningly, and Ki went on, "To-night we can still strike against the cartel. That is why I did not bring Jessie with me. She agrees with my plan." Ki raised his hand to ward off Moore's objections. "Hear me out," he demanded. "The slaves—meant for you, my friend, or supposedly for your father's lumber yards in Oregon—are worth much more to the cartel and the Tong than just another shipment of opium. If we can intercept their slave ship, rescue the poor souls locked within it, and then destroy the vessel, we will throw our enemies into turmoil."

"Without hurting the slaves?" Moore asked.

"Without hurting them," Ki promised. "Indeed, we shall give them back their freedom."

"Just the two of us?" Moore asked dubiously. Then he smiled. "Are you that good?"

Ki took another sip of brandy. "Are you?" he asked.

"You bet!" Moore laughed. "What the hell! Let's do it!" He raised his glass for a toast.

Ki did the same with his brandy snifter. "As you so aptly put it, my friend, 'What the hell!'"

"But why did you leave Jessie there?"

"Divide and conquer," Ki smiled. "Jessie told me that the bordello's madam blames Smith for babbling about the slave shipment while he was under the influence of opium. Now, since nobody saw me enter the bordello and speak with Jessie—"

"I get it!" Moore exclaimed. "As it stands, if something should happen to disrupt the shipment, Foxy Muscat is going to blame it all on Smith. She'll figure that he spilled the beans somewhere else, as well. That's beautiful," the detective said admiringly. "As long as Jessie stays in the bordello, nobody can suspect her."

"As far as they know, she's talked to no one," Ki agreed. "They will *have* to blame Smith for their misfortune."

"Greta Kahr and Chang will fight over who gets to slit Smith's throat."

The samurai nodded. "You'd better get ready to go," he said.

Moore went into his bedroom to change his clothes, leaving Ki alone with his thoughts. He stared into the fire, wishing he could see his future in the flames. Neither Jessie nor Moore had guessed at his ulterior motive for fostering the daring plan. What Ki had kept to himself was the fact that he intended to take the rescued coolies to Chinatown, to present them to Suling's family, and in that way prove himself worthy of her. Surely her family could no longer forbid Ki to see her, once he'd rescued so many of their fellow countrymen from a life in shackles?

And if her parents are won over? Ki asked himself. *Then what?* Could he possibly break the vow he'd so long ago made to Jessica's father? Could he possibly leave Jessie to fend for herself?

But perhaps he would not have to choose between his own happiness and his sworn duty. He could take a bride and still serve the Starbuck cause. But would he be as willing to risk his life in that cause, knowing that a wife—and perhaps a child—were waiting for him?

The swirling misery of his conflicting emotions was enough

to make Ki think that either his heart or his brain was going to explode. Here was a chance for happiness, but how was he to seize it, while still maintaining his honor?

Moore had quickly changed into a dark wool sweater, dark pants, and india-rubber-soled shoes. He carried a canvas jacket, and his gun and shoulder holster, but set them down on a chair as he stared at Ki, who was still sitting, seemingly oblivious to everything.

"What's wrong?" the detective demanded.

Ki stood up, shaking his head. "Nothing. We should go . . ."

"Don't give me that 'nothing' business," Moore scolded. "We're probably going to get killed tonight. The least you can do is tell me what's eating you!"

Ki stared down at the smaller man who was so brazenly confronting him. Then he smiled. "A fellow named Longarm, a federal lawman, has a saying: 'A man ought to eat an apple one bite at a time.' If all goes well tonight, I may ask your advice about something. If all does not go well . . ." Ki shrugged.

"Have it your own way," Moore sighed. He slipped on his shoulder holster, checked his Colt to see that it was fully loaded, and then put on his jacket. "But I'll tell you this. If you don't find somebody to open up to, one of these days you're going to explode."

"Jordan," Ki said earnestly. "One thing you should know. You will not die tonight. I will see to it."

"I'd better *not*, friend," Moore slipped extra ammunition, cigars, and matches into the pockets of his jacket. "If I do get killed, Jessie Starbuck is going to get one hell of a bill."

Chapter 13

The lightly rigged, ten-foot-long mosquito board that Moore had earlier secured for the mission skimmed across the inky waters of the bay. What little moon there was this night was suddenly hidden by a cloud. The four-man craft had no running lights, and was therefore invisible in the darkness.

"Damn!" Moore seethed through his chattering teeth. He wedged the tiller beneath his arm in order to more tightly pull his spray-drenched jacket around him. "Aren't *you* cold?" he glared at Ki, who appeared to be quite comfortable in just his shirtsleeves and vest.

"Cold is a state of mind," Ki remarked amiably. He pointed to their left. "There it is. The cartel's clipper."

The three-masted, square-rigged cargo ship loomed before them like an island. Glowing lanterns speckled the long craft. The sea winds roared and wailed in its billowing sails as the clipper cut a swath through the black chop and swell of the bay.

Moore glanced over his shoulder at the distant, twinkling lights of the waterfront. "We've got to do it before they get much closer," he announced quietly. "Hey! It just occurred to me. Getting all those coolies to shore is going to be a problem."

"We'll use the clipper's lifeboats," Ki cut him off. "When we're done, the crew will no longer have need of them."

"All right, then," Moore whispered. "The crew will number between twenty and thirty. There won't be a lot of guns about, but every man will have a knife, and know how to use it."

Ki nodded. "Do you have a knife?" he asked as the clipper's black silhouette grew before them.

151

"Ugh!" Moore shuddered. "Not me! I hate knives!"

"Odd," Ki remarked. "A knife is usually a skinny man's weapon . . ."

"Hey!" Moore laughed. "You're already going to be up against thirty men. In a minute it's going to be thirty-one!"

Ki reached into the satchel strapped across his shoulder, and removed several egg-sized objects painted different colors. "Here," he said, handing them to Moore.

"What's this? Food?"

Ki laughed. "Not unless you have a very strong stomach, my friend. They are called *nage teppo*," he explained. "They are bombs. The red ones create smoke. The yellow ones explode in a flash of light which is harmless but temporarily blinding. The green ones explode like dynamite."

"What about this white one?" Moore asked, examining the grenades.

"The white are filled with a substance that, upon contact with the air, erupts into flame," Ki told him. "All of the bombs need only to be tossed. Upon landing, their outer shells will shatter and the explosions will occur."

"Not bad," Moore chuckled as he slipped the deadly eggs into his pocket. "Hey! What if I should fall down and these things should crack?"

"Do not worry," Ki assured him. "It would be over so quickly you would never feel a thing."

Moore nodded. "That's a load off my mind. I've got my gun and these little toys of yours, but where are your weapons?"

"In this satchel I have many more 'toys,' as you call them," Ki replied. "I have *shuriken* throwing blades, and I have these." From his belt he extracted two eighteen-inch-long swordlike weapons. A pair of prongs, curved like the horns of a steer, sprouted from the hilt of each sword. "These are called *sai*," Ki explained.

"I wish you had something else in that bag of tricks," Moore sighed.

"What?"

"About ten more men!" He swung the tiller sharply to heave the mosquito boat around. Now they were running parallel to the clipper. "Get ready!" he hissed, as he angled their boat ever closer to the big hull of the cargo ship.

Ki took from his pocket the same spool of cord and multi-barbed hook that he'd used to aid him in his climb at the

152

bordello. As the distance between the two craft was narrowed, he began to swing the cord above his head the way a cowboy twirls a lariat.

Less than a yard now separated the tiny boat from the high, curved hull of the clipper, and they were being buffeted by the three-master's wake. "I can't hold us here much longer!" Moore warned as he clenched the tiller with both hands. "I'll either ram them or capsize—"

Ki stood with his legs braced against the bench seat of the bouncing mosquito boat. It was like trying to stand on the saddle of a galloping horse. He let the cord fly. The hook caught the clipper's gunwale.

"Done!" he called, while tying his end of the cord to one of the cleats mounted on the mosquito boat's prow. The clipper was now towing them along.

Groaning with relief, the detective levered the rudder out of the churning water. He collapsed their two small sails, and scrambled into the prow along with Ki.

The clipper's railing was fifteen feet above them. Ki hurled another hooked cord up to catch the gunwale. He made sure it was securely lodged, then offered the cord to Moore.

"What's that for?" the detective asked. "And how are we going to get up there?" He gestured toward the clipper's decks.

Ki pushed the cord at him. "Climb this, of course!"

Moore's eyes widened in disbelief. "That piece of thread? You've got to be kidding?"

Ki shook his head in exasperation. "Jordan," he hissed. "You cannot climb a rope?"

"I don't see a rope," Moore replied adamantly. "I see a thread! I can climb a rope . . . although I'd prefer a rope ladder . . ." he trailed off.

"Lock your arms around my neck," Ki ordered. "I will carry you up on my back."

"You can't carry me—" Moore began, but then he shrugged. "Sure you can . . ."

With the detective holding on for dear life, Ki hauled himself out of the mosquito boat and up the side of the clipper. "Stop kicking!" he ordered his squirming passenger.

"This is humiliating!" Moore complained.

"Stealth, and the element of surprise is everything," Ki warned. "Do not fire your gun unless absolutely necessary."

"Hey! What's going on?" A sailor, strolling along the middle

153

deck, was staring at them in astonishment. "Where'd you two come from?"

Ki chinned himself up past the deck rail, to let Moore scramble off his back, and then hauled himself over, landing lightly on his feet. As he began to move toward the sailor, the man pulled a pistol from his belt. A second later, a shot drove the samurai down to the wooden planking.

"Help!" the sailor shouted. "Intruders on the port side!"

"So much for stealth," Moore smirked.

"So much for their not having guns." Ki growled, hugging the deck as the sailor's second shot sent splinters into the air just inches in front of his face. "Shoot him!" he called, searching over his shoulder for Moore. "Where are you?"

"All you had to do was ask," the detective said. He drew his short-barreled Colt, gripped it in both hands, and squeezed the trigger. The big .44's detonation shattered the windswept night. Moore rode the pistol's recoil up, and then brought the gun's squat barrel back on target.

But there was no need for a second shot. The sailor was staring down at his bloody belly in amazed horror, his pistol clattering to the deck as he pitched forward.

Moore helped Ki to his feet. "You all right?" he asked.

Ki nodded, and at the same time shoved the detective aside. A *shuriken* star seemed to materialize in his hand. He sent it whizzing toward a second sailor who had just appeared on the center deck. The swab uttered a hoarse scream. He skidded and then fell out of sight, his fingers slapping at the cold steel Ki had planted in his chest.

Now sailors were popping up everywhere. They poured out from belowdecks through hatches, and swarmed out of cabin doors like ants massing to protect their nest. Moore's pistol flashed and boomed twice again, dropping two more of the enemy.

"This isn't working out the way we'd planned," the detective shouted over the commotion.

"You are a very good shot," Ki complimented him.

"You'd better hope so," Moore laughed. He swung his gun around to fire a quick shot that knocked back a charging, knife-wielding sailor. "But I've only got one round left. I've got to reload!"

"Run toward the stern," Ki ordered. He pulled one of the yellow *nage teppo* grenades out of his shoulder satchel. "Close your eyes!" he warned, and then tossed the egg over his shoulder.

There was only a dull thud, but the flash of light was enough to penetrate Moore's tightly clenched lids, so that his closed eyes saw bright red. When he opened them, he saw several sailors milling about blindly.

Moore clicked open the smoking cylinder of his revolver as he ran astern, ejecting the spent shells and feeding fresh rounds into his gun. He stopped short at the raised bulkhead of the main cargo bay. Were the coolies down there? The next thing he knew, he was flying through the air, his gun spinning out of his grip. He'd been tackled by a sailor lurking in the shadows.

Moore kicked and squirmed out of the sailor's grasp. He got to his feet along with his adversary, who was now flashing an extremely long, shiny knife.

"I'll cut your gizzards out, mate!" the sailor spat, rushing toward Moore.

The detective dodged the man's knife thrust at his stomach. He rammed his fist into the swab's thick midsection, doubling him over, then brought his left around in a swooping, downward cross that connected beneath the sailor's ear. The poleaxed swab fell while Moore hurried to retrieve his revolver.

Ki, meanwhile, was standing his ground, preventing a half-dozen sailors from getting past him. Each time the men tried, he'd dance sideways, cutting them off. Finally they formed a wary semicircle around the samurai.

"Watch yourselves, men!" came the gruff voice of their captain from behind the line of sailors. "I've seen his type in the Japans. He's a one-man army!"

Ki, grinning like a tiger, pulled his brace of *sai* from his belt. He twirled the two eighteen-inch-long swords like batons as he charged into the six sailors.

Two of the sailors lifted their own machete-like blades in order to swing them down at Ki's head. The samurai spun sideways to avoid the first man's deadly downward slash, and then crossed his two *sai* blades above his head in an X-block, catching the second man's knife between the trident-like prongs that curved outward from the weapons' hilts. Ki twisted his wrists to wrench the man's trapped blade from his grasp, and at the same time executed a forward snap-kick to the man's head. The sailor was somersaulted backward, his jaw broken by the incredible impact of Ki's steely, stiffened toes against his chin.

The entire maneuver was over in seconds. The first sailor had barely recovered his balance and was just raising his machete for another try at Ki's back, when the samurai spun one of his *sai* so that the blade was pointed to the rear, and then stabbed backward, running the sailor through. With his other *sai* he parried the thrust of another sailor's knife, before slitting the man's throat.

"It's no good," the captain swore. "Jimmy! Here's my keys! Open up the gun locker in my cabin. Arm the men!" He tossed the key ring through the air to the sailor he'd addressed, a man who seemed quite happy to quit the fight to do his captain's bidding.

It would not do to have the sailors armed with guns, Ki thought. He hurled one of his *sai* at the departing sailor. The blade penetrated the man's back, its momentum carrying the swab another few feet before his lifeless legs gave out and he thudded to the deck.

Now there were only two men left to confront him. The captain was hurrying toward where his keys lay tangled in the dead man's fingers. The samurai ducked beneath the slashing blade of the first man to attack him. He carefully grasped the point of his remaining *sai*, and used the pronged hilt to hook the other sailor's leg. One jerk of the sword sent that man sprawling on his back. Ki snatched up the fallen sailor's machete in time to drive it into the chest of the man who was still on his feet, but when he turned to use his *sai* upon the downed man, he was met with a plea for mercy.

"Don't kill me! P-please!" the sailor whimpered. His face was deathly pale, and his eyes were screwed shut. "I give up! Don't do it!"

Ki straddled the man, brought his blade up, and then started it on its downward plunge toward the sobbing man. But at the last moment, he baton-twirled the weapon, so that it was the hard round knob mounted at the end of the *sai's* handle, and not its razor-sharp blade, that came into contact with the swab's head, knocking him cold.

Muttering to himself, Ki stepped over the unconscious sailor, plucked his sai from the corpse of the man who had briefly held the captain's keys, then hurried on toward the stern.

He spied Moore being attacked from behind by a sailor who

looked to be twice the slender detective's size. Ki hurried to the scene, but it looked as if he was going to be too late. The big, burly swab had locked his forearm against Moore's throat and lifted him up into the air. The detective's gun fell to the deck as his legs dangled. Ki could not throw one of his *sai* or one of his *shuriken* blades—there was too great a danger of hitting Moore's body. He ran as fast as he could, but the samurai despaired that his companion's life would be choked out of him before he could arrive to lend a hand.

Then Ki stopped running, to watch in amazement as Moore managed to slam his elbow into his attacker's gut, driving the air out of him and forcing him to loosen his lock about Moore's throat.

"I'll murda ya, ya little rat!" the sailor spat, trying for another armlock around his opponent. "Stand still! Damn you!" He groped for Moore, like a bear being worried by a terrier.

Moore was simply too fast for the lumbering sailor. He ducked beneath the man's hamlike hands, to drive a set of fast uppercuts into the sailor's ribs. The big man's grunts changed into a squeal of pain as Moore quickly stepped behind the fellow in order to deliver a series of short, hard jabs into the man's kidneys.

The groaning swab was now desperate. He was swatting at Moore as though the detective were a stinging bee, but his blows caught only air. Finally he tried to backhand Moore, and that was the sailor's final mistake, for it left him wide open. Moore easily ducked the clumsy blow, and moved in for a try at the swab's chin. He locked his two fists together and brought them up in a sledgehammer swing that started at deck-level and picked up speed and power as it rose. Moore's aim was a trifle off. He missed the man's chin, but caught him square on the nose. There was a splatter of blood, and a surprised yelp from the sailor. He lost his balance and tottered backward, cracking the back of his skull against the cargo hold's hatch cover.

Moore himself had put so much shoulder into the punch that his swing carried him full around. His feet slid out from under him and he hit the deck on his belly. Ki couldn't keep from laughing as he helped Moore up.

"Showed that big palooka," Moore muttered. He glanced at Ki. "Hell, if I'd known how amused you'd be, I would've let the guy kill me. Where's my gun?"

"You are quite fast," Ki said. "And, of course, *he* was quite slow." He pointed at the fallen sailor.

"Speed is what it's all about," Moore said smugly, picking up his Colt.

"Until you come up against a *fast* big man," Ki teased.

Moore waved his gun. "I find it helpful to shoot big, fast men," he cheerfully replied. "I hate to change the subject, but look at what I found." He slid open the cargo hold's hatch cover.

Ki peered down into the hold. Twenty ragged, pitifully emaciated Chinese men fearfully looked up at him.

"My daddy in Oregon would be so pleased," Moore said quietly, "assuming I *had* such a daddy. Look at their backs, Ki. They've been whipped badly."

"That would be the captain's doing," the samurai said slowly. His voice trembled with fury. "I will pay him back for this cruelty. But why have their shackles been removed?"

"That's standard practice when a slave ship approaches its port," Moore explained. "It allows the circulation to come back into the coolies' limbs. Otherwise they would not be able to haul themselves out of the hold."

Ki nodded. "Well, it will make our task easier." He gestured down toward the coolies. "We must find a way to communicate with them. They must know that we mean to help them."

A shot thwacked into the hatch bulkhead. Both Ki and Moore took cover on the far side of the cargo hold.

"The captain has armed his remaining men," Ki said. "It is time to strike against the ship itself."

Moore did not answer him. Instead, the detective slowly read from a crumpled sheet of paper. The strange sounds he made were tentative and faltering, but they were definitely Chinese. The coolies nodded to Moore, and began to speak excitedly among themselves in their native tongue.

"What did you say to them?" Ki asked.

"While you were at the bordello, I copied this out of a phrase book I had in my library at home," Moore replied. "I believe I said, 'We are friends. We take you to freedom.' Either that or 'What time does the train arrive?'" Moore's eyes narrowed as he stared at the area where the sailors had regrouped. "It's the captain himself, and he's waving a white flag!"

"Get your head down," Ki ordered. "He may have a white flag in one hand, but he holds a revolver in the other!"

"You two better give up!" the captain shouted, standing up

behind a hastily erected barricade of crates. "Else you'll not leave this ship alive!" One of his men squeezed off a shot. "Hold your fire, men! Give them a chance to surrender!"

"He does not wish his men to fire because they may hit some of their human cargo," Ki began. "Jordan, you—"

But Ki was cut off by the loud report of Moore's Colt .44. The captain dropped his pistol, clutched at his throat, then fell out of sight behind the crates.

"Sorry," Moore shrugged. "But that bastard deserved to die for what he's done to these men." His smoking gun barrel gestured toward the coolies in the hold.

Ki nodded. "One of us had to kill him," the samurai acknowledged. "I grow weary of this. Let us finish it."

Panicked, and freed from restraint by the death of their captain, the sailors let loose a volley of gunfire. The rounds rattled against the bulkhead, sending splinters flying.

"Get ready to throw the green bomb I gave you," Ki instructed. "Ready? Now!"

As Moore lobbed his grenade, Ki let fly two of his own. The three *nage teppo* landed accurately, each exploding like a stick of dynamite. Shards of wooden crates and deck planking, as well as coils of rope and the mutilated bodies of several sailors, flew in all directions. The remaining sailors, now totally demoralized, flew belowdecks.

Finding themselves suddenly unopposed, Moore and Ki made quick work of getting the coolies out of the hold. Understanding what was expected of them, the coolies organized themselves into several gangs and lowered the ship's lifeboats. All in all, there were about fifty men distributed among the clipper's three boats. When all the boats were in the water, Ki ordered Moore, "You ride in the first boat, and I'll take the third."

As Moore nodded and hoisted himself over the gunwale, Ki said, "Give me your white *nage teppo*."

Moore handed it over, saying, "Don't be too long, now. I'd hate to have to leave without you. I don't understand why you have to burn the ship, anyway. It's been without a tillerman ever since the fight started, and it's bound to run aground."

Ki shook his head. "I want nothing left that the cartel could salvage."

"All right," Moore said, "but hurry. Most of these coolies are probably not experienced boatmen, and I don't know how long I can hold these boats together in these waves."

"Only a moment, my friend," Ki replied, hurrying off toward the open cargo hold.

After lowering himself into the hold, it took Ki only a moment to find an area where a number of barrels of lamp-oil were stored. Smiling, he hurled the deadly egg in the direction of the clustered barrels, but did not wait to see it land. He was already well on his way toward the ladder that led up out of the hold when the tiny grenade hit and cracked open with a deep *whump!* The flaming, sticky liquid inside the bomb spread quickly over the containers of flammable oil. Ki knew it would take a few moments for the oil to catch, but when it did...

He was on his way over the gunwale and into the last of the three boats when there came a muffled explosion from belowdecks, and he felt the wooden side of the big ship shudder. He dropped into the boat, and Moore and Ki cast off the lines holding their lifeboats to the ship. The coolies in the middle boat understood, and did likewise, and Moore guided the tiny convoy of refugees toward a stretch of dark shoreline some distance from the relatively well-lit waterfront and the crowds that would soon gather there to watch the funeral pyre of the cartel clipper.

As they put distance between themselves and the ship, Ki looked back and smiled again, in satisfaction, as an orange fireball erupted from the main deck, illuminating the stretch of dark water between the lifeboats and their dying mother ship.

A bit later, as Moore and Ki stood with the huddled Chinese on a sandy beach, watching the floating mountain of fire in the middle of the black bay, Moore turned to Ki and said, "You know, I'm afraid my friend won't be too happy about his mosquito boat."

"Don't worry," Ki replied. "You keep reminding us of how large your bill will be. I'm sure the cost of such a modest vessel will be easily absorbed. You have earned your pay, Jordan Moore. You are a fine warrior." He turned, and momentarily contemplated the huddled group of coolies. "I will take them to Chinatown now," he said finally.

"All by yourself?" Moore exclaimed. "Let me come with you."

"No, my friend. It will be all right. I know a shortcut." Ki motioned to the coolies, and they nodded and headed toward him, eager to get off the chilly, windy beach.

Moore watched Ki head off with his ragtag band until they were swallowed up in the darkness. *What's he being so all-fired mysterious about?* the detective wondered. *Well, if he wants to go off on his own, that's just fine. Two can play at that same game.*

Ki hustled his charges along the back-alley route that Su-ling had shown him the night she'd escorted him out of Chinatown. He had a hard time keeping the coolies from running off in fifty different directions once they'd reached the relative security of Chinatown's outskirts, but a few stern glances and barked orders kept them docile. After all, they'd seen what happened to men who made Ki mad.

It was just midnight when Ki and the coolies reached the Gold Coin restaurant owned by Su-ling's family. Due to the lateness of the hour, the place was empty of diners.

"What do you wish here?" the father scowled as he left the kitchen to confront Ki. "What are you doing with these men?" Behind him stood his wife, his young son, and the old grandfather, but Su-ling was nowhere in sight.

There was something wrong here, Ki suddenly felt. "Where is she?" the samurai asked softly.

The father's face was pale with grief. His eyes, Ki now noticed, were red-rimmed and raw. "I have to tell you nothing!" the father spat contemptuously.

Suddenly one of the coolies began to speak to the father in their own tongue. The restaurant proprietor listened intently. When the coolie was finished, Su-ling's father turned to regard Ki. "This man says that you rescued them from a slave ship. That you killed the captain and crew who mistreated them. That you burnt the ship itself." The father shook his head. *"Jibon-ren,* I do not understand. Why would you risk your own life for Chinese people?"

"The feud between us must be forgotten in this new country," Ki began quietly. "The old bitterness must be gone, like last night's dreams. Yes, I am a samurai. But I fight not for a warlord; I fight for all downtrodden people. In America, I am a samurai who fights for *you.*"

"Samurai," the father groaned in misery, "if you had come last night, things might have been different." He stared at the sawdust-sprinkled floor, unable to meet Ki's gaze.

161

"Where is Su-ling?" Ki asked gently.

"Last night, Chang came here with his men. He demanded payment from us. When he saw that we had no money—" The father's voice abruptly broke. "When he saw that we had no money," he now whispered, "he took our only daughter as payment. Took her to his white man's whorehouse. Took her there to defile her!"

Ki stood perfectly still. *Last night,* he thought. *It has already happened. Chang did this to her last night.*

If an enemy had happened to choose that instant to strike at Ki, the samurai might well have shattered into a thousand pieces. His body was rigid with anger.

"You did not fight for your daughter's honor?" he demanded. "You would not fight for her?"

"We all would have died!" the father said fiercely, but he too was now weeping, like the rest of his kin. "My whole family! I am not a skilled warrior like yourself. My whole family would have been slaughtered, and still Chang would have taken my daughter."

"She will be avenged," Ki whispered. He turned to go.

The horrified coolies had been watching all this. They knew no English, but words were not needed to comprehend Ki's agonized reactions to what he was being told. One of them now spoke to the father, who, in turn, translated the message for Ki. "They thank you for their freedom," the father said. "They hope that someday, someone will pay you back the boon—that someday, someone will unlock the shackles on your soul."

★

Chapter 14

"Wake up! Damn you!"

Jessie's eyes sprang open. She stared up at the gray, pinched face of Mrs. Fitzroy. "What? What time is it?" she yawned.

"Well after midnight," the matron replied. "You've been sleeping for hours. Foxy let you come up to your room for a nap, but she never intended for you to sleep the night away. Now come on!" She gathered up a lock of Jessie's hair and gave it a tug, pulling Jessie out of bed.

"Ow! All right!" Jessie exclaimed. "I'm up!" She hopped off the narrow bed, ruefully thinking about how Ki had been in the room just a few hours ago, and how she could have escaped with him then. Well, one more night of this, and it would be all over. "Where am I going?" she mumbled as she rubbed at her sleepy eyes.

"The client you've been promised to is here," Fitzroy said wickedly. "Your time has come, girl!"

"B-but—" Jessie stammered, trying to thing. "I was told it would be a few days," she pleaded. "You were going to teach me things..."

"Well, all that has changed," Fitzroy chuckled. "You'll be taught by the expert in these matters."

"Who is he?" Jessie moaned.

"He? Who ever said it was going to be a *man?*" Fitzroy said mockingly. "You were brought here to please a very important *woman*. She waits for you now. I'm to take you to one of our rooms upstairs. She will then join you." The matron smoothed Jessie's scanty gown. "This woman heads up a huge

163

business organization. Tonight that organization suffered an expensive mishap. One of their ships, along with its crew and cargo, was destroyed by her enemies. All the worse for you, I'm afraid."

"How so?" Jessie, frightened, stared at her captor. "What will she do to me?"

The matron's eyes glinted with cruelty. "At her best, she delights in inflicting pain upon her lovers. Tonight, the woman you belong to is in a *foul* mood." Fitzroy roared with laughter as she steered Jessie out of the sanctuary of her little bedroom. "Dear, sweet, Annie. When Greta Kahr is done with you, you may not have eyes left in your head to see the coming dawn!"

Ki climbed up the rear of the bordello. As he clambered up the thin cord he'd hooked into the house's roof, he took a moment to check Jessie's room. It was dark, and she was not in it. Very well, he would find her later. The plan had changed. She would have to come out with Su-ling and himself this very night. Ki did not intend to leave this house standing. He would burn it to the ground, the way he'd burned the cartel's clipper ship.

The layout Moore had earlier sketched for him showed that the third and fourth floors were reserved for the entertainment of the bordello's clients. Ki had already been on the third. The rooms there were small, and the walls flimsy. No, Chang most likely had a more luxurious retreat on the fourth floor. A bed-chamber fit for a Tong leader, Ki mused sourly.

The samurai climbed all the way to the roof. He would prowl the perimeter of the building until he found the room Su-ling had been taken to. Then he would swing down from the eaves to rescue her. He wondered if Chang and his guards were still in the bordello. Ki hoped that they were. Chang, and a lot of guards. The samurai knew he could not kill all of the men in the Steel Claw Tong, but tonight he intended to kill very many indeed.

Ki skipped lightly across the steeply slanted shingles with the agility of a cat. At each top-floor window he lowered himself by hooking his toes into the roof gutter and hanging upside down, like a bat. In this way he was able to peer into the various rooms. He found her in the second room he checked. She was alone, nude, lying on a big double bed with her back to him. The lushly appointed room was decorated with Chinese painted screens, jade carvings, and intricate ink-and-brush

164

paintings. This was, indeed, Chang's private hideaway.

The window was unlocked. Ki slid it open and jackknifed himself inside. Su-ling turned to face him. The expression on her face went from joyful surprise to a sadness so awful that Ki thought his heart would break.

"I have come for you," he said.

"No." She shook her head, frowning. "Please!" she began to cower like a whipped dog. "Do not look at me!" she begged. She laced her arms across her breasts. "They have taken my clothes. What they have left me is a whore's garb, but I will not wear it. Ki! No!"

But he had already crossed the room to hold her in his arms. "I have come for you," he repeated.

"Not for me," Su-ling murmured, pressing her face against his chest. "You came for who I *used* to be. But the Steel Claw has changed all of that. Look at me! At my face! Then tell me everything has not changed!"

Ki stared down at her. Her shiny black hair, her face, were both as lovely as ever. Then he gazed into her big dark eyes, and was forced to nod sorrowfully. They no longer held the serene glow that had captivated him; they were the tortured eyes of a slave.

I will kill him, Ki vowed silently, but the threat seemed so pitifully weak against the enormity of what Chang had done to Su-ling. Addressing her, Ki whispered, "For me, nothing has changed. We will leave this place and forge a life for ourselves."

"But I am ruined. Chang has taken my virginity," Su-ling wept. "I am now a whore—"

Ki cut her off with a kiss. His hands roamed across her finely sculptured buttocks, then rose to cup her small, delicately formed breasts. She moaned in his embrace, melted against him, and darted her hot, wet tongue into his mouth.

"Prove to me that nothing has changed?" she now begged him. *"Heal* me . . ."

Ki picked her up to lay her gently upon the bed.

Su-ling shuddered. *"He* had me on the bed. Make love to me on the carpet . . ."

Ki quickly stripped off his clothes, and once more wrapped his arms around her. Together they folded onto the thick, soft rug.

Ki nuzzled the sweet fragrance of her neck, licked and

165

sucked at her dark nipples that stood so pertly erect in worship of his flicking tongue. The room seemed to spin, so dizzy with desire was the samurai for this woman.

"I have bathed myself," she whispered bashfully as Ki's gentle fingers explored the wetness between her legs. "I want you so much," she moaned. "But do not think *his* taint is still upon me—*within* me—for I scrubbed myself to cleanse—"

"Silence, woman!" Ki pleaded. "It is in the past. It is a nightmare from which you have awoken."

"Please, prove that to me," was all she would say as she spread her legs for his pulsing hardness. "Heal me," was all she whispered as Ki slid into her, to the hilt.

They rocked together, saying nothing, but constantly staring into each other's eyes for long minutes. It seemed to him that just being inside of her, and having her long, lovely legs clamped about his back was sensation enough, and almost too intense to bear.

He used his strong back muscles to raise them both up, and then he moved into a cross-legged, sitting position. Su-ling's strong internal muscles kept him safely nestled inside of her while she settled herself upon his lap. She now began to moan. Ki gazed down at the rise and fall of her sweat-sheened breasts, and at the undulations of her soft, flat belly. His thighs felt the birdlike quivering of her satin-smooth bottom as her sweet center rose and fell upon his glistening, marble-hard shaft.

She cried out as she climaxed, her warm juices flowing to soak his loins. "The Steel Claw tried to wrench this moment from us," she whimpered between her shudders of pleasure. "Chang tried to tear this most precious prize from me. He took everything from me, but this he did not get. All last night and today, I kept my sanity by imagining how I might finally offer this to you..."

She began to ride him, *hard*. She seemed half mad in her frenzied desire to feel him spend himself inside her. Her tongue licked hungrily across his chest. She chewed and sucked at his nipples until they were exquisitely aroused, twin buttons of sensation. Her fingers herded shivers up and down his spine. Her supple hips gyrated against his lap. She rode him as though he were truly a steed who could carry her far away from this horrid bordello. She rode him until he began to feel his own orgasm coming closer and closer, like a boulder rolling down a mountain side, a boulder about to crush him beneath its awesome mass. When he came, it was all he could do not to howl as a wolf howls at the moon.

"I am healed," she told Ki as she kissed his closed eyes. "I will always love you, no matter what happens."

Ki thought her choice of words was ominous. He stared intently into her eyes. The fear seemed to be banished, to be replaced by some measure of their previous serenity, but all was not as it had been. Before, Su-ling's eyes had been those of a young girl. Now she had the eyes of an old woman.

But he *had* brought some peace back to her, the samurai reassured himself. With careful nurturing, who was to say that he could not coax back her original joyfulness? And if he couldn't, he would count himself lucky to have her as she was. Truth to tell, *his* eyes were no longer those of a spiritually young man...

"I thank you for healing me," she smiled. "You have given me back a sweet thing to meditate upon."

Ki wondered how to begin to tell her what he felt inside. All the words he could think of seemed so inadequate. Finally, all he could do was smile at her. "You have given me back my home," was what he said.

Jessie waited in anxious solitude. She'd been led by Mrs. Fitzroy to a dimly candlelit room on the fourth floor of the big house. The room was mirrored on all four walls, except for the window, and one narrow area where various leather whips, iron manacles, and riding crops hung from pegs. The ceiling above the double bed was mirrored as well. The bed was a four-poster. Jessie did not have to guess what those satin cords hanging from each post were for...

Well, here I am, the lamb waiting for the slaughter, she thought to herself. *But this is one lamb who's going to fight back*.

She tried the door, hoping that she might be able to sneak downstairs to the second floor and retrieve her gun, but Mrs. Fitzroy had locked it securely. Jessie gazed about the place. There were whips and things that she could use as weapons, but first she would have to get close enough to Greta Kahr to get the drop on the woman. That wasn't going to be easy. Kahr knew what Jessie looked like. The Prussian would walk in here, take one look at her "prize," and shout bloody murder!

Jessie wandered over to the wall to inspect the various implements of torture so conveniently arranged for Greta Kahr's pleasure and her own anguish. As she fingered the hard, black leather braid of one of the riding crops, she thought back on what Ki had said concerning his experience with Kahr after he'd unknowingly rescued the cartel leader from those purse-snatchers. According to Ki, she liked to *feel* pain during love-making, not *inflict* it . . .

But maybe that's how she is with men, Jessie mused as she lifted a black leather hood from its place on the wall. *Maybe Kahr wants men to hurt her, but likes to hurt women . . .*

The hood had slits cut for one's nose, mouth, and eyes, and an opening at the top, for ventilation, Jessie imagined. As she stared down at the face, carved into the leather the way a jack-o'-lantern's face is carved into a pumpkin, she began to formulate her plan . . .

A half hour later, Jessie heard the door to the room being unlocked. She was all ready. She'd shucked her thin chemise, and had put on the leather mask. She'd taken a kneeling position on the carpeted floor, angling her uplifted, shapely, and quite bare bottom toward the door. Her masked chin was resting between her hands upon the carpet, but she was able to gauge the reactions of her visitors by watching their reflections in the wall mirror opposite the doorway.

In came Greta Kahr, flanked by Foxy Muscat and Mrs. Fitzroy. She was the same auburn-curled, middle-aged woman Jessie had spied at the after-hours club Jordan had taken her to. Kahr was dressed in a low-cut gown of green velvet. Around her shoulders was a full-length cape of mink that matched the reddish-brown shade of her hair. As on that previous evening, she clutched a tightly furled umbrella.

Kahr's violet eyes widened in surprised glee as they feasted upon Jessie's angled and splayed bottom. Watching them all in the mirror, Jessie sardonically noted that Mrs. Fitzroy, too, was licking her lips.

"Allow me to introduce—" Foxy Muscat began, but Greta Kahr cut her off imperiously with a wave of her finely manicured hand.

"Leave us," the Prussian commanded. "No introductions are necessary."

"Yes, ma'am," Foxy said meekly. Both she and Mrs. Fitzroy left, closing the door behind them.

Jessie waited until she felt certain that the duo had reached the stairway and were out of earshot. Then she stood up.

"Ah, but I did not give my slave permission to rise," Kahr chuckled. She set her umbrella down upon the bed, then shrugged off her cape, carefully letting it drop to the floor.

Jessie watched the woman sashay across the room, to the wall of whips and crops. Kahr selected the braided riding crop and then turned to face Jessie.

"You must be punished for your impertinence..." Kahr sneered. Beads of spittle collected upon the thick red gloss that colored her mouth. She approached Jessie. Kahr's purple eyes ran the length of Jessie's nude body, lingering on her full breasts and the golden-red thatch of hair between her thighs. "With this"—she waved the riding crop in front of Jessie's masked face—"I will teach you obedience!"

"You and who else?" Jessie shot back, pulling off her hood.

Kahr stared in disbelief. "Jessica Starbuck?" she gasped. The riding crop fell from her hand as she made a mad dash for the bed, where she snatched up her umbrella.

The umbrella! Jessie realized. *Of course!* Jessie picked up the riding crop, moved into position, and whipped it down hard upon Kahr's hand as the woman turned, with the long, thin, gleamingly sharp rapier inside her umbrella already more than half drawn. Kahr screamed as the harsh leather bit into her hand. The umbrella-sword fell to the carpet. Jessie let the riding crop fall beside it. Before Kahr could open her mouth to scream again, Jessie knocked her cold with a right uppercut that landed flush against the Prussian woman's weak chin. Kahr fell across the bed, her violet eyes showing their whites as they fluttered and then rolled up into her head.

Jessie grabbed the woman's mink cape and clasped it around her shoulders. *Lord above,* she thought happily. *It does feel good to have substantial clothing on again!* She stared down at the sword sheathed in the woman's umbrella. Clearly this was the weapon Kahr had used to stab poor old Shanks, Moore's partner, to death.

Jessie went to the door and opened it partway, peeking up and down the corridor to make sure she could escape undetected. There was nobody around. She darted down the hallway to the stairs, and then sneaked quietly down to the second floor. Once she thought she heard footsteps behind her, but when she turned, the corridor was empty.

Inside the little bedroom, she dragged the mattress off the

169

bed frame and tore open the ragged stiches she'd sewn. She removed her revolver and extra ammunition, stashing her spare rounds in an inside pocket of the mink cape.

She held her gun beneath the cape as she left the bedroom. She was about to make her way downstairs when a gruff male voice suddenly commanded, "Freeze!"

He couldn't have seen my gun, she reminded herself. *I've got the element of surprise . . .*

She whirled, bringing up her Colt. *"You* freeze!" she retorted, snapping back the hammer of her double-action .38.

Jordan Moore laughingly held up his hands.

"How'd you get in here?" Jessie sighed in relief. She lowered her gun and gave him a big hug.

Moore squeezed her tightly. "Hey," he chuckled. "You don't have anything on under this fur."

"How *did* you get in here?" Jessie repeated, smiling up at him.

"I'm a very important client," Moore reminded her. "I just put on my 'Oregon wastrel' outfit, and dropped by for some fun. I hired one of the girls to take me upstairs, and then I began to search for you. I heard the commotion, and followed you down to your bedroom."

"How do *you* rate the *fourth* floor?" Jessie teased.

"Well, they *do* want to make me happy," Moore smiled mischievously. "They're trying to butter me up. They were *so* apologetic about not being able to deliver the slaves my daddy wants." The detective winked. "Seems that somebody sank their expensive old boat."

"I heard about that," Jessie giggled. "You said you were with some woman. Won't she sound the alarm about you wandering around unescorted?"

"Don't worry about Ruthie," Moore replied. "I left her bound and gagged on the bed."

"That's awful!" Jessie scolded him. "She must be petrified."

"Ruthie *loves* being bound and gagged. It's her specialty."

"I don't want to hear it," Jessie sighed. "Come on, let's see what's going on downstairs."

The duo crept down the stairs, to the landing just above the first-floor-front parlor. The big sitting room was now empty of both girls and clients. The bartenders were gone, as was the kindly black piano player. Mrs. Fitzroy and Foxy Muscat were both seated on one of the long, black leather sofas. Guarding the door to the room were two Tong bodyguards armed with pistols shoved into the belts of their long blue cotton tunics. Sitting on a straight-backed wooden chair in the center of the room was a quite unhappy-looking Commissioner Smith. His hands were tied behind his back. Standing above him was Chang, the Steel Claw, leader of the Tong.

"I swear it, Chang!" Smith whined. "I told no one about tonight's shipment."

"That's not true!" Foxy called out. Her childish voice made her sound like a tattling schoolgirl. "He told one of my girls all about it while he was drugged on opium."

Chang nodded to the bordello's madam as he shrugged off his suit jacket. The gaslight chandelier's bright glow was reflected slickly from his bald yellow skull. His expressionless black lizard-eyes glittered like wet coal. The Tong leader's thick shoulders and chest were even more impressive now that he was just in his shirtsleeves. The gleaming, five-taloned claw that was his right hand seemed to have some evil life of its own as Chang thrust it beneath the petrified Smith's quivering nose.

"She says you told what you knew of our plans to a girl," Chang hissed. His voice was dry and husky. It rattled in his throat like ancient ivory dice in a leather cup. The Tong leader glanced at Mrs. Fitzroy and Foxy Muscat. "Could this girl have informed on us?"

"The girl is just a child," Fitzroy said from her place on the couch. "She's talked to no one since serving *him*." She pointed an accusing finger at the weeping Smith. "Now she's with Greta Kahr."

Chang nodded, chuckling. "Punishment *enough*, in any event."

"My God," Smith moaned. "I don't even remember the girl."

"Yes, I know," Chang said. "Your brain has become so riddled with opium smoke that you remember nothing. So. You *could* have told our business to others. How would you *know*, Commissioner?" He prodded his victim with his claw.

"Oh, please, Chang, don't . . ." was all the broken man could whimper.

Watching it all from their hiding place, Jessie and Moore exchanged horrified looks. It was evident that Smith was about to die. Jessie had to remind herself that this poor, frightened man was one of the enemy. But still—how could she let him be murdered?

"Jordan," she whispered. "We've got to do something."

Moore began to nod, but before he could reply, Chang once again addressed the commissioner.

"You have outlived your usefulness to my Tong!" he cried. He raised his steel claw—then thrust it into Smith's chest!

The waterfront commissioner shrieked as the needle-sharp talons pierced his flesh. Slowly, Chang locked his elbow and began to raise his arm, lifting Smith, still tied to his chair, up into the air. The commissioner hung suspended upon the metal hooks dug into his body. Chang held him aloft like some awful trophy, until the man's moans faded and his head lolled loosely upon his neck. Only then did the Tong leader set the dead man's chair back upon the carpeted floor. He braced his foot against Smith's slack body to wrench his claw out of the dead man's flesh.

Moore looked at Jessie. *"Strong* son of a bitch," he murmured thoughtfully. "I think we should get out of here—"

"It's a bit late for that," Greta Kahr sneered behind them. "Put up your hands!"

Jessie felt the cold, sharp point of the woman's rapier tickling her ear. Slowly she raised her hands. Her Colt was snatched out of her fingers by the Prussian, who dropped it on the landing.

"I can't believe you didn't tie her up!" Moore hissed to Jessie, as Greta herded them down the stairs.

"I forgot," Jessie shrugged.

"You had every kind of bondage implement known to mankind in that room. What do you mean you forgot?" Moore insisted.

"Look," Jessie retorted impatiently, "my mind doesn't work that way!"

"Silence!" Greta Kahr commanded.

"What is going on here?" Chang demanded as he eyed Moore and Jessie. "Greta? Have you taken leave of your senses?"

"That's the girl I mentioned," Foxy Muscat offered helpfully. "Her name's Annabelle Willis—"

"Fool!" Greta Kahr cut her off. Her jaw was discolored by an angry purple bruise, the result of Jessie's punch. As she spoke, she winced in pain. "This woman's name is Jessica Starbuck."

"B-but how could *I* have known?" Foxy simpered, before glaring at a perplexed Mrs. Fitzroy.

"It is beginning to make sense," Chang smiled. He wiped his bloody claw upon Smith's suit jacket, and then turned his reptilian face toward Moore. "And you are not who *you* have pretended to be, correct?"

Jessie thought quickly. No one had yet searched Moore for his gun. If she could manage to distract them, she might be able to keep them from remembering to do so. "Jordan, that rapier is the weapon Kahr used to kill Shanks!" she said.

"Ah, so you are Jordan Moore, the detective..." Chang nodded in satisfaction. "The late Mr. Shanks's partner..."

Moore was too busy glaring at Greta Kahr to answer the Tong leader. His face paled with anger as he looked down at the sword in her hand.

"I am surrounded by fools!" Kahr ranted. "Chang! How dare you kill Smith without my permission!"

Chang scowled. "I need no permission! I kill who I please, woman! This is my town!"

Kahr could not meet the Tong leader's icy gaze. "But we still need him. Or someone like him."

"It will be no problem to buy another official," Chang said. "But why do we quarrel, Greta? Tonight we have lost a battle, but won the war! Jessica Starbuck is in our control!" He threw back his head and laughed.

"Perhaps," Kahr mused. "But there is still the Japanese to contend with." She gestured with her rapier toward Jessie. "Wherever *she* goes, the Japanese is not far behind."

Ki cautioned Su-ling to remain quiet. They were crouched behind the bannister railing of the staircase's landing. It was the same hiding spot recently vacated by Jessie and Moore. Ki was so intent on gauging the scene in the parlor below he did not notice Jessie's Colt lying in the corner. Su-ling, however, kneeling behind him, did see the gun. Silently she picked it up, to clutch it behind her back.

It was Smith's death cry that had drawn them out of their room on the fourth floor. Ki had given Su-ling his cotton shirt to wear. It was big enough to quite modestly cover the diminutive Chinese woman. He himself was wearing just his jeans and his sleeveless leather vest.

Ki now removed two *shuriken* throwing blades from his pockets. "Su-ling, stay here, and keep yourself covered!" he warned. "I shall dispose of the two bodyguards, and then attack Chang. I suspect that Jessie and Moore can handle that sword-wielding bitch!"

"Before you begin," she whispered into Ki's ear, "I want you to remember something—"

"Nothing shall happen to me," Ki impatiently interrupted. "We will have much time later to talk." He stood up, his hands rising to hurl his deadly blades.

"Remember that my honor is as precious a thing as yours!" Su-ling cried, standing up beside him and aiming at Chang with Jessie's revolver. "Steel Claw! I avenge myself upon you!"

Startled, Ki paused before sending his blades toward the bodyguards. The two Tong henchmen were well-trained and devoted men. They drew their pistols and fired not at Ki, who was only threatening them, but at Su-ling, who was aiming at their master, Chang. Their two shots punched the slight Chinese woman backwards, so that the one shot she managed to fire went wild. A moment later, the two Tong henchmen were themselves falling backward, Ki's steel blades lodged in their throats.

Jessie, meanwhile, had launched herself at Greta Kahr. The Prussian slashed wildly at her attacker with her rapier, but Jessie ducked beneath the slicing arc of the deadly sword, to drive her shoulder into Kahr's belly. The rapier went flying as the Prussian sat down hard upon the floor, the wind knocked out of her. Jessie tried to pin her, but Kahr managed to free herself of Jessie's grasp. The Prussian crawled on her hands and knees to snatch up one of the fallen Tong bodyguards' pistols. She was just bringing it to bear on Jessie when the room once again exploded with gunfire.

Kahr looked horror-stricken as she dropped her gun. She blotted wildly at the fast-spreading crimson stain marring the front of her green velvet gown, as if it were a glass of wine she'd carelessly spilled upon herself. She rose up on her knees, as if in supplication, and then toppled over. She was a corpse before her head hit the carpet.

"That was for Shanks," Moore said. He turned his smoking

.44 toward Chang. "Hold very still," he warned the Tong leader.

Ki stared down at the lifeless, staring eyes of Su-ling. Blood seeped from the two bullet holes in her chest. He knelt down beside her body, and gently kissed her forehead. "I salute you," he whispered tenderly. "Your death was a good one. Without honor there is nothing."

The samurai was just descending the stairs when Chang made his move. His left hand flashed up to hurl a tiny blade, much like Ki's own *shuriken* weapons, at Moore. The little knife caught the detective in the right shoulder.

Moore clutched at the knife hilt protruding from his upper arm. His Colt fell from his trembling fingers. "Stop him!" he cried as Chang bolted for the door.

Ki was upon the man in a flash. He spun Chang around, at the same time delivering a *shuto-uchi,* or "knife-hand strike," to the Tong's leader's neck. It would have killed any normal man, but Chang was not a normal man.

He shrugged off Ki's blow, and raised his taloned weapon in order to rake it down across Ki's face. Ki managed to lock his own left hand about Chang's extended right wrist.

"*I* took what *you* wanted, Japanese," Chang mocked as the two men struggled together, testing each other's strength. "I had her, and spoiled her—"

"And now I shall avenge her," Ki said quietly, but his almond eyes burned. He began to squeeze Chang's wrist.

The veins cording the Tong leader's bald head began to bulge and throb, and sweat began to stream down his lizard-skinned face. He stared up at his steel claw, but he could not move it. Ki kept applying his awful pressure around Chang's wrist.

"L-let go!" Chang at first demanded, and then began to plead. The first clicking sounds of his wrist bones being crushed were heard by the now silent, awestruck witnesses. "My wrist! Let go-o-o!" Chang wailed. His steel claw now hung from the end of his outstretched arm like a dead leaf on a withered branch. Chang's wrist bones had been squeezed into shards by Ki's steely fingers.

Ki released the Tong leader, stepped back, and drove his fist full force into the man's solar plexus. Blood spurted from Chang's mouth as he fell forward, to twitch facedown upon the carpet for several seconds, before settling into death.

"You—you tore his heart open with that punch of yours . . ." Foxy Muscat whispered fearfully from her place on the couch. She and Mrs. Fitzroy were huddled there together beneath Jessie's watchful scrutiny.

Ki slowly stared up at Su-ling's body on the landing. "It is fitting," he said softly. "Chang has torn mine . . ."

Chapter 15

Jordan Moore waited for Jessie in the lobby of the Palace Hotel. His stitched-up right shoulder ached slightly, and the sling the doctor was forcing him to wear to cradle the injured limb was a nuisance, but his arm would be as good as new in a couple of weeks.

The detective managed awkwardly to extract a cigar from the sling-shrouded breast pocket of his gray herringbone suit, and struck a match on the heel of his boot. He'd blown no more than one smoke ring before a waiter appeared to proffer a clean copper ashtray to replace the one Moore had "dirtied" with his spent match.

Moore thanked the man, and at the same time shifted in his armchair, trying to ease the pressure of the Colt .44 wedged into his waistband. Wearing his gun this way was a worse nuisance than wearing the sling, but at least he'd be able to paw it out with his left hand, should the need arise. He was a clumsy shot with his left, but a clumsy shot was better than nothing. Since Chang's death, the Steel Claw Tong had dissolved into ten feuding clans bent on waging war with each other over the disputed Chinatown territory. Most likely, they'd end up killing each other off, but until that happened, Moore wanted to make sure he could handle the situation if some opium-crazed Tong fellow should decide to avenge his master's death . . .

He glanced at the front page of the newspaper spread out on the table before him. It was filled with stories about the "opium and sex murder" of Waterfront Commissioner Smith.

Between himself and Arthur Lewis, they'd been able to pull enough strings to keep Jessie's name out of the stories. The dead bodies of Greta Kahr, Chang, and Smith were certainly not going to implicate her, and both Foxy Muscat and Mrs. Fitzroy were more than willing to go along with whatever was required of them, in exchange for train tickets out of San Francisco. Their bordello had been closed down. The scandal had put the house off limits to the wealthy clientele who had frequented the bordello and enjoyed its pleasures. Of course, another house would soon be open. After all, this *was* San Francisco . . .

Moore flipped through the paper until he reached the business section. Taking up a quarter-page was the sweetest news of all, as far as he was concerned. It was a large advertisement, offering for sale the waterfront warehouse of the Prussian cartel. Jessie had told him that with Greta Kahr's death, the loss of their clipper, and the scandal brought on by the exposure of their links with the Tong and opium trafficking, the cartel had lost all of their legitimate business connections. They'd declared their local offices bankrupt. The Prussians were finished in San Francisco.

Moore stood up as Jessie crossed the lobby and approached his table. The detective couldn't help noticing how every man in the lobby followed her with his eyes, but Moore had long ago given up any thoughts of jealousy. It made no sense for a man to think he could ever own Jessica Starbuck.

"You look beautiful," Moore grinned as Jessie kissed his cheek. "Do we have time for a drink?"

"Later. I want to go down to the waterfront. You've got to see the cartel's warehouse!" she chattered excitedly.

"But why?"

Jessie tapped the newspaper lying on the table. "That ad the Cartel placed is old news, Jordan. We've already bought up their waterfront holdings!"

"I'd think the last thing the Starbuck business needs is another shipping dock," Moore replied, now genuinely puzzled.

"You'll understand when you see it," she laughed, tugging him along out of the sitting area of the lobby, to the area where they could flag a carriage.

Moore considered himself a tough interrogator, but he was no match for Jessie. She successfully resisted all his questions until their hack was wheeling its way along the Embarcadero.

178

"Oh, *we* don't need the property," Jessie finally began as their carriage came to a halt. "Actually, buying it was Ki's idea."

They exited the carriage to stare at the ramshackle dock building. "Great!" Jessie exclaimed. "We were just in time!"

Moore watched as the cartel's pennant was lowered from the building's flagpole, and as the Starbuck flag was hoisted up. The Circle Star emblem looked lovely, fluttering in the breeze against the clear blue sky. The detective looked around. "Jessie!" he suddenly blurted. "All the workers are Chinese!"

"Yes!" she laughed. "That's Ki's idea. He suggested that we sublease the building to Chinese workers. They'll handle the loading and unloading of our ships, and we'll pay them a percentage of the profits, until they've saved enough to buy the building outright. Then they can go into business for themselves."

"Ki thought up all of this?" Moore asked slowly. "For the Chinese? Unusual behavior for a samurai . . ."

"Oh, well," Jessie assured him. "He's a very special man. Ki says that this way, Chinese Americans can begin to establish themselves outside of Chinatown and, at the same time, maintain their dignity." Jessie paused. "His exact words were, 'their sense of honor . . .'"

It was hidden deep in the darkest place of Chinatown. It was hidden in a subbasement, and reachable only by a rickety, steep, twisting set of wooden stairs.

One had to pass through several locked and barred doors to get to it. No white man had ever been down there. Indeed, there were many Chinese who had no inkling of its existence.

No Tong headquarters was so securely hidden; no opium den enjoyed such security. But if one were allowed to descend the rickety steps and pass through the doors, one would find oneself in another world.

It was a world of dim candles and sweet smoke wafting through the air, a world where men quietly sat in trancelike states of awareness. The smoke here, however, rose not from opium pipes, but from sticks of burning incense, and the men were not drugged. Far from it, for this was a Buddhist prayer hall.

Today it was crowded, for all of the monks who belonged to the sect were anxious to catch a glimpse of the stranger who had been brought here to pray for his loved one's departed soul. For a white man to be in this Chinese place was astounding, for a Japanese to be here was incredible, but for a half-white, half-Japanese—

Well, all of the shaven-headed, burlap-robed monks knew that the samurai named Ki was indeed an astounding and incredible man. Word of his exploits on their community's behalf had spread all across Chinatown. It was illogical, but nonetheless true—even Zen masters had a hard time accepting it:

A Japanese had proven himself the champion of the Chinese. He was their samurai.

Ki sat cross-legged on the polished wooden floor. He'd refused the offer of an interview with the hall's master, just as he'd refused to light the ceremonial incense. He was not sure why he had come to this place. He was not a religious man, but a warrior. He meditated not for enlightenment, but the more forthrightly to meet the enemy...

He was not sure why he came here. Temples were bad for warriors. Too many *kami,* too many ghosts could surround one. So many...One blade could never cut them all...

Su-ling, Ki thought. *See what I have left for you: Many of your people will prosper. They will be your children...*

He wondered what to tell her next. He wondered *how* to say it. All the while, he dreaded the time when he would have to say farewell to her hovering spirit.

It was then that one of those ghosts out of his past found him.

It was his old teacher, the master samurai Hirata. *What is this?* the *kami* scolded gruffly. *Weeping? That will never do! Do not mourn, but see to your blades! A samurai's blades can never be too sharp to cut through this world!*

Smiling, Ki rose to leave the prayer hall. *One's* karma *is one's* karma, he mused. *One learns to live with it, and live it out.* There were many adventures left for Jessica Starbuck and himself to enjoy. Ki was ready and willing to confront them all!

Ki walked out of the prayer hall. As he left, there was not one monk who did not touch the floor with his forehead in homage to *their* samurai.

45